ALL WAS BEING SUND[...]

The organization for wh[...]
Emperor Smith was a w[...] prisoner of his own
government. And Remo was determined more than
ever to find his past.

This last worried the Master of Sinanju more than
any of these other events, significant as they were.
This time, Remo would not give up. This time, he
was driven by the spirit of his own mother. This time,
he would not rest until he knew all.

And if he succeeded, if he should be reunited with
the man from whose loins he originally sprang,
would there be any room in his new life for the old
man whom he called Little Father?

Also available in this series:

#95 High Priestess
#96 Infernal Revenue

Created by
WARREN MURPHY
and RICHARD SAPIR

THE Destroyer™

IDENTITY CRISIS

A GOLD EAGLE BOOK FROM
WORLDWIDE.

TORONTO • NEW YORK • LONDON
AMSTERDAM • PARIS • SYDNEY • HAMBURG
STOCKHOLM • ATHENS • TOKYO • MILAN
MADRID • WARSAW • BUDAPEST • AUCKLAND

First edition November 1994

ISBN 0-373-63212-6

Special thanks and acknowledgment to
Will Murray for his contribution to this work.

IDENTITY CRISIS

For Walter Von Bosau, longtime Friend
of the House.

And for the Glorious House of Sinanju,
P.O. Box 2505, Quincy MA 02269.

1

Dr. Harold W. Smith harbored no thoughts of suicide as he pecked his wife of forty years on the cheek, exited his Tudor-style house in Rye, New York, and climbed into his battered station wagon. Not his suicide, not anybody's. Not today, not tomorrow. Hopefully not ever.

Mrs. Smith called after him from the open door. She was a frumpy woman with blued hair and the body of a comfortable sofa chair.

"Harold, will you be working late again?"

"I believe so, dear."

"Shall I leave your meat loaf warming in the oven or in the icebox for you to reheat?"

"In the icebox, dear," said Harold Smith, starting the car.

He barely noticed the unmarked white van parked across the street and had no inkling that he was being videotaped by a hidden camera. Had he known, he might have given some thought to taking his own life—even in front of his sad-faced wife, who stood in the open door, her hand fluttering in its usual good-bye wave.

When Smith pulled out of his driveway, the van stayed put. A burgundy Ford Taurus at the end of his street slithered after him when he turned left. It followed him through the center of town, and when Smith stopped for gas, it kept going.

He paid for the gas with two crisp one-dollar bills and thirty-seven cents in exact change counted out from a red plastic change holder. The minute Smith put the gas station behind him, a delivery truck got in front of him and took the same wooded road that led to Smith's place of work. Smith thought nothing of this, either. It was a well-traveled road up to the fork in the road. Many vehicles took it.

When the delivery van reached the fork, it cut left. Smith kept to the right and had the winding wooded road all to himself, as he did virtually every morning of his six-day work week.

The road was secluded. On either side the black-and-white pillars of poplars stood in lonely ranks, their dead leaves a carpet of yellow and brown on the ground. They were as naked as the telephone poles that switched by every hundred yards or so.

Smith spotted the telephone lineman up on a pole a quarter mile before he came upon him, and was prepared for the NYNEX repair van parked on the soft shoulder of the road. Slowing, he eased past it, wondering if there was a problem with his lines. The poles served his place of work exclusively. It never occurred to him to look beyond the obvious or question the work the lineman was doing.

Smith noticed everything and yet nothing. He had been taking this identical, unvarying route for some thirty years now. There were other ways to reach the winding road to Folcroft Sanitarium, but Smith never used them. He was a man of stultifying but comfortable routine.

The same road, the same exact minute of departure and the identical time of arrival. These things never changed. Smith also wore the same gray three-piece suit to work every day. It was early autumn, so a gray porkpie hat covered the gray hair that was too thin to protect his head from the chill. Since it had been his habit to wear a hat in cold weather all of his adult life, the fact that the hat was twenty years out of fashion seemed beside the point.

When he sent the rust-eaten station wagon through the unguarded brick gate to Folcroft Sanitarium on the shores of Long Island Sound, he didn't have to look at his ancient Timex wristwatch to check the hour. He drove like a machine, and like a machine he invariably arrived at work at the exact same time.

Thirty years, and only once had Harold Smith been more than sixteen seconds late by his self-winding Timex. He took a secret pride in that record. That one exception was due to a flat tire which he had fixed himself and still managed to arrive, technically, on time. That had been on November 24, 1973. The date had remained burned into his memory. He promised himself it would never happen again. Smith had kept that promise.

Smith parked in his comfortable reserved parking spot in the east parking lot and emerged carrying a worn leather briefcase that looked like a hand-me-down.

Being an unimaginative man, he felt no eyes on him. There were boats out on the sound. He noticed them because he noticed everything, but they were ordinary speedboats. He had no inkling that from those boats, six pairs of Bushnell binoculars followed him to the main entrance.

Smith nodded to the lobby guard and took the elevator to his second-floor office, where he greeted his personal secretary with a curt "Good morning, Mrs. Mikulka." His voice sounded the way lemons taste, sour.

His secretary said, "No calls, Dr. Smith."

It was exactly 6:00 a.m. Of course there were no calls at this hour. But over the years, Harold Smith had always asked, and so Eileen Mikulka got into the habit of answering the unspoken question in lieu of a greeting.

"Is there a problem with the phone lines?" Smith asked.

"Not that I am aware."

Frowning, Smith passed on.

"Oh, Dr. Smith."

Smith paused. "Yes?"

"Dr. Gerling reported another one of those mysterious incidents last night."

"The drumming?"

"Yes."

"Which patient reported it?"

"Why, Dr. Gerling himself. He claimed that he stepped off the third-floor elevator and the drumming started up immediately. He chased it around a corner to a utility closet, but there was nothing in the closet when he opened the door. By then, the drumming had stopped."

Smith pressed his slipping glasses back into place. "Odd. Did he say anything else?"

"Yes, he thought it sounded familiar."

"Familiar how?"

"He didn't say, Dr. Smith. Dr. Gerling couldn't place it, but he was certain the drumming was something he had heard before."

Smith made a prim mouth. "When he comes on duty, ask Dr. Gerling to report to me."

"Yes, Dr. Smith."

Smith closed the door behind him and crossed the Spartan office toward the desk that faced away from the one concession to Folcroft's scenic location, a picture window framing Long Island Sound.

The speedboats were still clustered out there. Had Smith been aware that they were filled with men fighting the focusing rings of their binoculars and barking into walkie-talkies in frustration, he might have suffered a heart attack right then and there and been spared the need to take his own life. But he was oblivious and so pressed the hidden button under the edge of his desk. The window behind him was made of one-way glass. He could look out, but no one could see in.

The top of his desk was a slab of tempered black glass. The instant he pressed the concealed button, an amber computer screen sprang into life under the black plate. The buried monitor was set at an angle so only the man seated at the desk could read the tilted screen.

Smith brought his thin fingers to the desktop. Their nearness illuminated the dormant keys of a touch-sensitive keyboard. He went to work, tapping the thin white letters, which flashed with each silent stroke of his fingers.

The computer booted up soundlessly. Smith waited while the virus-check program ran and silently announced that the banks of mainframes and WORM array disk drives that toiled under lock and key in the basement of Folcroft Sanitarium were secure and virus free.

ON ONE OF THE BOATS out in the sound, a man scanned Folcroft with an electronic device designed to pick up radio transmissions from any monitor in the building and duplicate the display on a portable screen. He got white noise. There was only one monitor in all of Folcroft, and Smith's office walls were honeycombed with a copper mesh designed to soak up all radio emanations, shielding it against such sophisticated electronic eavesdropping.

Two miles down the road the man dressed as a telephone lineman was hanging from a safety harness and listening to the tap on the Folcroft phone lines, unaware that he was wasting his time. The critical telephone lines left Folcroft though an underground conduit not found on any AT&T blueprint.

Five minutes later the white van, the burgundy Taurus and the delivery truck that had shadowed Harold Smith on his drive to work pulled up to the telephone pole, and a man in a dark blue suit got out and called up. He had a head that was pinched in at the temples and tapered down to a shovel-shaped jaw. His eyes looked too small for his angular skull.

"Catch anything?"

"No, Mr. Koldstad. The lines are quiet."

"Sever them."

"Yes, sir," said the lineman. He pulled a cable cutter from his leather tool belt and simply cut the lines with three quick snaps.

The man in the blue suit turned and said, "Time to take this place down. Listen up. We go in tough, make a lot of noise, and this operation should go down exactly as scenariod."

Guns came out. Small arms. Ten mm Delta Elites and MAC-10s. They were checked, their safeties latched off, and held tightly or placed within easy reach.

The convoy of vehicles started up the oak-and-poplar-lined road, picking up speed. They passed unchallenged through the gate of Folcroft Sanitarium, which was unguarded except for the severe countenances of twin stone lion heads set on each brick post.

OUT ON THE BAY, a red-bearded man in a blue windbreaker leaned over the technician hunkered above the radio receiver.

"No computer activity?"

"No, sir."

"Anybody spot our man?"

Another man shook his head negatively. "The sun is coming right off the windows," he said. He passed over his binoculars. "See for yourself."

"Figures." The red-bearded man lifted the binoculars and asked, "What are those things circling the building?"

Five pair of binoculars lifted in unison.

"Looks like vultures," someone suggested.

"Vultures! In these parts?"

"Too big to be sea gulls."

The red-bearded man grunted. "Screw it. We can't wait all day." He picked up a walkie-talkie and barked, "The word is go. Repeat, the word is go."

Immediately the three speedboats sprang into life. Engines revved, the sterns dug into the foaming water, and the lifted noses of all three craft converged on a rickety dock jutting out from the grassy slope of the east side of the Folcroft grounds.

Black hoods were hastily pulled over heads. Weapons were pulled from stowage and handed out. Shotguns predominated.

From time to time, the red-bearded man brought his binoculars to his eyes and tried to focus on the three circling birds.

It was weird. Very weird. They were approaching their target at over ten knots, and the three circling vultures refused to come into clear focus.

He decided it must be an omen. He didn't like omens. He dropped his binoculars and checked the safety on his machine pistol, thinking, I don't need vultures to tell me Folcroft Sanitarium and everyone in it is dead meat.

OBLIVIOUS to the forces converging on him, Harold Smith continued working at his computer. Then he received his first warning of danger.

An amber light began winking on and off in the upper right-hand side of the desktop screen. Smith tapped a function key, and the program instantly displayed a warning message picked up by the roving computers two floors below. Routinely they scanned every link in the net, from wire-service computer-message traffic to the vast data banks of the FBI, the IRS, CIA and the other governmental agencies.

For Folcroft Sanitarium, a sleepy private hospital dedicated to patients with long-term chronic problems, was not what it appeared to be. And Harold W. Smith, ostensibly its director, was not all what he seemed, either.

The program was designed to work off key words and phrases, extract the data and reduce it to a concise digest. It was the first order of each day for Smith to scan the overnight extracts for matters requiring his attention.

But certain key words bubbling up from the net meant a security problem that couldn't wait for Smith to discover it.

Smith's tired gray eyes—he woke up with eyestrain even after a full night's rest—absorbed the terse data digest and began blinking rapidly.

It was headed by a key phrase that under normal circumstances should never appear on the net.

The phrase was: "Folcroft Sanitarium."

Smith had no sooner read it a second time with incredulous eyes and a cold spot forming in the pit of his stomach than the amber light flashed again. By sheer reflex—Smith was all but paralyzed in his seat by what he had just read—he tapped the function key, and a second digest replaced the first.

It too was headed: "Folcroft Sanitarium."

"My God," said Harold W. Smith in a long groan that sounded as if it had been pulled out of his stern New England soul.

Beyond the soundproof walls of his office, the screech of burning tires, the roar of speedboat motors, the slamming of doors and the crackle and rattle of gunfire blended into a single ugly detonation of sound.

Smith stabbed at his intercom button.

"Mrs. Mikulka," he said hoarsely. "Alert the lobby guard."

"Dr. Smith, there's a terrible racket going on outside!"

"I know," Smith said urgently. "Tell the lobby guard to retreat to a safe place. Folcroft is under attack."

"Attack? Who would—"

"Call the guard! Under no circumstances is he to return fire. This is a private hospital. I will tolerate no violence."

"Yes, Dr. Smith."

Smith returned to his computer. He typed one word: SUPERWIPE.

Below, the multipurpose computers geared into high speed. Tape after tape, disk upon disk, offered itself to be erased. The unerasable optical WORM drives came under the glare of powerful lasers, melting them on their spindles. It took less than five minutes to execute. Then a secondary program kicked in and began writing nonsense strings onto every intact disk and tape, making data recovery impossible.

His secrets safe, Smith tapped the button that shut down the desktop monitor.

When they burst in, there would be no trace of the desk being anything more than an executive's desk. Smith reached for the fire-engine red telephone that normally sat on his desk. Then he remembered that he had placed it in the bottom drawer after the direct line to Washington had been severed. If they found it, it would prove nothing. Smith lifted the receiver of his desk telephone, intending to call his wife. But there was no dial tone, and suddenly he understood what the telephone lineman had been up to. Bitterly he replaced the receiver. There was no other way to tell her goodbye.

There was one last book to be closed. Smith pulled out a preaddressed envelope from a drawer and hastily scribbled out a note in ink. He folded it in threes and slipped the note into the envelope. Sealing it with his tongue, he tossed it into his Out basket.

It landed with the name of the addressee facing upward. The name was Winston Smith.

That done, there was no time left to do anything except what Harold W. Smith had to do.

Smith stood up on unsteady legs. With two fingers he reached into the watch pocket of his vest, extracting a white coffin-shaped pill. He stared at it with sick eyes. He had carried that pill in his watch pocket every day of the past thirty years. It had been given to him by a President of the United States who was then as young as Harold Smith had been. They had belonged to the same generation—the generation that had fought World War II. The only difference was that Harold Smith had lived to grow old in the responsibilities the chief executive had set on his bony shoulders. The young President had been cut down by an assassin's bullet, and so remained eternally youthful in the collective memory of the nation they both served.

Harold Smith was lifting the poison pill to his blood-drained lips when the pounding of feet on stairs came through the thick office door. Mrs. Mikulka screamed once shortly.

And Smith took the pill that would end his life into his dry-with-fear mouth.

2

His name was Remo, and he never visited the grave with his name on it.

For that matter, he never visited Newark, New Jersey, where he had grown up in Saint Theresa's Orphanage as Remo Williams. For all he knew, he had been born in Newark. All the nuns knew was that one morning there was a baby on the doorstep, and the anonymous note said he was Remo Williams. They raised him under that name and, when the time came, they sent him out into the world, and he became Remo Williams, beat cop. Young, honest, he was a good cop, and Newark was his world. Except for a hitch in the Marines, he stayed inside that world. He died there, too.

It had been more than twenty years now. A pusher had been found beaten to death in a Newark alley. Next to the body lay a cop's badge. Remo Williams's badge. It had been an unusually fast jump from suspicion to trial and conviction. Remo had found himself sitting in the electric chair almost before it had sunk in that he hadn't been put through a show trial to satisfy Internal Affairs. He had been deliberately framed, but no one believed him. There had been no one on his side. No fancy lawyers, no last-minute appeals or stays of execution. It would have been different had it taken place today. But it hadn't. Remo finally understood he'd been framed. And then he'd been executed.

But the electric chair hadn't worked. It had been fixed. Someone else now lay in a grave marked with Remo Williams's name, and Remo's face had been fixed by plastic surgery, and fixed and fixed again. It was possible to go back to Newark with a new face, but Remo got tired of seeing new faces in the mirror every other year, so there was one last face-lift, and Remo had his old face back. More or less. That meant he could no longer walk the streets of his childhood anymore. Because the people who had framed him, and the people who had fixed the electric chair so that Remo Williams would be legally dead, couldn't let that happen.

So Remo had never paid his respects to his old self.

Arriving at sunset, Remo now stood looking down at his own grave for a very long time. His strong, angular face with its high cheekbones and deep-set brown eyes might have been a death mask for all the emotion it revealed. Remo stood perfectly still. For nearly an hour he stood without moving a muscle.

The headstone had been bought on the cheap. There was his name, an incised cross, but no dates of birth or death. No one knew his birthday anyway. Not even Remo. Wildwood Cemetery was not exactly Potter's Field, but it wasn't much of a step above it.

A nameless hobo lay buried in the dirt under his feet. But Remo wasn't thinking of him. He was looking at all that was left of his old life. A name on a granite stone, a cross and nothing more. The leaves of autumn lay scattered about the ground, and from time to time the wind sent them chasing one another like frisky squirrels. For most of his life he had lived like one of those leaves, rootless and disconnected.

After a while Remo crossed his legs at the ankles and scissored down into a lotus position before his own grave. His body compressed the dry, dead leaves of the season, and they crumpled silently under him because he had perfect control over his body and was trained to make no sounds he didn't want heard.

Resting his unusually thick wrists, one on each knee, he let his loose fingers dangle. Remo closed his eyes.

The one who had trained him told him many years ago that all the answers he sought in life lay within him. It was true. He had learned to breathe correctly, not to put the processed poisons civilization called food into his body and to use all five of his senses fully and without succumbing to illusion. And once those things had been mastered, Remo Williams truly began to master his mind and body.

One day, when he was whole in mind and spirit and flesh, Remo had sat before his Master and asked, "I know how to breathe."

"Because of me."

"I know how to kill."

"Because I have taught you the blows."

"I know myself fully."

"Except in one way."

"Yes," Remo had replied, and was surprised. He was always surprised by his Master. "I don't know who I am."

"You are my pupil. You are next in line after me. You are of Sinanju. Nothing else matters."

"Knowing where I came from matters."

"Not to my ancestors who have adopted you in spirit."

"I am honored, Little Father. But I must know who I am if I am to go forward."

"You must go forward because to do otherwise is to wither and die. If on the path before you, you discover the answers to these unimportant questions, this will be good."

"Knowing who my parents were is not unimportant."

"If your parents did not deem you important enough to keep, why do you wish to honor their neglect?"

"I want to see my parents' faces."

"Look into a mirror, then, for no adult can do so and not see the familiar ghosts of those who came before him."

Remo had tried looking into a mirror and saw only disappointment written on his strong features.

Returning to the Master of Sinanju, he'd said, "The mirror told me squat."

"Then you do not wish to see the truth it holds for you."

"What do you mean?"

"In your face is reflected the face of your father. In it also is reflected that of your mother. But they blend in you, so that you may have the eyes of one and the nose of the other. It is necessary to separate the elements to determine the truth. For often a child takes more after one parent than another."

Remo had felt his face. "I never thought about it that way. Is there any way to figure out who I look more like—my mother or my father?"

The Master of Sinanju had shrugged helplessly. "With a Korean, yes. In your case, no."

"Why not?"

"One baboon looks much like any other. Heh heh. One baboon looks much like any other."

Remo had frowned but pressed on over the Master of Sinanju's self-satisfied cackling at his own joke.

"I still want to find my parents."

"Then look into the mirror of memory—your own mind. For no child is born into this world without seeing the faces of at least one of his parents. And while one's first memory may be buried deep, it is never buried forever."

"I don't remember my parents at all."

"But your mind does. You have only to unlock the memory."

Remo had gone away and meditated for five days, eating only cold rice and drinking only purified water. But no faces appeared in his mind's eye.

When he complained to the Master of Sinanju later, Chiun had dismissed his complaint with a curt "Then you are not ready."

"When will I be ready?"

"When your memory allows itself to be unfolded like chrysanthemum petals."

For years after that, Remo had shoved the question of his parents into the furthest recesses of his mind. He told himself that they must have died in a car accident, that he had not been abandoned, that there was a good reason someone had set him, an infant, in a wicker basket on an orphanage doorstep. To think otherwise was too painful.

Now, so many years later, Remo felt he was ready.

So he sat before his own grave and closed his brown eyes. If necessary, he would meditate all night until he had his answers.

The leaves swirled about him, and the rising moon was caught in the creaking copper beech branches that lay against the night sky like dead nerve endings. An owl hooted. He hooted again, and again and again until his calls became part of the lonesome night.

Remo looked deep into himself. Images came and went. The first face he remembered belonged to Sister Mary Margaret, her smooth face framed by the wimple of her habit. She, more than any of the other nuns, had raised him. She was quick with a ruler on the knuckles, but even quicker with a kind word.

The day he had left the orphanage to make his way in the world, the kindly light in her eyes was replaced by the glow of pride. But that was all the warmth she would give Remo Williams that day.

"God go with you, Remo Williams," she had said, shaking his hand with a firm detachment that said,

"We have done our best with you. Visit if you like, but this is no longer your home."

The coolness had stung. But in later years Remo had understood. He was responsible for himself now.

Other faces came. He saw his police-academy instructor, his Marine D.I., Kathy Gilhooly, whom he planned to marry before his old life had ended. The judge who sentenced him appeared. So did his lawyer. They had been bought off—although Remo hadn't known it then. The bitter lemony features of Harold W. Smith, the man who had engineered the frame, swam into view. Remo made him go away. He skipped over the wrinkled countenance of the Master of Sinanju. He would be of no help now.

A laughing little girl's face came after a while. Freya, his daughter by Jilda of Lakluun, the blond Viking warrior woman he had encountered during one of his trips to Korea. They were far from him now, safe from the dangerous life Remo led. Remo's face softened as he looked upon his daughter again. He hardly knew her, really. And in his mind's eye, Remo thought he could see a little of his own face in hers.

There was something about Freya's face that struck a deep, half-forgotten chord. Remo held the little girl's features before his mind's eye, turning the image sideways, trying to pin the inkling down.

It was there. Something was there. But it was elusive.

Remo refused to let it go.

In the gray hours before dawn, he thought he saw a new face. A woman's face. He had never seen the face before. Not as an adult. But it was familiar to him somehow.

Her face was an oval, and her hair hung down long and straight and black. It was a good face, with warm, loving eyes and a high, intelligent forehead. It reminded him of Freya's face. They had the same eyes.

His own eyes still closed, Remo reached out as if to touch her.

The image faded. He tried to summon it again. But it wouldn't come.

Then a voice spoke. "If I could stand up..."

It was a woman's voice. But it wasn't in his mind. It was here. It was near him. His heart rate picking up, Remo opened his eyes.

There was only the grave with the name on it that might or might not be his true one.

Remo started to close his eyes again when the voice came again.

"If I could stand up where I lie..."

The voice was behind him. His ears told him that. But his other senses, the ones that had been raised to the pinnacle of human ability, told Remo there was no living thing behind him. His ears detected no beating heart, no crackle of rib cartilege from expanding lungs, no subtle friction of blood coursing through arteries and lesser veins. The bare back of his neck and arms detected no warning of human body heat.

But the voice sounded real. His sensitive eardrums still reverberated from its echoes.

Remo came to his feet like an unfolding telescope, whirling, alert and ready for anything.

The woman looked at him with infinitely sad yet warm eyes. Her hair was pulled tight off her high, smooth brow, but it was as black as the hair of the woman in his mind's eye. Her eyes were the same deep brown.

"Who—"

The woman continued, as if reciting a tone poem.

"If I could stand up where I lie, I would see mountains in all directions. There is a stream called Laughing Brook. If you find my resting place, you will find me."

"Huh?"

"If you find me, you will find him."

"Who—"

"You must find him, my son."

"Son?" Remo felt his heart jump like a salmon. "Moth—" The word caught in his throat. He had never called a woman that.

"It is too late for me, but your father lives."

"Who is he?"

"He is known to you, my son." The woman lifted a hand and reached out toward him.

Remo started forward, his right hand up and trembling.

Just before his fingers could touch hers, she faded from sight. Remo swept the empty air with his hands, but caught up only dead leaves.

The owl that had been silent for the past hour resumed its eerie call.

"Hoo...hoo...hoo."

Remo Williams stood at the foot of his own grave and trembled from head to toe. He had not trembled from fear since Vietnam. He had not trembled with anticipation since the last time he had known true love very long ago. And he had not trembled with any longing since he had come to Sinanju.

Now he trembled with all those emotions and more. He had seen his mother. She had spoken to him. He knew this with a certainty that rested not in his brain, but burned hot in the pit of his stomach.

He had not been forsaken after all.

Remo sank to his knees and wept tears of relief into the cool loam of the grave that was not truly his and slept until the rising sun sent its rays through the pink of his eyelids, snapping him to instant wakefulness.

He walked without a backward glance to his waiting car.

He had looked into the mirror of memory and saw true.

It was time to find himself.

3

Jack Koldstad hated jeopardy seizures.

They were the worst, nastiest, most dangerous operational responsibilites in his capacity as special agent for the Criminal Investigation Division of the Internal Revenue Service. Citizens were ordinarily touchy about being dunned for unpaid taxes or having liens put on their homes and bank accounts. *Touchy* wasn't the right word, actually. They often went bug-nuts, throwing insane screaming fits, threatening murder if they didn't get their way and promising suicide if that didn't work. The whole psychotic nine yards.

But at least they had some warning. The thirty-day letter. Then if they ignored that, the ninety-day letter. Followed by no-nonsense telephone calls. A series of firm, escalating steps designed to wear down the deadbeats and promote compliance with the tax code. Usually people came across. It was hard to stay mad at someone for months at a time—especially a faceless arm of Uncle Sam like the IRS.

But where a high risk of asset flight was indicated, the IRS was allowed by law to set aside its rules concerning seizure of assets and swoop down without warning. Jeopardy seizures, as the official terminology put it. The question was: jeopardy for whom?

You went in armed with a warrant, breaking down doors if necessary, and confiscated the disputed assets while the tax violator typically screamed for his lawyer. No polite notice. No warning. No nothing.

Usually the noncompliant taxpayer had the living shit scared out of him, and that was more than enough to cut the bull.

Sometimes it was the other way around.

Jack Koldstad had seized the private homes of Mafia dons, corporate criminals and other high-risk tax cheats many times during the course of a long career. Only rarely did he have to negotiate a standoff or swap fire.

Over the past dozen years, that had changed for the worse. It changed with the coming of cocaine and its derivatives, crack, crank and all that evil stuff. It changed with the rise of the drug kingpin with his unlimited financial power and his ruthless willingness to use that power to preserve his empire of white powder. The drug lords were the only group that never learned to fear the cold arm of the IRS.

Once the service began going after the drug barons, the rules of the game changed. Bulletproof vests became standard IRS issue. So did 9 mm side arms, shotguns and—this was an IRS first—casualties. Agents began dying in the line of duty. Some were targeted for assassination. The IRS had instituted a policy of allowing agents to interface with the public under sanctioned on-file aliases to protect them from retribution. It was a whole new ball game.

Which was why Jack Koldstad had come to hate jeopardy seizures. Who the hell wants to take a bullet for the tax code?

So there were precautions he had learned to take. Go in in overwhelming numbers, cut off all escape routes and make damn sure the phone lines are down. Otherwise, you could knock on a door, and while your troops are spreading out, the cheat is calling for reinforcements—or worse, the cops. More than once Koldstad had had police officers draw down on his men, thinking they were black hats or some damn thing.

Folcroft Sanitarium offered a model scenario. One route in and one out. Off the beaten track. And the phone lines were up on poles, not buried in underground pipe.

It should have been a textbook seizure. Go in hard and loud, and flash the warrant. Shout down any resistance. Get the job done.

Folcroft was a private hospital, for Christ's sake. It should have gone by the book.

It started going wrong the second they raced through the open gates, Koldstad's burgundy Taurus in the lead.

They had surveyed the area by helicopter the day before. The fact that the hospital fronted Long Island Sound had been worrisome, but no escape boat was tied up at the dock. Hell, the dock was so decrepit, it looked all set to fall into the water.

A water escape was ruled highly improbable.

But when they came through the gates, Koldstad was shocked to see boats converging on the same rickety dock. Sleek white Cigarette boats, the kind popular with your basic drug runner.

It was Koldstad's absolute worst-case scenario. They had sailed into the middle of a drug drop.

"What do we do?" asked the trainee, Greenwood. "We're outnumbered."

"Too late to worry about that," Koldstad bit out. Into his walkie-talkie, he shouted, "It's a damn drop! We gotta take them down before we can secure the site. Everybody out—now!"

The vehicles screamed, slewing to a crowded stop. Doors popped. Agents piled out, weapons coming up. They crouched behind their vehicles, pistols steady in two-handed marksman's grips. Koldstad took up a kneeling position with his arms stretched out, the butt of his 9 mm Taurus resting on the hood of his car, the engine block protecting his body. Beside him Greenwood copied the stance. He licked his dewy upper lip nervously.

The boats didn't bother with the dock. They ran aground on the shelf of mud below the grass, and men jumped out in blacksuits and cradling Uzis and shotguns. Their faces were masked—black pullover hoods that covered the entire head except for a filly oblong around the eyes.

From behind the shelter of his Taurus, Koldstad called out, "Drop your weapons!" He didn't say IRS. The manual called for it, but hard experience had taught him those three letters usually incited a non-compliant taxpayer to greater violence.

The men from the boats dropped to their bellies and out of the line of fire before a single warning shot could be squeezed off.

"Damn!" Koldstad said. He got down and tried to see under the car. There was no sign of them. They were good.

Greenwood leaned down, his voice excited. "I think I can reconnoiter over to their position by crawling on my belly, sir."

"Quiet!" Koldstad snapped.

Then the first perforated gun barrel poked over the slope of the grass. It angled around like a questing snout.

Greenwood got down on his hands and knees, trying to peer around the right front tire.

Koldstad opened his mouth to warn him. Too late.

The questing perforated snout popped once.

A bullet came and shredded the tread before it mushroomed into Greenwood's brain. It exited, carrying away a piece of skull and scalp the size of a human palm. Greenwood rocked back as if kicked, splaying onto the ground like a beached starfish.

"Open fire!" Koldstead screamed.

After that it was bedlam. The air shivered and shook with screaming rounds. Hot shell casings rolled smoking on the ground. The grassy clods at the edge of the lawn jumped like stung frogs. The return fire was murderous. Punch holes began appearing on the other side of the official IRS vehicles.

The IRS with their handguns and small arms were no match for the superior fire being directed at them. Their only advantage was in having the high ground. Koldstad ordered his men to lay down a sustained fire so the enemy didn't dare poke their heads up to aim.

That didn't stop them. The enemy just angled their weapons up and fired blindly. The sedan, van and delivery truck took most of the damage. Safety glass showered in nuggets. Tires burst and hissed until they were flat. Under the blazing onslaught, the three vehicles actually drummed and rocked on their springs.

"Get behind your engine blocks!" Koldstad ordered.

A man, moving to obey, caught one in the ankle. Screaming, he grabbed himself.

Koldstad shot to pieces a hand trying to angle an Uzi at them in return. That only seemed to make them madder because there came a lull while the enemy regrouped, and suddenly they were coming up over the grass slope, yelling and firing like damn Comanches.

"What's that they're yelling?" Koldstad cried over the din.

No one answered. They were too busy firing back.

Koldstad joined the fire storm. He picked a man at random and perforated his thigh. The man stumbled and rolled. On the black front of his battle suit, there was a white smudge. Koldstad caught a glimpse of it as the man fell. It was unreadable, but familiar.

"Cease fire! Cease fire!" Koldstad ordered.

An agent man turned to call, "What?"

"I said cease your damn shooting!"

But it was too late. No one paid any attention. His men were too busy trying to preserve their lives.

"IRS! IRS!" Koldstad shouted. "Dammit, we're with the Internal Revenue Service!"

The window glass was really flying now.

Abruptly Koldstad fell on the body of Greenwood, stripping him of his blue windbreaker with the letters IRS stenciled on the back. The letters were stained with blood now.

Koldstad took a chance. He reached up and snapped off the car antenna. A bullet gouged the car hood less than a foot from his eager fingers. Then he hung the jacket on the thing and with both hands paid it up so it stuck up above the line of the hood.

It began kicking and twitching under the lash of bullets.

"Dammit, read the letters!" Koldstad said through too-tight teeth.

Then, to make matters worse, his agents began running out of ammo.

They looked at him with sick, confused eyes.

Koldstad dropped the antenna and, as the gunmen in black came surging around from both directions, he lifted his hands above his head.

"We surrender!"

His men, helpless, followed suit. Except for those who were trying to hide under the chassis of their vehicles.

A thick-set man in a shapeless white hood came around with a shotgun.

"Freeze!" he yelled, finger white on the trigger. "DEA!"

"IRS!" Koldstad screamed back. "We're the goddamn IRS!"

There was a moment of stunned silence. Jaws dropped slowly, and faces turned gray and then drained bone white.

A DEA man vomited violently. Others began retching. His own face fish white, Jack Koldstad climbed to his feet. But only after the white finger on the shotgun trigger relaxed and turned pink again.

"You in charge here?" Koldstad demanded.

The thick man stripped off his white hood to reveal a shaggy red beard and no-nonsense eyes. "Tardo. Drug Enforcement Administration."

"Koldstad. IRS. You just shot the shit out of three official cars, not to mention my trainee."

"You drew down on us first," Tardo pointed out, his voice surly.

"You barbarians were storming ashore like this was the beach at Normandy," Koldstad said hotly. "Of course we drew down on you first. We thought you were drug runners."

"Like hell."

"We're seizing this hospital for failure to report income in excess of ten thousand dollars and for violating Title 21, Section 881 of the United States Code."

Tardo's blunt face darkened. "This is a suspected turkey-drug factory. It's ours."

"What do you base that on?"

"A telephone tipoff that large wire transfers go through the Folcroft bank account regularly."

Koldstad blinked. "That's what red-flagged us, too. But we have jurisdiction."

"No way. This is our bust."

The two men stepped up to each other until their noses almost met. They glared. Around them their men fingered their weapons uneasily.

"I've got three wounded," Tardo said. "That makes this mine."

"And I have one wounded and one dead agent. Trump that ace."

Tardo showed his teeth as he ground them in anger.

"We gotta cover each other's butt on this," he said, low voiced.

"I'm prepared to let the chips fall exactly where they will," Koldstad said. "Exactly."

"Tell you what. You get the medical equipment and any loose cash. We take the bank account, vehicles and, of course, any drugs we find. And DEA goes in first. Fair enough?"

"We already have a lien on the bank account," Koldstad said. "And a DEA bullet in a dead IRS agent. IRS goes in first."

Tardo scratched his beard thoughtfully. "That building looks to be worth a cool ten mil. It's yours uncontested if we can keep the mutual embarrassment to a minimum. What say?"

"Done."

Tardo offered his hand. "Shake on it?"

"Greenwood does all my hand shaking for me."

"Which one is he?"

"The one with his brains fertilizing the damn grass," Koldstad said tightly.

4

The Master of Sinanju usually awoke with the sun.

But there was no sun where he slept. All was dark. There were no windows in this place of gray walls and bad, musty air where the sun never shone.

He was old—so old that in almost the entire history of the human race a man was counted fortunate if he lived half of the current life span of the Master of Sinanju, who had already seen one hundred winters—even if he now slept on a simple reed mat in the lowermost dungeon of the brick fortress of his emperor, which was called Folcroft.

But it was necessary, and so Chiun, Reigning Master of Sinanju, endured it.

And he did not need the rising sun to inform his senses that a new day had arrived. His perfect body told him that. His clear brain accepted the knowledge, and so he awoke each morning at the correct hour.

On this morning his body still slept when his perfect ears were assaulted by rudeness.

Without hesitating, his upper body snapped upward, his mind and eyes coming open simultaneously, as if a spring had uncoiled.

The walls of the Folcroft dungeon—called by Westerners a basement—were thick and made of the ugly sand-and-mud concoction called concrete. Still, sounds could penetrate it if they were loud enough.

These sounds were.

The sharp reports of pistols punctuated by the rattle of the noisier weapons carried by Westerners so incompetent they could not even kill with a single correctly delivered bullet reverberated dully. Men yelled in the coarse manner of the West, their voices high and hoarse.

"Boom sticks!" Chiun squeaked. "My emperor needs me!"

And he flung off his simple linen sleeping kimono, taking up the night black silk one that lay neatly folded at his bedside. It cracked open like a parachute before settling over him like a shroud. His tiny feet slid into simple black sandals.

Face determined, the Master of Sinanju cried aloud.

"Beware, defilers of Fortress Folcroft! Your doom has awakened!"

Then he hesitated.

"What if they have come for the gold?" he squeaked.

The gold lay in neat stacks on the other side of a triple-locked basement vault. Only Emperor Smith possessed the keys—not that Chiun would need keys to get at the gold, which was his payment for the coming year's worth of service. Normally it was shipped directly to the village of his ancestors. But the gold had been hijacked from the submarine conveying it to Sinanju, on the rocky and forbidding coast of North Korea, and had been recovered only with great difficulty.

Since the Master of Sinanju had recovered the gold himself, it was considered salvage. This was replacement gold, offered to seal the latest contract between America and Chiun, who headed the greatest house of assassins in human history, the House of Sinanju. Practitioners of the first and greatest martial art, also called Sinanju, the Masters of Sinanju had served the greatest thrones of the ancient world and now served the most powerful nation of the modern world, America.

While Smith—whom Chiun called emperor because it was traditional to do so—made arrangements for another submarine to convey this gold to Korea, it was being kept in the Folcroft basement. And as long as it remained upon American soil, Chiun had vowed to guard it with his life every waking moment. This was the reason he slept in ignominy.

Chiun regarded the triple-locked door, worry written in every spiderweb wrinkle in his parchment features. What to do? His emperor needed him. But emperors were mortal. Gold endured forever.

The firing continued. It was getting worse.

"What if they have come for the gold?" he squeaked. "I must remain here to guard it."

A man screamed, mortally wounded.

"But if they have come for Smith, it is my sacred duty to protect his life. For if I fail, the gold of America is forfeit."

The Master of Sinanju formed ivory yellow fists with his long-nailed fingers. He stood rooted to the dusty concrete of the floor, his body immobilized by the dire necessity of racing to the side of him whom he had sworn to protect and the equal need to safeguard the gold he had yet to earn. The wispy tail of his beard quivered with his torment. The puffs of snow over each ear likewise trembled. His hazel eyes squeezed into walnuts in his pain.

In the end the Master of Sinanju left the gold.

There was nothing else to do. His ancestors would either honor him or revile him after the events of this day. He did not know. But he would do his duty, and if his decision was a wrong one, a severe penalty would be exacted upon those who forced this odious decision upon him.

THE MASTER OF SINANJU padded purposefully up the sloping concrete floor to the corrugated steel door of the loading dock. He did not slow as he approached it. Instead, he lifted one hand, extending his index finger with its long, curving nail that looked so delicate.

Chiun brought the nail up and then down, and when it came into contact with the steel corrugations, the metal squealed and parted vertically.

Taking the sharp edges of the rip in his hand, the Master of Sinanju exerted simple opposing pressure. The vertical rent exploded apart. He stepped through onto the loading dock.

Chiun disdained the steps and dropped off the dock, his black skirts billowing as he landed with a grace that belied his great age.

Keeping to the edges of the building, he moved along the walls, turning corners like a floating black rag dragged by a stick. Even in the clear morning light, a watcher would have not read his movement as those of man, but as something fitful and inanimate.

Thus did the Master of Sinanju come upon the invaders of his emperor's fortress, unheralded and unsuspected.

They stood around the entrance, relaxed in their manner, their weapons lowered.

The faithful guard in blue knelt at their feet in abject surrender, his holster empty, his hands tied behind his back with a plastic loop. It was shameful to behold. The man should have given his life before allowing this to come to pass.

The invaders in their black garments stood watch, obviously confident that their fellows had captured their prize. By their manner, it was already too late. Folcroft had fallen. The way their eyes fell voraciously upon the steel vehicles in the parking lot told him this.

Chiun withdrew. Stealth was called for now, not death. The Master of Sinanju would deal out death in his own time.

The walls of Folcroft were of brick. Coming to a point where he would not be seen, the Master of Sinanju stopped and took hold of the bricks where they met. He began climbing upward, hands and feet bringing him effortlessly to the second floor.

He paused on a windowsill, and the fingernail that had been hardened by years of diet and exercise and will showed that it could defeat glass as well as steel. Chiun traced a circle in the pane with a swift motion that compressed the squeak of the glass into a short bark that might be mistaken for a dog's.

Still, it was a sound, and it carried.

A man entered the room, gun in hand. His eyes swept the room and came to rest upon the figure of the Master of Sinanju floating on the other side of the window glass.

Bringing a weapon from under his coat, he identified himself.

"IRS!"

Tapping the circle, Chiun reached in in time to catch the circle of glass before it fell. He flicked his wrist. The disc of glass sailed across the room and through the open door, neatly separating the man standing there from his head.

Chiun entered through the circular opening and padded past the invader who lay quivering in two parts, an expression of wonderment on his upturned face. Chiun erased the expression with the heel of his sandal. It erased his face, as well.

"Barley drinkers," Chiun hissed.

Moving down the corridor, his ears captured sounds.

"Get a doctor," a man yelled. "He's choking!"

"Anybody know the Heimlich Manuever? Get him to cough it up!"

The shouting was coming from the direction of Smith's office.

Chiun picked up his pace. His feet seemed to but brush the floor, but they propelled him along like a gazelle. His pipe-stem arms churning in his swishing kimono sleeves, and his pumping legs made his silken skirts swirl in agitation.

No one heard his approach; no one sensed his growing shadow.

They would not be aware of him until his hands were at their vitals—and the moment in which they would recognize their doom would be as brief as a spark.

FROM THE MOMENT he stepped into Folcroft Sanitarium, it only got worse for Jack Koldstad.

The lobby guard was standing in front of his desk, his hands in the air, his revolver at his feet. His arms trembled.

"These premises are hereby seized by order of the commissioner of the Internal Revenue Service," Koldstad barked.

"Okay by me," the guard said, his voice quavering. "Dr. Smith said to do whatever you fellas say."

An agent stiffened. "Did you hear that? He knew we were coming!"

"Where is Smith?" Koldstad barked.

"Second floor. Right off the elevator. Can't miss it."

Koldstad turned to his aide. "Hand this flunky off to DEA. It'll give them something to do besides scratching themselves while we secure the building."

Koldstad led his men up the stairs. An elevator could be stopped by cutting the power. It had happened to him twice before he learned to take the stairs even if it was fifty flights up.

There was an ample-bosomed woman about fifty years old trembling behind a second-floor reception desk. Her hands were caught up around her throat.

Koldstad flashed his ID in her jowly face. "IRS. Where's Harold W. Smith?"

"Dr. Smith is . . . is in his office."

They went in, guns drawn. Koldstad took point.

They found Harold Smith behind his desk, clutching his throat and lunging for something behind him.

"Freeze! IRS!"

His face turning purple, Harold Smith ignored the order.

"Dammit, I said 'Freeze!' "

Someone shouted in Koldstad's ear. "He's going for a gun!"

Koldstad fired a warning shot past Smith's gray head. It struck the plate-glass window behind him, bringing it down in large, dangerous shards.

A flat triangle of glass struck Smith on the head. He went down.

Koldstad rushed to his side, knocked the glass away and turned him over.

Smith's face was a strange color—purple gray. The gray was giving way to the purple hue.

"He's going into cardiac arrest!" an agent said.

Koldstad saw the crumpled paper cup in Smith's hand and noticed the water dispenser. "Dammit, he's choking. Get him some water!"

While an agent struggled with the water dispenser, Jack Koldstad fought to pry Harold Smith's strong jaws open. Smith set his teeth, and his jaw muscles hardened to stone.

"Stop fighting me, dammit! I'm trying to save you!"

Smith clenched his teeth all the more. He was coughing violently, and the cough had nowhere to go except out his nose. Expelled air mixed with hot mucus spattered Koldstad across the face.

"Dammit, Smith. I'm trying to help you!"

His eyes rolling up in his head, Smith clawed Koldstad's face with blunt fingernails.

"Give me a hand here!" Koldstad shouted.

Two agents dropped to their knees in the cramped space behind Smith's desk and fought to hold the elderly man down.

"What's wrong with this guy? He doesn't want to be saved."

"Maybe he swallowed poison," an agent suggested.

"Where's that doctor, dammit? Who knows the Heimlich maneuver? We can't have another casualty. It'll be our pensions."

Then a voice like a brass gong filled the room.

"Hold!"

All heads turned toward the sound. Koldstad's head came around. And he couldn't believe his eyes.

A tiny Asian man stood in the room. He was hardly more than five feet tall, looked older than God and wore a kimono that belonged on a geisha. The door was blocked by two armed IRS agents. Yet he had gotten past them. The twin dumbfounded expressions roosting on the guard's faces told that tale.

"Who the hell are you?" Koldstad said hotly.

"I am Chiun, personal physician to that man you are manhandling. Stand aside, barley drinkers, for only I can help him."

"Barley—"

"Make haste if you wish to spare his life."

Koldstad hesitated. Smith let go with another violent suppressed cough, and the hot mucus that splattered across the front of Koldstad's coat decided him.

"Give that man room to work."

The agents withdrew as the tiny Asian knelt.

"O Smith, speak the words I wish to hear."

Smith opened his mouth.

"Kkk—"

"I do not understand you, Smith."

"Kikkk—"

"He's trying to say something, but there's something caught in his throat," Koldstad said.

And as Koldstad watched, the tiny Asian used two delicate-looking fingers to pry apart Harold Smith's jaws. Koldstad had tried the same thing, and his strength hadn't been near enough.

But the old guy acted as if he were picking apart the petals of a rose. Smith's jaws parted. He hacked.

Keeping the jaws apart with one hand, the tiny Asian reached into his mouth to get at the obstructing object lodged deep within.

"You'll need to Heimlich him to get it out, whatever it is."

"Silence! I need silence to save this man."

Then the old guy began massaging Smith's angular Adam's apple with a caressing thumb.

Smith heaved out a violent hack, and something seemed to pop up from his mouth. It was white, and Koldstad tried to track it with his eyes. He lost it as it sailed past the old doctor's shoulder. Koldstad blinked. It seemed to disappear in midair. He approached, face quizzical. He hadn't heard the sound of the white object falling to the floor. The floor was polished pine. There should have been a click.

While Koldstad was searching the floor, Harold Smith subsided.

"Speak, Smith."

"Kikk—"

"Swallow. It will ease your throat."

"Here's some water," said Koldstad, handing over a cup filled with water.

Smith swallowed. There were tears in his eyes.

The first word he got out was "Kill..."

Koldstad asked, "What did he say?"

"I do not know."

"...me..." added Smith.

"Hush, Smith. You are distraught. You require rest."

"Kill me," said Harold Smith. "Please." His gray eyes were locked with those of the old Asian. They pleaded.

"Did he just ask you to kill him?"

"He has been under great strain of late. We must get him to his bed to rest."

"Not before I finish official business," Koldstad said, looming over the stricken man. "Harold Smith, I am seizing this hospital for willful failure to pay income taxes, concealing income from the Internal Revenue Service, violating the Money Laundering Control Act of 1983 by illegally importing into this country income in amounts exceeding ten thousand dollars and failing to pay the lawful taxes thereon."

Smith suddenly fainted. He collapsed onto the floor as if defeated. There was no warning. He had started to sit up when the old Asian simply touched the center of his forehead as if to flick a bead of sweat away. Instead, Smith all but fell apart under the touch.

"Damn," said Koldstad.

The old Asian arose. "Summon a doctor to take him to his bed of rest."

Koldstad narrowed suspicious eyes. "I thought you said you were his doctor."

"You misunderstood. I am his adviser."

"Financial adviser?"

"Adviser. I am called Chiun."

Koldstad whirled on his men, red faced. "Somebody confirm this. Drag that weepy secretary in here."

Mrs. Mikulka was brought in trembling.

"Why are you people doing this?" she asked tearfully. "Dr. Smith is one of the—"

"—lowest forms of life on the planet today," Jack Koldstad said harshly. "A suspected tax evader."

"Suspected! Is that any reason to come into a hospital with drawn guns?"

"Where tax revenue is concerned, Uncle Sam doesn't take prisoners." Koldstad pointed to Chiun. "Do you know this man?"

"Yes, that is Mr. Chiun."

"So you know him?"

"Yes. He is a former patient who often returns to Folcroft."

"Patient?"

"I understand he is completely cured of his delusions."

"What delusions?"

"I don't know exactly. But he has been known to refer to Dr. Smith as 'Emperor.'"

"Emperor of what?"

"Of America, of course," replied the old Asian named Chiun.

All eyes went to him. Koldstad strode up to the tiny Oriental, towering over him. "Did you say America?"

"Yes. Smith secretly rules this land."

"What about the President?"

Chiun shrugged his black silk shoulders. "A mere puppet. Disposable and unimportant."

"And you're his adviser?"

"I stand by his throne and protect him from his enemies."

"Get a real doctor in here!" Koldstad shouted. "Fast. And place this little yellow nut under arrest."

"Catch me if you can," squeaked Chiun.

And in a swirl of skirts, he turned, making for the door.

"Stop him!"

The IRS agents at the door gave it their best. Their best involved dropping into a crouch, hands splayed as if to catch a fumbled football. It looked like a good strategy. But they were playing the wrong kind of ball.

The Master of Sinanju struck them like a black bowling ball. They cartwheeled in midair like tenpins, only to fall clutching one another in the mistaken impression they had grabbed their intended target.

Koldstad stepped over them and looked up and down the corridor. Something reached up and pulled him down by his navy blue necktie. His face struck the floor with so much force he bounced back to a standing position and had to be helped over to a couch.

"Dammit, what kind of madhouse is Smith running here?" Koldstad barked through bloody fingers that clutched his bruised nose.

"This *is* a sanitarium," Mrs. Mikulka pointed out timidly.

5

Remo Williams noticed the circling birds first.

There was something wrong about the birds. He couldn't put his finger on it as he drove up the wooded road to Folcroft Sanitarium, but the birds were wrong. Very wrong.

His senses had been developed to the pinnacle of human achievement and beyond. His eyes could spot a deer tick making its way along its host from a distance of half a mile by the near-imperceptible movement of the deer's guard hairs.

The birds circled Folcroft in high, lazy spirals like condors. Remo thought of condors. Condors were not native to North America, so they couldn't be condors. Vultures, probably. Their wingspreads were too great for hawks, their bodies too small for sea gulls.

As Remo negotiated the winding road, his eyes kept going to the circling birds. They were black against the rising sun, and that made it harder for even his eyes to make out their color and nature.

Vultures, Remo decided. Vultures for sure. But why were they circling Folcroft as if it was dead?

As he got closer, he began to smell blood. The metallic tang hung in the early-morning air. There were other smells—death smells. Sinanju had not taught him to proceed cautiously when he smelled them. He had learned that as a Marine, back in Nam.

Pulling over to the side of the road, Remo got out. There were leaves underfoot. Without having to look down, his feet avoided them perfectly. That he hadn't learned in Vietnam. That was Sinanju, and so deeply ingrained it was second nature.

Remo moved on to the trees, easing from bole to bole until he found an oak tall enough to do him some good. He went up it.

Half the leaves were gone, but there was foliage enough to conceal him provided he didn't move.

From the branches Remo spotted the unguarded gate to Folcroft. There was a sign on one of the brick gate pillars. It read:

NO TRESPASSING
GOVERNMENT PROPERTY
SEIZED BY ORDER OF THE
INTERNAL REVENUE SERVICE

The black block letters were printed over the IRS seal.

"Damn, damn, damn," Remo said.

In the early days of his work for CURE, the supersecret agency that didn't exist, there had been a number of standing orders. Paramount among them was what to do if Folcroft was compromised in any way: disappear. Since Remo was CURE's enforcement arm, his very existence was a security secret.

In the old days Remo had taken security seriously. The years had taught him differently. He had been officially dead more than two decades now. Although thanks to the succession of plastic surgeries and the strange effects of his Sinanju training, he looked almost exactly the same now as he did then. For all intents and purposes, Remo hadn't aged. That very fact meant that if any old friend from his past ever came across him, knowing Remo had been executed by the State of New Jersey, he would naturally have leaped to a logical conclusion: Remo was his own son.

Remo had never had a son. Had never been married. But the days when he had to stay away from New Jersey and his past were long over. No one would assume that Remo Williams was above ground. Even if they did, the world wouldn't come to an end. Remo could be in the witness-protection program for all anyone knew. It was all Harold Smith bullshit.

Remo had had enough of Smith's bullshit. That was why he had quit CURE the week before. Technically he was a free agent, but he had agreed to stick around for the duration of Chiun's next contract on one condition: that Smith use CURE's massive computer outreach to help Remo locate his parents, living or dead.

Smith had agreed. Chiun, surprisingly, had gone along with it all. But Remo was serious this time. A year hence he would kiss Harold Smith, CURE and Folcroft Sanitarium goodbye. Forever.

Chiun, he would worry about then.

But as he hung in the crown of the oak, Remo understood that something unexpected had happened, something that promised to cheat him out of the one chance he had to unearth his roots.

CURE was under stress as the result of an effort by an old enemy—a superintelligent artificial-intelligence microchip called Friend—to destroy the organization. Friend, whose programming was dedicated to the mindless making of profit and the unremitting accumulation of wealth, had struck at CURE in a brilliant three-prong attack calculated to render the agency nonfunctional.

It had come at a critical time. Chiun had just negotiated the contract for the coming year. The gold had been shipped to the village of Sinanju on the West Korea Bay by submarine. A renegade North Korean frigate captain had commandeered it, destroying the sub and seizing the gold. Without gold, the contract was void. Without gold, the Master of Sinanju had withdrawn his services, along with Remo's.

At the same time Friend had struck at Remo indirectly. By a subtle manipulation of the data in the CURE computer system, a man's name had bubbled up to catch Smith's attention. A fugitive hit man, long wanted by the authorities. Exactly the kind of hit that Remo routinely handled between higher-priority assignments.

Remo had tracked him down on Smith's orders. And killed what was later discovered to be an innocent man in front of his wife and daughter. Their horrified faces still haunted Remo, shocking him enough to question his role as a secret assassin for an even more secret arm of the United States government.

When Chiun had balked at another year's service because of the missing shipment of gold, Remo already had one foot out the door.

The trouble continued piling up from there. CURE's computers became unreliable. Something somehow had managed to sever Harold Smith's direct telephone line to the President of the United States. CURE was cut off from the one U.S. official who knew it existed.

It was a masterful plan, and CURE should not have survived. But it had. The gold had been recovered. Friend had been deactivated as he was consummating a brilliant attempt to blackmail the U.S. government through computer manipulation designed to paralyze the federal banking system.

But the damage had been done. CURE had been hobbled, and all Remo cared about now was uncovering his past. The future would take care of itself.

And now this.

Remo wondered if the President had had something to do with this. Smith hadn't been getting along with the new President. They were like oil and water. And Friend had managed to divert the last of CURE's operating funds from its offshore bank. Smith had been trying to trace the lost taxpayer funds for over a week now. The President had not been happy to hear about that. The very existence of CURE offended him.

Maybe, Remo mused, he had decided to lower the boom this way.

Stepping to the ground, he decided to find out.

Moving low, Remo made his way to the sound. He eased into it, the cool water swallowing his bare feet. He had stepped out of his Italian loafers. The water drank his thighs, his waist and, after his dark hair dipped into the cool blue surface, the water regathered as if he had never been there.

No disturbance marked Remo's progress. He swam effortlessly, arms trailing loosely, feet kicking easily. So quiet was his progress that a sunfish failed to notice him until Remo had already passed his line of sight. Then it twisted away in staring-eyed panic.

When the rotting piles of the Folcroft dock—a relic of some long-ago period before Folcroft had been built—came into view, Remo arrowed toward the ground.

He came out of the water like a seal, on his stomach. The entire operation was soundless.

Lying on the mud, Remo lifted his head.

The smell of blood was still strong. Over the L-shaped brick building that was the headquarters for CURE, the three circling birds still described their tight looping pattern. Remo focused on them.

For the first time since he had embraced the sun source called Sinanju, his eyes failed him. The birds remained black against the sky of the new day, like living shadows. Remo couldn't make out their true color, never mind their markings and distinguishing features.

Not sea gulls, not vultures, not really like any birds he knew.

The skin along his bare forearms tightened with a vague fear.

Remo shifted his gaze to the window he knew was Harold Smith's. He didn't expect to see into it. The opacity of the one-way glass defeated even his sharp eyes.

The window was broken. Through the angular hole in the pane, Remo spotted figures moving about. Men in suits. Men who didn't belong in Harold Smith's office.

There was no sign of Smith.

Remo shifted his gaze. The water was draining from his clothes, and he was willing his body temperature to rise by fifteen degrees. That would take care of the remaining dampness in his clothes.

There were Cigarette boats beached in the mud not far from him. They were empty. The ground around the rise when the mud became high ground had been chewed up by feet and something more vicious.

The air was thick with stale gunpowder smell, Remo noticed. Digging his fingers into the tiny burrow in the mud, he pulled out an intact 9 mm round.

Someone had attacked Folcroft by boat. That much was clear. But who had fought them back? Although Folcroft was technically one of America's most secret installations, Smith had never installed sophisticated security systems. There was only a single lobby guard, no barbed wire or electrified fences, no motion-sensing detectors or other such safeguards. Smith believed that installing such trappings would merely serve to advertise Folcroft's importance. He might as well string up Christmas lights that spelled out Secret High Security Installation. Do Not Enter.

It was Smith's New England sensibleness that betrayed him. Folcroft had been assaulted and taken. It had never happened before.

When Remo's clothes were dry enough to leave no dripping trail, he got up off his flat stomach and started to reconnoiter.

There were men standing about the Folcroft entrance, men in black fighting suits with various assault weapons slung from shoulders and belts. They smoked nervously. The way they hung their heads and slumped their shoulders jarred.

Their bodies screamed failure, not victory.

Remo spotted the letters DEA on the back of one man's jacket.

It didn't exactly clarify the situation, so he moved off to the southern exposure.

He knew Chiun had been sleeping in the Folcroft basement, guarding the gold he had wrangled from Smith until arrangements to ship it to Sinanju could be finalized. The Master of Sinanju had not let Remo forget it. Remo was supposed to take the day trick. And he was a half hour late.

Remo figured Chiun would be with the gold. When he found Chiun, he would start to find some answers.

Remo made it to the freight entrance without being spotted. Once he passed a DEA agent pissing behind a parked car. The man never so much as smelled the odor of sea salt clinging to Remo's clothing.

The corrugated freight door looked as if King Kong had punched his fist through it. The force was clearly outward, not inward. Chiun leaving. Only the Master of Sinanju could split corrugated steel so neatly down the middle before forcing the hole open.

Remo went in anyway.

The basement was dim and musty. The concrete floor sloped downward. There were no sounds or smells of intruders.

Remo reached Chiun's sleeping mat, found the hastily discarded sleeping kimono on the floor and understood that the assault had come with the dawn. Chiun had been lying here when the shooting had started and flung his sleeping kimono aside in his haste. Normally the Master of Sinanju was too fastidious to toss it aside so carelessly.

Remo went to the triple-locked door in an otherwise blank concrete wall. In the dark his eyes saw true. The locks were secure, the door closed. That meant the gold was safe. It was probably the chief reason those DEA agents were lounging about the front lawn and not floating as dismembered body parts on the sound being nibbled at by the fishes.

From behind the door came a bitter tang. Not blood. Certainly not gold, which hadn't a specific smell, although Chiun had long insisted that he could smell gold at a distance of six Korean *ri*—about three miles.

Remo eased up to the door. He retreated suddenly, holding his nose. The smell was burned plastic. Smith's computers. He had destroyed them. Not a good sign. Smith would sooner take the poison pill he kept in the watch pocket of his vest than destroy his precious mainframes.

The realization hit Remo then. "Damn!"

Reversing, he made for the stairs. The worst had happened. Smith was by now either dead or dying.

"Damn that Smith," Remo hissed. "What the hell's wrong with him? The IRS isn't the KGB."

He glided up the stairs.

There goes my last hope of tracking down my parents, Remo thought bitterly.

An IRS agent was standing guard at the top of the stairs. He made the mistake of challenging Remo.

"Halt. Who goes there?"

Remo went for his wallet, intending to flash one of his many fictitious ID cards supplied by Smith. He was wondering if he should try to outrank the IRS agent with his Remo Eastwood Secret Service badge or bluff him with his Remo Helmsley IRS special agent's card.

The point became moot when the agent pulled out a 9 mm Glock.

Remo yanked the Glock out of the agent's hand and inserted the blunt barrel into his mouth. The IRS agent looked surprised, then bewildered, then a thin golden stream began to come out of his left pant cuff to cut into the high polish of his cordovans.

"I'm an innocent citizen," Remo grated. "Who are you?"

The agent managed to get the mushy letters *IRS* past his chipped teeth and plastic side arm.

"Since when does that give you cause to shoot at an innocent hospital employee?"

The man's explanation refused to get past the Glock, so Remo removed it, keeping the barrel hovering menacingly. The agent understood Remo had no intention of shooting him. His finger wasn't even on the trigger. But having felt the impact on his teeth, he recognized the threat.

"You can't do this to the IRS."

"The IRS did it to me first. Now I want answers."

The thin stream petered out as the agent got his answer organized. "This hospital has been seized by IRS order."

"I saw the sign. Why? And don't tell me for deducting his 900-number calls. Harold Smith is as honest as the day is long."

"The days are getting shorter. Smith failed to report over twelve million dollars of income. That makes him a money launderer. Maybe a drug dealer."

"Drugs! Smith?"

"This is a private hospital. A perfect cover for illicit drug dealing."

"That why the DEA is standing outside, scratching themselves?"

The IRS man nodded. "They landed just as we pulled in through the gate. There were two separate operations. We got the worst of it, fortunately."

"What do you mean, fortunately?"

"Well, we lost a man, but he was only a trainee. And another agent took one in the ankle. That gave us the moral high ground to claim jurisdiction."

"That's gotta be worth a man and an ankle," Remo said dryly.

"Without tax revenue, there is no America," the agent said in a wounded voice.

"Tell it to Thomas Jefferson."

"Who?"

"The founding father who said something about taxation without representation being tyranny."

"Never heard of him."

"Do tell. Where's Smith?"

"They took him to intensive care."

"Dead?"

"We don't know what's wrong with him. He's stiff as a corpse. Paralyzed, but his eyes are open." The agent repressed a visible shudder.

"Sounds scary," Remo remarked.

"I wouldn't want that to happen to me."

"Perish the thought," said Remo, reaching up to tap the man on the exact center of his forehead, where his third eye was supposed to be. The man went out like a human light. Remo grabbed him by his tie and eased him to the floor.

Remo left him lying flat on his back, stiff as a board. But not before he stopped to peel back the agent's eyelids and remove the opaque glass dome from an overhead light so the harsh bulb glare struck him full in his unprotected eyes.

Maybe the guy wouldn't go blind when he came to again, but he'd be wearing sunglasses for the next year.

Remo went up the steps. He met Mrs. Mikulka, Smith's longtime private secretary, who was carrying down a cardboard box. She was fighting back tears.

"What's going on?" Remo asked.

She caught at her throat. "Oh, you startled me."

"Sorry."

"I've been fired."

"Smith fired you?"

"No. The IRS."

"How can they fire you?"

"They have taken over the hospital. I barely had time to get my things together." She showed him the cardboard box, whose top flaps hung open and forlorn.

Remo looked into the box. "It's empty," he said.

"They confiscated my personal effects."

"Why?"

"They called them assets. My poor son's graduation photo was all they let me keep. And only because I fought them for it."

"Look," Remo said sympathetically, "I'm sure we can get this straightened out. You go home and wait for the all-clear."

"Poor Dr. Smith is in intensive care. They burst in on him as if he were some sort of criminal. But he's not like that. Not at all. He's the dearest man. Why, when my son passed away—"

"Smith up on the third floor?"

"Yes."

"Go home. Someone will call you when everything gets straightened out."

On the third floor Remo eased the fire door open. The buzz of voices was a blur. He couldn't make out any one voice in particular. He was in the process of zeroing in on one voice when he became aware of a subtle warmth on the cool stairwell.

Remo whirled.

The Master of Sinanju stood regarding him with brittle eyes.

"What happened?" Remo asked.

"Idiots happened. Why are you not guarding the gold?"

"I could ask the same of you," Remo said pointedly.

"It was our agreement that I sleep with the gold and that you pass your idle waking hours guarding the gold. When I was awakened by rudeness and ignorance, you were not there."

"I was paying my respects."

Chiun made a disgusted face. "You have no respects. Not for yourself. Not for the one who exalted you above all others of your stumbling ilk." Chiun's hazel eyes narrowed suddenly. "Respects to whom?"

"To myself. I went to the grave last night."

"Only a white would mourn for himself."

"I looked into the mirror of memory."

Chiun cocked his birdlike head to one side. "And?"

"I saw a woman's face. She had Freya's eyes." Remo lowered his voice to a whisper. "Chiun, I think it was my mother."

"You did not see your father?"

"No."

"How could you summon up your mother and not your father?"

"Because my mother appeared to me."

"Like a spirit?"

"Exactly."

"What was this lying wench wearing?"

"That's no way to speak about my mother, dammit."

Chiun clapped long-nailed hands together. Dust filtered down from the ceiling in response. "Answer!"

"I don't remember," Remo admitted.

"You have the eyes of a hawk and you do not remember common clothes?"

Remo thought about that a moment. "I don't think she was wearing any."

"Your mother was naked?"

"No. I can't explain it. I don't remember her being naked, but I know she wasn't wearing clothes."

Chiun's hazel eyes narrowed thinly. "You did indeed see your mother, Remo."

"She was trying to tell me how to find my father. She said if she could stand up where she lay, she could see mountains and a stream called Laughing Brook."

"Your mother is dead, Remo."

"I know," Remo said softly.

"But your father is not."

"She thought it was important for me to find him."

"Then it is. But first we have work to do."

"Without Smith, I don't have a prayer of finding anyone. What the hell's going on?"

"I do not know. I awoke to rudeness and boom sticks booming, and then the barley drinkers were swarming over Folcroft."

"Barley drinkers?"

"The lesser English."

"Lesser?"

"The Irish terrorists. Those who break knees and mothers' hearts with their cruelty."

"You mean the IRS?"

"Exactly."

"Little Father, the Irish terrorists are called the IRA. Irish Republican Army. The IRS is the Internal Revenue Service."

Chiun squeaked, "Those who tax! The taxing ones?"

"Exactly."

"They must not find my gold. Quickly! We must go to guard it."

"What about Smith?" asked Remo.

"I have placed him in the sleep from which only I can awaken him. The fool attempted to end his life with poison."

"Just because the IRS landed on him?"

"No doubt he is guilty of skimming vast sums from his overseers. That can await. The gold must be moved."

"We move that gold, and the IRS will be on us like white on rice—excuse the expression."

"Then we must dispatch these IRS confiscators."

"We can't do that," said Remo.

"Why not? If we kill them all, they will leave us alone."

"You don't know the IRS. They'll keep sending out agents until they get what they want."

"Then we will kill them all!" Chiun proclaimed.

"They'll just keep swearing in more agents. It's a bottomless pit. Forget it, Little Father. We gotta solve this some other way."

"What other way?"

"I don't know, but we can't hang around this stairwell forever. Let's make tracks."

"I would rather make IRS bodies."

But the Master of Sinanju followed Remo down the stairs on cat feet.

On the way down, they heard a steady beating like a drum.

Doom doom doom doom . . .

"What the hell is that?" Remo wondered aloud.

"I do not know and I do not care," sniffed Chiun.

"Sounds familiar."

"We have more important matters before us than some lunatic beating an animal skin."

Remo stopped abruptly in front of a fire door. "Sounds like it's on the other side."

But when he flung open the door, there was only a deserted corridor. And the drumming had stopped.

Shrugging, Remo started back down. They reached the basement undetected.

Chiun flew to the triple-locked door and saw that it was secure.

"We must guard this with our lives," he said grimly.

"Look, can you hold the fort for an hour or so?" Remo asked, anxious voiced.

Chiun looked up at him suspiciously.

"Better than you, but what is so important that you would leave the one who raised you up from the muck of Christianity and other Western nonsense to defend the gold of his village alone?"

"There was something else my mother said," Remo said.

"What was it?"

"She said I knew my father."

"Then she is not your mother, for she lied to you."

"Her exact words were, 'He is known to you, my son.' She called me 'son.' I gotta find out who she is, Chiun."

And seeing the troubled light in his pupil's dark eyes, the Master of Sinanju said, "I give you one hour. But what do you expect to accomplish in so brief a time?"

"I'm going to get her picture," said Remo in a strange voice.

But before the Master of Sinanju could question his obviously demented pupil further, he slipped out the side door.

Chiun took up a position before the triple-locked door, his face stern, his eyes troubled. Far more troubled than those of his pupil.

For he knew what Remo Williams did not. That he had met his father, unknowing, and must not learn the truth of his parentage. Otherwise, the Master of Sinanju might never be forgiven for concealing this truth.

*Ferr he knew what it would mean: his end. Just the
time . . .*

6

Harold W. Smith heard the federal magistrate's
charges from his hospital bed.

He was awake. They could tell that by his eyes. The
attending physician had proved that he was awake
even if he could not move his body by getting Smith to
blink once for yes and twice for no.

It had been half a day now. A half day since the
combined raids by the IRS and the DEA had over-
whelmed Folcroft's virtually nonexistent defenses. A
half day since the Master of Sinanju had thwarted his
attempt to ingest the suicide pill that was Smith's last
resort in the event of catastrophic compromise. Once
before, he had been forced to take that pill. Chiun had
stopped him then, too. Didn't he understand? Once
CURE was no more, Smith would have to die.

Perhaps it was the memory of that last wrenching
failure that had caused Smith's mouth to go dry as he
took the pill into his mouth. Perhaps it was the suspicion that it was the new President's way of shutting
down CURE and making certain it stayed shut down
that had brought on the raids.

Smith could only surmise these things. Whatever the
case, the pill would not go down his dry throat, but

had lodged there instead. Chiun had caused it to pop out with his irresistible manipulations, and with that thoughtless act went Smith's final chance to end it all.

Now he lay paralyzed. Again the Master of Sinanju had been very clever. He understood that Smith would find a way—any way—to end his life if he had the strength and mobility to do so.

But as the federal magistrate droned out the charges—the titles and sections and subsections of the Revenue Code—which had come crashing down on his head like a rain of hard brick, Smith began to realize the absurdity of it all.

They thought he was some kind of drug merchant and money launderer. Where could they have gotten so ludicrous an idea?

"These charges include the willful and deliberate failure to report some twelve million dollars in income that were surreptitiously wire transferred to the Folcroft Sanitarium bank account—an account that you, Dr. Smith, have sole control over. No currency-transaction report was generated, and there was no rendering to the IRS of estimated tax payments. How do you plead to these charges? Guilty or not guilty? Blink once for guilty, twice for not."

Smith blinked twice.

"Since you have waived the right to counsel, I hereby place you under house arrest. You are not to leave these premises under any circumstance."

I am completely paralyzed, Smith thought bitterly. What is that man thinking of?

"Pending a federal trial, I have agreed to the petition of the Internal Revenue Service that they take complete operating control of this hospital pending the outcome of said trial. You may of course file a petition with the tax court if you feel this seizure is baseless or excessive."

Smith would have groaned if his throat would let him.

They would search Folcroft for contraband, if they hadn't already done so. They would find the CURE computers. Even with their data banks erased, this would raise unanswerable questions. And there was the gold stored with the computers. It had belonged to Friend. Its recovery by the Master of Sinanju and Remo meant CURE had operating capital for the coming fiscal year. It would be impossible to explain away.

As impossible as the twelve million dollars that now lay on deposit in the Folcroft bank account.

The amount could not be a coincidence, Smith realized.

During Friend's multipronged attempt to neutralize Folcroft so he could blackmail the U.S. banking system, the relentlessly greedy VLSI chip had infiltrated the computer links that governed the Federal Reserve wire-transfer system. Money began disappearing from bank computers all over the nation, including the CURE operating fund in the Grand Cayman Trust headquartered on Grand Cayman Island in the Caribbean.

The money had disappeared. Smith had coerced Friend into returning all the rerouted funds before shutting him down for good. He had forgotten to specify the missing CURE money. It was a serious oversight, committed at the end of a very taxing operation.

Now Smith understood where the missing funds had gone to. Friend had wire transferred them to the Folcroft account. It was a final scorpion sting from an old foe who had refused to die. Folcroft was already being audited by the IRS. Friend's doing once again, Smith now realized.

No doubt Friend had also dropped a dime with the DEA.

Thus, from the oblivion of his electronic grave, Friend had exacted his final revenge upon CURE and Harold W. Smith.

There was no way to explain away twelve million dollars in the operating account of a sleepy private hospital. No doubt the bank that handled the Folcroft business account itself was under great scrutiny.

CURE was finished.

Harold Smith lay on his hospital bed prison wishing for the strength to finish himself, too.

But only the Master of Sinanju had the power to fulfill that particular wish.

JACK KOLDSTAD was wondering exactly what kind of madhouse Folcroft Sanitarium really was.

After six hours it was very clear that it functioned—at least outwardly—as a private hospital. Its patients were generally chronic convalescent cases, older and from moneyed families prepared to warehouse their sick until the inevitable end of natural life. None of that Dr. Kevorkian crap here.

There was a psychiatric wing for the mentally ill. He hadn't checked into it yet. A subordinate had done that. Koldstad wasn't sure he wanted to deal with those kinds of people. He had enough problems on his hands.

First there was Dr. Smith's paralysis. None of the Folcroft physicians could explain it. The man was obviously alert and conscious. His eyes were open. But he couldn't even twitch. Koldstad wondered if it was psychosomatic, so he had slipped into Smith's room when no one was looking and jabbed Smith in the cheek with a needle.

Smith hadn't flinched. He had batted his eyes and glared at Koldstad. But not a twitch otherwise.

Just to make sure, Koldstad had inserted the needle in a couple of other tender places with the same disappointing result.

He didn't try the technique on his own agent. They had found him on the first-floor stairwell on the floor, eyes staring, stiff as a board, but alive and thinking. Koldstad ordered him into an available room and gave instructions to keep a lid on it.

No one could explain him, either.

And no one could explain the drumming.

Koldstad had first heard it while going through Dr. Smith's desk. He'd found a wide array of antacid pills, foams, aspirin and other common remedies—much of it marked Free or Sample—but no drugs or incriminating papers.

The drumming had come from Smith's private washroom.

It was a steady, almost monotonous drumbeat. *Doom doom doom doom.* It had continued while Koldstad fumbled for the washroom key, and it was still going when he'd jammed it into the lock.

When the door was flung open, the drumming had stopped.

There had been nothing in the washroom, either. Koldstad had checked everywhere, including the toilet tank, which was a common place to hide contraband.

When he closed the door, the drumming had started all over again.

Doom doom doom doom...

It had stopped when he'd thrown the door open.

Three times the phenomenon had repeated itself. Koldstad figured there was some mechanism involved. Close the door, the drumming starts. Open it, it stops. He had gone over every inch of the door and its jamb and found nothing even after he'd removed the door from its hinges. There had been no sign of wiring or strange devices. Not even a microchip. He knew you could buy greeting cards that played little musical notes when you opened the cards, activating a pressure-sensitive microchip.

But there was no microchip to be found, and the sound was too loud for a tiny chip or even a big chip.

Then there were the damn vultures that kept circling Folcroft.

They had been doing that since Koldstad first rolled through the Folcroft gates at dawn. It was approaching dusk now, and they were still at it. No one could explain what they were or how they came to be there.

They never broke off for food or rest or even to take a dump. It was infuriating. It defied all logic, all rules.

Jack Koldstad was a stickler for rules. So he had one of his men fetch up a scope-mounted Ruger rifle and personally went out on the grass to bring those damn birds down.

He went through an even dozen clips. Sure, he missed a time or three. But they were flying lazy circles. Impossible to miss time after time. Yet not a pinfeather came fluttering to earth.

Most unnerving was the fact that they looked exactly the same through the scope as they did to the naked eye. Dark. Indistinct. Unidentifiable.

Koldstad jerked out the twelfth and last clip from the rifle and threw it away in disgust.

"You!"

A G-12 flinched under the lash of his call. "Sir?"

"You have bird duty."

"Sir?"

"Watch those birds. They have to tire sometime. When they do, follow them. Follow them and kill them if you can."

"But why?"

"Those damn birds are flouting the authority of the almighty Internal Revenue Service. That's why!"

"Yes, sir."

Koldstad stormed into Folcroft. This was ridiculous. They'd been on-site for most of the day already and they hadn't completed the search yet. It was all the fault of the damn DEA. They were fighting the IRS every step of the way. The unshaven bastards. Where did they get off trying to usurp IRS authority?

He took the elevator to the second-floor office that bore the legend Dr. Harold W. Smith, Director on the door. When he opened the door, a blast of chilly mid-September air struck him. Hunching his shoulders, Koldstad went in and took the cracked leather executive's chair behind the desk, whose top was a slab of tempered black-tinted glass.

The cold air coming through the break in the picture window made the close-shaven skin on the back of his neck creep and bunch, but Jack Koldstad ignored it.

It was time to report in to the local office, and Jack Koldstad wasn't looking forward to it. Still, he dialed the number without hesitation, even if his dialing finger did quiver a little.

"Mr. Brull's office," a clipped female voice announced.

Koldstad cleared his throat. "Jack Koldstad calling for Mr. Brull."

"One moment."

The voice that came on the line a moment later sounded like two stones grinding together.

"What's your report, Koldstad?"

"We're still in the inventory stage," Koldstad said.

"What the hell?"

"This is a big place, sir. And with the DEA to contend with—"

"Who's the DEA honcho on the ground there?"

"Tardo. First name Wayne. Middle initial *P.*"

"Social Security number?"

"I haven't developed that information yet, sir."

"Doesn't matter. How many Wayne P. Tardo's can be working out of the New York DEA? Did you ask him the question?"

"I did."

"His reply?"

"He informed me that no, he had never been called in for a tax audit, Mr. Brull."

"The bastard sweat when he answered you?"

"No. But his upper lip twitched noticeably, and since then he's been on the quiet side."

"Then you have no excuses. Get Folcroft buttoned up and locked down. I want answers. What has been going on down there, how long has it been going on, and how much money is the service owed?"

"Understood, Mr. Brull. What about the DEA?"

"Those bastards would seize a rendering plant if they knew it would come up for a government auction three months later. They're seizure happy, and that makes their people all ripe for a field audit. You won't be bothered by the DEA once I make some calls."

"Very good, Mr. Brull."

"And your estimates had better be damn high or I'll bust you down to extractor by the end of this fiscal quarter. Between that dead G-12 trainee and the wounded, this operation is going to send the service's risk-insurance premiums into orbit. Make damn certain that Folcroft revenue more than covers the losses. Revenue neutral won't cut it.''

"Guaranteed, Mr. Brull.''

The line went dead. Jack Koldstad replaced the receiver with sweaty palms. There was only one man on earth who could set his pores leaking, and that was Dick Brull. God help Jack Koldstad if he didn't squeeze every drop of money out of Folcroft Sanitarium. And God help anyone who got in his way of fulfilling his quota on this one.

The trouble was, so far Folcroft showed no signs of illegal activity outside of that twelve-million-dollar bombshell in the bank account.

As he got up to set the downsizing of Folcroft Sanitarium in motion, his heel struck a piece of the broken picture window lying on the floor. The shard cracked underfoot.

Swearing, Koldstad reached down to pick up the glass. He froze.

The fragment of glass had broken into three pieces. Three separate mirror reflections of Jack Koldstad's grim face stared back at him.

Koldstad scooped up the largest piece. It was a mirror. But when he turned it around, he could see his fingers through transparent glass.

"Damn!''

He went to the fractured window. The hole was large enough for his head but the edges were too sharp to risk it, so he stuck his hand out, holding the piece of glass mirror-side in.

The mirror's own reflection showed up in the glass. Koldstad should have seen himself reflected. The other side of the window was obviously a mirror, too.

"A damn one-way window," Koldstad growled. "Folcroft isn't so innocent after all."

He dropped the shard into a wastepaper basket as he strode out of the office, his squeezed-in temples making him look like a man with the most excruciating headache in the universe.

7

Desk Sergeant Troy Tremaine had seen it all.

During his thirty years on the Port Chester, New York, police force, he had seen every human aberration, every nut case, nut job, dimwit, chuckle head and dip-shit loser come through the frosted-glass front doors and step up to his old-fashioned high precinct desk.

The skinny guy with the thick wrists didn't look like one of those. In fact, he looked very sincere. There was great sincerity in his deep-set brown eyes. They were veritable wells of sincerity. Sergeant Tremaine would have staked his pension on the skinny guy's high sincerity quotient.

He walked up, squeezed the front edge of the desk with his fingers and said in a very sincere voice, "My wife is missing."

Tremaine, who had a wife himself, immediately felt for the poor guy. But business was business.

"How long?"

"Two days."

"We need three days before we can file a missing-person report."

"Did I say days? I meant weeks."

Tremaine's hot button should have gone off right
then. But the guy was so sincere. He looked exactly as
though he was heartsick over the loss of his wife.

So Troy said, "You said two days."

"I'm upset. I meant weeks."

"Her name?"

"Esmerelda."

Troy looked up. "Esmerelda?"

"It was her mother's name, too. Esmerelda Lolobrigida."

"That would make you . . ."

"Remo Lolobrigida." And the skinny guy produced an ID card that said he was Remo Lolobrigida,
private investigator.

"You try looking for her yourself?"

Remo Lolobrigida nodded soberly. "Yeah. For the
past week." His voice dripped sincerity.

"But you said she was missing two."

"I was out of town one week. Look, this is serious.
I gotta find her."

"Okay, let me hand you off to a detective." He
craned his bull neck and lifted his voice to a passing
uniform. "Hey, who's catching today?"

The answer came back. "Boyle. But he's out to
lunch."

"Damn. Okay, I'll take it. Give me the particulars,
friend."

"She's about, I'd say twenty-eight."

"Say?"

"I think she lied about her age before we married.
You know how women are."

"Right. Right."

"She's brown on brown, slim, wears her hair long."

"Recent photo available?"

"No. She was camera shy."

Oh, great, Tremaine thought. He kept it to himself. "How do you expect us to find your wife, buddy, without a recent snapshot?"

"Is there a police artist around? I know I can describe her pretty well."

Tremaine chewed on that as he erased something he had written.

"Guess we can try that." He picked up a phone and said, "DeVito. Got a guy out here who's missing his wife. Yeah. No recent photo. In fact, no photo at all. Want to take a crack at it? Sure."

Tremaine pointed to a door. "Go through there. DeVito will help you. Good luck, pal."

"Thanks," said the skinny guy, walking away. Only then did Troy Tremaine think that it was damn cool out there to be walking around in a T-shirt. By then it was too late.

POLICE SKETCH ARTIST Tony DeVito thought nothing of the skinny guy's light attire, either. He waved him into his office and said, "First I want you to look at some head shapes. Just to get us started."

The skinny guy went through the book and picked out a nice oval. Tony transferred the oval to his sketch pad and said, "Let's start with the eyes. What kind of eyes did—I mean does—your wife have?"

"Nice."

Tony winced. "Can you be more specific?"

"Sad."

"Sad but nice. Okay," Tony said, rolling his own eyes. Why did people think it was possible to draw nice? "Were they long, round or square?"

"Round."

Tony sketched round eyes. "Eyebrows?"

"Thick. Not plucked. But not too thick."

Tony drew Brooke Shields eyebrows, figuring he could subtract hair later on.

"Now the nose. Snub? Ski? Or sharp?"

"Neither. More of an Anne Archer nose."

Tony closed his eyes in thought. Anne Archer had a nice face and a memorable nose. He drew it from memory.

"Can you describe the mouth?"

"Not too full, not too wide."

"Good. More?"

"It was nice. Kind. Kind of motherly."

"I can draw kind, but not nice," he said tightly. "Do better than that."

They argued over the mouth for another ninety seconds before settling on a Susan Lucci mouth.

Tony started to put his pencil to the sheet and couldn't for the life of him remember what Susan Lucci's mouth looked like. Her legs, yes. Her eyes, sure. Her mouth, no.

"Any other actress besides Susan have a mouth like your wife's?" Tony asked.

"Minnie Mouse."

"Her I can draw."

The face came out surprisingly well for a first try. It was a nice face, even if the eyes were on the sad side.

"All we need is the hair," Tony said.

"Long in the back, but combed off the forehead."

"That's easy to do."

In the end Tony turned the sketch around and asked, "How close is that?"

The citizen frowned. "No, that's not her at all. The mouth is too thin, the nose too sharp, and the eyes are all wrong."

"Other than that it's a good likeness, right?" Tony asked dryly.

"The hair looks about right," Remo Lolobrigida admitted.

Great, Tony thought. It's a style twenty or thirty years out of date, but I'm right on the money with it.

"Okay," he said, "let's try tweaking the facial elements." He began erasing. "How about if I do this to the eyes?"

"She looks angry."

"Okay, she looks angry. Does she ever look like this when she's angry?"

"I never saw her angry."

"Married long?"

"No."

"Okay, how about this?"

"That looks about right."

"Let's bring the nose down, too."

It took twenty more minutes, but in the end the distraught husband said, "That's her. That's exactly her."

"Sure? This is going to go on posters everywhere. We want it exactly right."

The worried husband took the sheet of paper from Tony's hand and stared at it for an unnaturally long time. He was searching the face as if seeing it for the first time in a very, very long while.

"It's exactly her," he said in a wistful tone.

"Okay, let's get this on the wire."

Tony started to stand up. The worried husband reached out with an absent hand, his eyes never coming off the sketch. The hand caught him by the right knee and locked. Tony felt as if a pair of steel pliers had taken hold of him. The plierslike hand forced Tony back into his hard wooden chair with inexorable strength.

"Hey!"

The hand let go and found his throat. The man had gotten up, his eyes still locked with those of the woman in the sketch.

Everything went dark after that for Tony DeVito. When he came to, he was slumping in his chair and the desk sergeant was throwing water into his face.

"What happened?"

"What do you mean, what happened?" Sergeant Tremaine exploded. "You were out like a light. You tell *me* what freaking happened!"

"I was doing this sketch for that guy, Lolobrigida. And he started acting hinky." Tony looked around. "Where is he?"

"Where is he? He never came out!"

Then they noticed the open window. A very cool breeze was blowing in to disturb the papers on Tony's desk.

"What kind of guy goes to the trouble of having us sketch his missing wife and then walks off with the sketch?" Tony wondered dazedly.

"A nut job," barked Tremaine. "I knew he was a nut job the minute he walked into the place."

"He seemed perfectly normal to me."

Tremaine slammed down the window. "It's gotta be forty out there, and he's walking around in a stupid T-shirt. A nut job. Just like I said. I can spot them coming from three miles off."

"Then why didn't you warn me?"

Troy Tremaine shrugged. "Hey, he had a legitimate beef, and I can be wrong about people. But not nut jobs."

"What do we do?"

"Me, I don't do nothing. You, start sketching. I wanna post that nut job's face on the squad-room wall so the uniforms can see it."

8

Dr. Aldace Gerling was nervous. Very nervous.

As chief of psychiatry at Folcroft Sanitarium, he was an expert on neuroses, psychoses and every other form of mental illness known to modern man.

He could not account for what was happening to him.

It was a drumming. Others had heard it before him. Unfortunately those others were all patients in Folcroft's psychiatric wing. An orderly had been the first person not institutionalized in Folcroft to report hearing the drumming noise.

Dr. Gerling had dismissed the orderly's report as a mere auditory hallucination. So many others had reported the sound that the staff had begun listening for it. It was only natural that someone would hear something that made them think of drumming. It was the power of suggestion at work. Nothing more.

And then Dr. Gerling had heard it.

It was a distinct drumbeat, slow, steady. Oddly familiar, too. Gerling had raced to the spot, only to find the drumming noise racing ahead of him. Around every corner just ahead of him. As fast as he could waddle, the measured drumbeat outpaced him, its source annoyingly elusive.

Finally Dr. Gerling had turned the last corner on the psychiatric wing and thought he had the drumming trapped in a utility closet.

He had opened it, but there was nothing there. The drumming had stopped cold. There was nothing inside that could have produced the phenomenon. Not even remotely.

Still, Dr. Gerling had felt it incumbent on him to report this event to Dr. Smith, and did.

As he made his rounds, Dr. Gerling wondered if Dr. Smith had ever gotten his report. He wondered if Dr. Smith would ever receive any report at all, considering the regretful state he was now in. Gerling had looked in on him and went pale at the sight. Smith appeared to be in some form a paralytic state. Utterly unmoving, eyes wide, every muscle rigid as if struggling to escape his useless body.

Dr. Gerling paused in front of the door of one of the more difficult patients at Folcroft, Jeremiah Purcell.

Purcell was a thin, pale young man with long cornsilk hair and almost no mind to speak off. When he had first been brought to Folcroft, he was a complete imbecile. He could not feed himself or dress without help, and had regressed to childhood so completely his toilet training had to be redone.

Thankfully he could now take care of most of those personal chores himself. Nevertheless, he seemed frozen in a state of utter befuddlement, watching cartoons and other such childish programs for hours and

hours on end. There was no character disorder on
record to explain it, so Dr. Gerling had coined one:
adult-onset autistic regression. He would have written a paper on this new frontier in mental illness, but
Dr. Smith frowned on any publicity that directed a
spotlight upon Folcroft, no matter how positive.

Dr. Gerling observed his remarkable patient
through the tiny square window in the steel door.
Purcell sat in a big comfortable chair, intense neon
blue eyes glued to the TV screen, long canvas sleeves
buckled to the back of his straitjacket. From time to
time he giggled. He seemed very pleased with his program, so Dr. Gerling made a remark on his clipboard
that the patient was in elevated spirits today. On the
clipboard, he prescribed only half of the daily forty
milligrams of haloperidol.

He passed on.

The next patient was not in good spirits. He had
been a resident of Folcroft for a much shorter time.
About two years.

The man was perfectly normal intellectually, but he
suffered from a character disorder whose chief symp-
tom manifested itself as delusions of grandeur. The
patient thought he was Uncle Sam Beasley, the famous cartoonist and founder of the Sam Beasley entertainment empire, which included a movie studio
and a chain of theme parks around the world.

He was dressed as a pirate, right down to the rakish
black eye patch and swashbuckler boots. Why a person who imagined he was a twenty-five-years-dead
cartoonist would wear pirate clothes was beyond Al-

dace Gerling's understanding, so in his first interview with the man he probed these matters.

The patient had growled, "Go fuck yourself."

What was interesting was that the voice sounded exactly like that of the long-dead Uncle Sam Beasley—except, of course, the real Beasley would never have descended to such harsh language.

As Dr. Gerling peeked in, the patient—he was listed as Sam Beasley on Gerling's patient roster by order of Dr. Smith—was seated at a card table sketching. The walls of his room were littered with sketches. They depicted the patient climbing down a rope of knotted bed sheets though a broken Folcroft window and making his escape from the sanitarium. It was quite a detailed series of drawings, and included a self-portrait of himself cutting Dr. Gerling's throat with his pirate hook. The hook was real. The patient had been brought in with his right hand a blunt stump, so Dr. Gerling had taken the liberty of having a hook fitted. It was currently under lock and key because Beasley had tried to cut the throats of two different male nurses, after which Dr. Smith had decreed that the hook was too dangerous to remain attached to the patient's wrist stump.

Dr. Gerling had protested. "Removing the hook will only force the man to withdraw into himself, to become uncommunicative."

"The hook goes," said Smith, who placed a written reprimand in Dr. Gerling's file for endangering the staff.

So it went. Dr. Gerling had never agreed with the decision, but it wasn't his to reverse. As director of Folcroft, Dr. Smith ruled with an iron hand.

Still, the patient was doing quite well with his good hand. His drawings were excellent. It was amazing how deeply and thoroughly he had thrown himself into the role of Uncle Sam Beasley. The drawing looked uncannily like the real Beasley's work. Dr. Gerling had asked the patient to draw him a Monongahela Mouse, and the likeness was exquisite, right down to the perfectly matched black lollipop ears.

"You could easly find work in the Beasley animation studios," Gerling had clucked, unthinking.

"I built the Beasley Studio, you quack," the pseudo-Beasley roared back, snatching the drawing from Gerling's hand and tearing it to shreds between his good hand and his teeth. The look of animal ferocity in his one good eye was frightening to the extreme.

As these memories passed through Dr. Gerling's mind, the patient caught sight of him.

"You! Quack! How is Euro Beasley doing? Is the attendance up or down?"

"Down. Sharply."

"Damn those pip-squeaks. Can't they run anything in my absence? Tell them they're all fired. They should have known better than to try to appeal to those snobby French. Damn frogs think Jerry Lewis is some kind of creative genius and they dismiss me as a mere cartoonist."

"I will see you tomorrow," Dr. Gerling said pleasantly.

"And I'll see you hanging by your stethoscope," Beasley ground out, returning to his drawings.

"Remarkable case," Dr. Gerling murmured as he passed on, scribbling a note to the head nurse to increase the patient's dose of Clozaril, along with a reminder that his blood be tested every week in the event his white count bottomed out from the powerful drug.

The remaining patients were unremarkable. As he looked in on them, Dr. Gerling's thoughts drifted to the events of the day.

Folcroft lay under a very dark cloud. There was a problem with the Internal Revenue Service, which had swooped down like buzzards with guns at the crack of dawn.

When Dr. Gerling had arrived for work, he found a dead man lying on the lawn, and the wounded—who had included Dr. Smith, technically speaking—had been placed under the care of Folcroft's finest physicians.

Dr. Gerling had been challenged by representatives of the Drug Enforcement Administration and the IRS. The two agencies had fought over the right of first interrogation—whatever that was. The DEA had won. And so Dr. Gerling had submitted to a grueling three-hour interrogation, which consisted of repeating the same denials over and over again.

Finally the representative of the DEA had been forced to surrender him to the IRS. There ensued another long interrogation consisting of the same tiresome questions and heated denials.

At the end of it, he was told to report to work.

He had found Folcroft in tatters, staff wise. The lower-echelon staff had been told to go home, and a number of personnel, including Smith's trusted secretary, Mrs. Mikulka, had been terminated.

Dr. Gerling wondered if he too was going to be fired when all was said and done. It was a distinct possibility, he decided.

In the interim, he made his rounds. Perhaps nothing dire would happen and all would be restored to the status quo.

But he knew in his heart this was unlikely. The Internal Revenue Service and the Drug Enforcement Administration both had come down on Folcroft Sanitarium like avenging angels. It could not all be a mistake. These were very powerful, very important, very professional governmental agencies. They did not make mistakes.

And if there had been any doubt in Dr. Gerling's mind, it was dispelled by Dr. Smith's state.

He had been asked to evaluate it and, after conferring with the Folcroft doctors—who could find nothing organically wrong with Smith—Gerling was forced to conclude one thing.

"It appears psychosomatic," he'd told the IRS agent named Jack Koldstad.

"You mean he's faking?"

"No, I mean that his mind has created this condition because Dr. Smith cannot face an unpleasant reality."

"What causes this usually?"

"Different external problems. Fear. Depression."

"How about guilt?"

"Yes, guilt. Guilt is a very strong emotion. It could be guilt over something in his past."

"He's guilty of evading Uncle Sam's lawful levies, that's what he's guilty of."

"I do not think I have ever heard of a patient who would fall into a paralytic state over underreporting federal taxes."

"You just said guilt. I'm writing up guilt in my report."

"Yes, I said guilt. But it is a possibilty and no more. Dr. Smith might have other emotions causing this condition."

"Guilt makes sense to me. We found evidence he's guilty of tax evasion. We confronted him with it. He's guilty—end of story."

"Should not that be for a court of law to decide?" Dr. Gerling had asked.

"The IRS decides who is guilty of tax evasion," Jack Koldstad had snapped as he turned away. "Not the damn law."

That was when Dr. Gerling gave up all hope for Harold Smith. The man must be guilty, after all. It was too bad. He was an excellent administrator, even if he was a nickel-squeezing tightwad.

Completing his rounds, Dr. Gerling was walking back to his office when he heard a sound that made his heart skip a beat.

It was the drumming. *Doom doom doom doom doom* over and over again. Monotonous, relentless and distressingly familiar.

Reversing course, he made a beeline for the sound. It was coming from very close by, but the sound was muffled. The skirts of his white physician's coat flapping about his knees, Dr. Gerling moved with a waddling alacrity, his round head swiveling from side to side.

Very close, yes. The sound was close enough that he could almost reach out and touch it.

Gerling slowed his gait. Yes, quite close. Then he had the sound fixed. It was apparently coming from Purcell's room.

Cautiously Aldace Gerling slipped up to the square window with its thick wire-mesh-reinforced glass. Trying to keep from being seen, he used one bespectacled eye to look inside.

Jeremiah Purcell was watching television. Whatever it was, the program made his pale face light up with glee, and a cackle dribbled from between his laughing lips.

The drumming was definitely emanating from this room.

Dr. Gerling angled his head around, trying to spot it.

Then he saw it. The television set was the source of the monotonous drumming. A commercial. Dr. Gerling caught the last few seconds of it, just as the plush pink bunny narrowly escaped being trampled by a giant gorilla.

He marched into the sunset beating on his drum, the battery on his back showing.

"My word!" said Gerling. "I wonder if it was that silly commercial making the drumming after all?"

He decided not to speak of this to anyone else. The IRS had control of Folcroft Sanitarium now, and there was no telling on what flimsy grounds they would terminate someone.

Or worse, Gerling thought with a shiver, audit them.

After all, if a man were judged not in his right mind, would not his tax returns also be suspect?

9

In the basement of Folcroft Sanitarium, the Master of Sinanju fumed and paced like an impatient hen.

Where was Remo? He had promised not to be gone long. And it was his turn to guard the gold that now belonged to Sinanju.

The door at the top of the stairs opened. Perhaps this was he.

The clump of footsteps coming down told otherwise. Even in his most crude days, back before the grace of the sun source came upon him, Remo had not climbed like that. This was the tread of a clod, and so the Master of Sinanju glided from the triple-locked door of the basement vault room to meet this interloper.

"Who intrudes?" he challenged.

A stiff voice responded. "IRS. Who's down here?"

"No one. Go away."

"I am an agent of the IRS. We never go away."

"Never?"

"Never."

"That is too bad. No doubt you are here to confiscate wealth."

"What's down here?"

"No gold, despite what you may have heard."

"Gold? Who said anything about gold?"

The agent had reached the bottom of the steps and was splashing the beam of a flashlight about like a blind fool.

"No one said anything about gold," Chiun countered. "And if you turn around and poke your long nose elsewhere, no harm will befall you."

The agent was dashing the light about, trying to pin down the source of the Master of Sinanju's voice. He seemed not to realize that it was impossible to touch the Master of Sinanju even with a harmless beam of light if the Master of Sinanju did not choose to be touched.

Still, he persisted with both his light and his prying questions. "What's down here?"

"It is a simple basement. No more."

"I smell something funny...."

"It is beef. You reek of it."

"Smells like burned plastic."

"You have a good nose, considering its length."

"Look, as an agent of the Internal Revenue Service, I order you to stop horsing around and step into my light."

"This is an order?"

"It is."

"I hear and obey."

The Master of Sinanju stepped into the light. It touched his chest, swung up and illuminated his wise face.

The man blurted, "You're that crazy Chinaman."

"I am neither crazy nor Chinese, beef-brained one."

"I hereby place you under arrest."

"You cannot do that."

"As an agent of the Treasury Department, I am empowered to detain any United States citizen."

"Then it is too bad that I am not a United States denizen."

"You'll have to prove that in court. You're under arrest."

The Master of Sinanju said, "Cuff me, if you dare."

"I don't carry handcuffs." And the white man from the IRS reached out to profane the Master of Sinanju's outstretched wrists with his unwashed hands as if to haul him away like some common thief.

The Master of Sinanju made quick, dazzling motions with his hands that momentarily confused the white clod, whose fingers became entangled in one another. It was plain from the look on his face that he did not understand what was happening to him.

And so when the Master of Sinanju sent out a tiny fist that was as hard as a wooden mallet, the white's dull wits never saw the blow coming that struck his chest and jellied his heart.

He collapsed, his nostrils leaking a sigh like a balloon losing air.

The Master of Sinanju left him at the foot of the steps as a warning to others of his ilk that to trespass into the basement of Fortress Folcroft was to die.

He hoped he would not have to dispatch too many before they understood the meaning of this act. White corpses emitted the most disagreeable odors after the fourth day, and he did not want his gold to pick up the stink, like butter left near beef.

"You KILLED an IRS agent," Remo exploded when he nearly tripped over the body at the foot of the stairs. "For God's sake, why?"

"He offended me," said Chiun, turning away.

"You don't kill a government agent because he offended you."

"I did not kill the wretch," Chiun sniffed. "He killed himself. He reached out to profane the Master of Sinanju's personage with his grubby hands. Were he educated, he would have understood such an act to be the equal to committing suicide. It is the fault of your public schools, where they teach useless trivia like geometry and speaking the tongue of the French."

"So you're just going to leave him here?"

Chiun made a dismissive gesture with the flapping sleeve of his kimono. "Of course. Let it be a warning to the others."

"Warning? They're the IRS. You can't wave them off. They keep coming and coming. Like killer bees."

"I do not fear their sting, for I am not an American denizen, and thus not subject to their burdensome taxes."

"Yeah? Well, if they find that gold down here, they're not going to tax it. They'll confiscate it all."

Chiun whirled, face hard. "They cannot do that. It is my gold."

"Some of it is Smith's, remember? He got his share of Friend's gold, too. And some of it is mine."

Chiun made his tiny mouth tinier. "The smallest portion is yours."

"Thanks to you gypping me out of it."

Chiun shooed the comment away. "He who dwells in the past has no future."

Remo waved a piece of paper in Chiun's averted face. "Check this out."

Chiun took it. "Where did you obtain this drawing?"

"A police artist. It's my mother."

Chiun looked up from the drawing. "She is very beautiful, Remo."

Remo's face softened. "I think so, too."

"Therefore, she cannot be your mother," said Chiun, tossing the drawing over his shoulder.

"Hey!" Remo said, snatching it from midair between two fingers. "Watch what you're doing to my mother. This is the only picture I have of her."

"That is not your mother."

"Look again. She has Freya's eyes. Or Freya has her eyes."

Chiun peered at the drawing, which Remo held up at a safe distance from the Master's sharp fingernails.

"Pah!" said Chiun. "Coincidence. Besides, you describe the eyes you wished to see. It is a fragment of your imagination."

"That's 'figment.' And this morning you were convinced I saw my mother's ghost."

"This morning I was beside myself with worry over the gold. Now I am serene in the knowledge that it is safe from the confiscators because it is being protected by the greatest assassin to walk the earth since the days of the Great Wang."

"I want to show this to Smith."

"Why?"

"Maybe he can help me find who this face belongs to."

"If she is dead, what good would that do?"

"I don't know. All I know is that Smith owes me and I mean to collect."

"Very well. I have business with Smith, as well."

"You bring him out of it yet?"

"No."

"Why not?"

"Because I know what he will do himself in if I restore to him the means to do it."

"Good point. We gotta find a way to get Smith back behind his computer terminal so he doesn't take himself off."

"It will not be easy," squeaked Chiun, taking the stairs with his hands clasped before him, concealed by the joined sleeves of his kimono.

10

Harold Smith lay in the darkness, cursing the darkness.

Folcroft was quiet. The night shift moved past his door, down the two-tone green corridors with the slow, shuffling feet of zombies. No light came through the chinks in the door frame, so in his hospital room Smith lay in darkness, unmoving.

He still could not move, except to open and close his eyes. His stomach churned. The ulcers that had tormented him for years were flaring up, the result of the strain of the past week.

There was no doubt in Smith's active mind that CURE was through. It was ironic. Only a week before, he had, through his vast resources and superior mind, outwitted one of CURE's most implacable foes. The Friend operation designed to destroy CURE had nearly succeeded. Smith had blocked it, countered it, then smashed it utterly.

It was one of his greatest victories—measured by how close to the brink the supersecret organization had all come.

In the end it turned out to be a temporary respite from a plan that continued beyond the grave of its originator.

By now Folcroft must have been turned upside down in the IRS's blind determination to uncover Folcroft's supposed illicit secrets. In ordinary times there would have been so little to uncover. The secret terminal in Smith's desk. The computers, rendered mute and forever dumb by the Superwipe Program. Nothing more. He had run a totally paperless office. The true secrets of CURE were stored in his own perishable brain.

But there was the gold in the basement. Even if Remo and Chiun had been able to remove their portion, Smith's own would remain. It amounted to several million dollars in pure bullion. Millions in gold ingots in a sealed room in the basement of a sleepy private hospital, while American citizens were forbidden by law from owning gold except in the form of jewelry.

There was no way to explain all that gold away.

So Smith lay in darkness, cursing the darkness and wishing—actually willing—his heart to stop beating.

And without warning, the darkness around him seemed to swell.

At first Smith thought it a trick of the irredeemable darkness.

It was too dark for shadows. He might as well have been set in a block of breathable basalt.

But the blackness swelled on either side of his hospital bed, even though his frantic, darting eyes couldn't make the shapes resolve. His rimless glasses lay on the side table. Without them, the universe was a painful blur.

A light flicked on, blinding him.

And over the needle of pain in his brain, he heard a voice.

"Hiyah, Smitty."

Remo!

"Greetings, Harold the Resolute."

And Master Chiun.

"If we let you sit up," Remo was asking, "will you promise not to make a fuss? Blink twice for yes."

Smith was still trying to get his eyes to stop blinking from the sudden light. He squeezed his eyes shut and tried to make his face relax.

"Is that a no?" Remo asked Chiun.

"I do not know. Let us bring him out of his sad state anyway, for I know his heart is filled with words intended for our ears alone."

And Remo tapped Smith on the exact center of the forehead once, lightly. His motor functions instantly returned.

Smith sat up groaning. Blurred hands placed his eyeglasses onto his sharp patrician nose.

"You have failed CURE," he said bitterly.

"Now, is that any way to talk?"

"And you have failed your country, Remo. And you, Master Chiun, have failed your emperor. You above all know that once CURE is compromised, certain instructions are inviolate."

Chiun stiffened. "There is always time to die, Smith," he said in a frosty voice. "If it is your wish, it will be carried out."

"It is my order."

"Hold the phone," Remo interjected. "You're not going anywhere until you pay off a debt."

"Debt?"

"You promised to help find my parents."

Smith frowned. "That debt is cancelable by death."

"Then don't plan on dying."

"What Remo says is true, Emperor. You owe my adopted son a debt that must be discharged ere you can be granted the boon of oblivion."

"CURE security supercedes personal obligations," Smith snapped.

Remo shook his head. "Not to me. I gave twenty years of my life to the organization. It took my old life and my future from me. It owes me some answers."

Smith fell back on the pillow, his tired eyes closing. "I am sorry, Remo, but I can no longer help you in your search."

"Why not?"

"I erased the CURE data banks the minute the IRS and DEA burst in. Without them, I have no resources."

"We'll buy you a new computer," Remo said.

"With your own gold, of course," Chiun added hastily.

"Why is the DEA in on this, too?" Remo asked.

"Evidently Friend dropped a dime on us before he was destroyed. As you both recall, he had a three-pronged plan of attack to destroy the organization. I was so busy dealing with the simultaneous loss of the submarine with the gold, the failure of the Folcroft computers and Remo's distress over having killed the wrong target that it never occured to me that the IRS's sudden interest in Folcroft was anything other than a routine field audit. No doubt, the DEA investigation was under way without arousing suspicion on my part. Clearly that insidious little artificial intelligence left nothing to chance. We were set up from all angles."

"Remind me to go to that office building down in Harlem and pick through all those computer chips until I find that little creep. I'll crush his circuitry to powder," Remo said, demonstrating by grabbing the bed rails. The steel tubes seemed to melt under the touch of his fingers. They creaked once sharply, and when his hand came away, two fist-sized sections of tubing had been squeezed down to the thinness of wire.

"Friend is no longer the problem," Smith said. "The IRS is. Have they found the gold?"

"Not yet."

"It is only a matter of time," Smith said dully.

"Smitty, what do we have to do to get the IRS off your back and set things right?"

"You don't understand, Remo. The IRS is remorseless. Evidently Friend wire transferred the CURE operating fund from the Grand Cayman Trust to the Folcroft bank account. I never suspected it. When he restored the banking system to normalcy under my threat of destruction, he left those funds where he knew the IRS auditor would find them. It was exceedingly clever. Tantamount to a doomsday device. He knew I could never explain away such a vast sum, especially from an offshore bank of such dubious repute.''

"I do not understand this mumbo jumbo,'' Chiun said tartly.

"You don't have to,'' Remo said quickly. To Smith, he said, "C'mon Smitty. We've been in deeper holes than this.''

"Never. The IRS is effective, inexorable, remorseless and a law unto itself. Even if you are not guilty of any wrongdoing, they can ruin an individual or a business. Unlike our judicial system, the burden of proof lies with the accused, not the accuser. In IRS eyes, the twelve million dollars and the gold in the basement constitute unreported income that can never be explained away. Folcroft is compromised, CURE is finished, and my life and career are over. I will not live out my remaining years in a federal penitentiary.''

Smith's voice was emanating from his barely moving mouth like the last breath from a corpse. There was no life in it.

"We can set up elsewhere,'' Remo suggested.

"Where? We have no funds.''

"Hey, our credit cards are still good. We can go on the float.''

"You do not understand, Remo. The White House may have written us off. For all we know, even if the President knew of our predicament, he might simply let matters play out.''

"Want us to ask him?''

"No!" said Smith, his gray eyes snapping open. "CURE was not meant to operate indefinitely. It is just that the end of the line has come with much work unfinished."

Remo folded his lean arms. "I'll say. You can't send your kid to school without risking he ends up in a body bag. Guns are everywhere. Drugs are everywhere. And the police can't be everywhere. It's practically the fall of Rome all over again."

"The problems of this county have grown too great, too deeply woven into the fabric of American society, for CURE to remedy," said Smith.

"Fine. Given. But our problems are solvable. Somehow."

Chiun spoke up. "Remo is correct, O Emperor. We are not defeated. Surely there are ways around these tax terrorists."

Smith closed his eyes again and lay in thought for so long they began to wonder if he had fallen asleep.

"I do not know how we can solve these problems," Smith said at last, his voice tired and tentative. "But I will agree on a course of action to minimize our exposure."

"Shoot."

"First move the gold to a safe place."

"Done."

"Second we must cover our tracks."

"What tracks?"

"The CURE money trail."

"Just say how," said Remo.

"No currency-transfer report concerning the twelve million-dollar wire transfer to the Folcroft bank account was filed with the IRS. That means the people at my bank, the Lippincott Savings Bank, were either negligent or unaware of the transaction. If the president of the bank can be persuaded to testify that this was accomplished without my knowledge or express permission, it may be possible to evade IRS sanctions."

"Count on him being persuaded," Remo said tightly.

"If he so testifies, he may fall under IRS sanctions himself."

"He'll testify."

"The CURE funds were wire transferred from the Grand Cayman Trust. I visited the president, Basil Hume, during my investigation of the banking crisis Friend instigated. He knows my face and can link me to the missing twelve million. He must not be allowed to do so."

"I will be pleased to wring the neck of this parasite."

"Parasite, Chiun?" said Remo.

"Banks are inventions of the Italians, who as a race can only make their way in the world by levying illegal taxes upon others. Remind me to tell you about this sometime, Remo."

"Pass," said Remo.

"Spurner of wisdom."

Remo addressed Smith. "Okay, Smitty. We're in business again. We'll catch you later."

The light went out. And Harold Smith thought for a dark moment that he would have his freedom again. But a finger—he had no idea whose—tapped him on the exact center of his forehead, and his body froze in an excruciatingly awkward posture.

Hours later he still lay awake, his right arm going to sleep, cursing the darkness.

But at least he now had hope.

11

Jeremy Lippincott's silver Bentley circled the bank bearing his name three times before he received the high sign signifying that it was safe for the president of the Lippincott Savings Bank to enter.

"My usual spot, Wigglesworth," Jeremy said tartly.

"Yes, Mr. Lippincott."

The Bentley purred into the space, and Jeremy waited for the door to be opened by his brown-liveried chauffeur before alighting.

He noticed a slightly loose button on Wigglesworth's tunic. It dangled from two threads.

"Have you no personal pride?" Jeremy Lippincott, scion of the Lippincott family wealth, complained in his clipped lockjaw accents. "That button is dangling."

Wigglesworth looked down. His thin face went ashen. "I had no idea, Mr. Lippincott," he gulped, clapping the button close to his barrel chest.

"I believe you know the inviolate rule about faultless attire."

Wigglesworth puckered up his face in perplexity. "I don't believe I do, sir."

"Faultless attire earns one's salary. Attire at fault results in the docking of a day's salary for the day the sartorial lapse was committed, and for every day thereafter if it is not satisfactorily corrected."

"But Mr. Lippincott—"

"Stop sputtering, you latter-day hackney driver, and beat my usual path to the door."

Wigglesworth set his teeth and turned smartly on his booted heel, walking ahead of his master and opening the door for him.

"That will be all, Wigglesworth."

"Yes, Mr. Lippincott."

"Remain with the machine in case there is a sudden need for flight. But do not use the heater. In fact, why don't you stand at attention before the passenger door until instructed otherwise?"

"Might I point out that it *is* a tad nippy today?"

"If you catch your death, no doubt that loose button will make a fit epitaph," Jeremy drawled as he passed into the marble-and-brass bank lobby.

The Lippincott Savings Bank was the picture of an old-money bank. Oils hung high on the crackled and faded marble walls. The half-open bank vault had the look and feel of an old pocket watch magnified by the passing of years. The decor was so staid that even the red crushed-velvet guide ropes were gray.

All looked sound, Jeremy saw. Tellers were busy telling. The loan staff seemed under occupied, but perhaps it was a seasonal quirk. No need to lay off anyone prematurely. Too difficult to break in new stock, and with the hiring quotas these days, there was no telling what color person one would be forced to employ. Better a slacker with some pedigree than some low Mediterranean type.

Rawlings, the manager, met him at his office door.

"What took you so long?" Jeremy hissed. "I had to circle the block three times."

"I expected you at ten-thirty, not eleven, Mr. Lippincott," Rawlings said apologetically.

"I lingered over my scones and tea," Jeremy said. "One must eat a hearty breakfast if one is to endure the travails of this trade."

"Yes, sir."

"Speaking of travails, have those rotters been about?"

"The IRS? No, sir."

"Are we rid of them, then?"

"I doubt it, Mr. Lippincott. They were not satisfied with my explanations."

"Then give them explanations they *are* satisfied with, you unmitigated dunderhead!"

"It is not as simple as that."

"Exactly *how* simple is it?"

"As I have tried explain to you, Mr. Lippincott, it is not simple at all. The bank is in violation of several strict laws governing wire transfers, including the Bank Secrecy Act and the Money Laundering Control Act. Not to mention IRS reporting requirements regarding the transfer funds in excess of ten thousand dollars from other banks. I'm afraid we've failed to exercise due diligence."

"And whose responsibilty is that?"

"For the hundreth time, sir, these funds simply appeared in our system overnight. I brought this to your attention at the time, and you said to ignore it. And so I did. Emphatically."

"You obeyed my instructions?"

"Yes, sir. Implicitly."

"And thereby called down the combined wrath of the Federal Banking Commission and the Infernal Revenue Service!" Jeremy thundered.

"Please, sir. Not in front of the staff."

"The staff be hanged! This is your mess. Clean it up or clean out your desk."

"Yes, Mr. Lippincott," said Rawlings as the cherrywood door with the brass nameplate slammed shut in his face.

"Carry on," he told his staff in a voice as weak as his knocking knees.

JEREMY LIPPINCOTT crossed his cherrywood-paneled office in a blind tizzy. The nerve of that man, Rawlings. Trying to foist his personal failings on a Lippincott. Why, the Lippincotts had landed on Plymouth Rock in the first ship. The Rawlings were easily three sails back, yet he had dared stand up to his betters and speak as if an equal. After this ugliness was done with, he would suffer summary dismissal if Lippincott Savings had to replace him with an Italian—or worse, a damn Irishman!

By the time Jeremy Lippincott had doffed his slate gray Brooks Brothers suit and climbed into his habitual workaday attire, he had revised his thinking. It might be better if Rawlings only went to jail for his failings. That way it might be possible to hold his post open for him and avoid hiring a common type for the long term. Certainly the barbarous equal-hiring laws allowed an employer to hold a spot in reserve for a convicted felon like Rawlings. It only made sense. Rehabilitation and all that nonsense.

Jeremy Lippincott idled the difficult first hour of the working day before lunch by indulging in some witty repartee with one Mistress Fury on the Leather Line 900 number and had nearly recovered his good humor when the sounds of commotion came from the other side of his closed office door.

"You can't go in there!" Rawlings was protesting.

"No, you can't," Miss Chalmers chimed in. "That happens to be Mr. Lippincott's office. And we have express instructions to admit no one when the door is locked."

"So open the door," an unfamiliar voice said. It sounded rather lower-class. Rough would not be too strong a descriptive.

"Only Mr. Lippincott can open that door."

"Then I'll open the door."

"Are you with the IRS?" Rawlings demanded with positively nervous solicitude. The utter coward!

"Worse," returned the impatient voice.

"What is worse than the IRS?"

"The people who sent me. Now, get out of my way."

"I must see proper identification," Rawlings insisted. Good man, that Rawlings. His job was secure once the unfortunate prison interlude was out of the way.

"I left it in the car."

"I will not see anyone without proper identification," Jeremy shouted through the door. For good measure, he repeated it into his intercom, where it was certain to be heard by the intruder. He used his most stentorian voice—the one he employed to berate young Timothy—for additional intimidating power.

"Proper identification coming right up," the voice called back.

Jeremy did not like the way that sounded.

A moment later Rawlings began entering the room, yet the door remained firmly shut. Jeremy would have thought there was no way anyone could enter his office with the door locked.

But there was Rawlings's hand. He recognized it at once, despite its distressingly flattened condition. The man's plain wedding band was unmistakable, as was the inferior fabric of his coat sleeve.

The flattish hand was followed by a very flat arm, and the screams Rawlings emitted were quite shocking to the refined ear.

"Is this ID enough?" the crude voice demanded. "Or do I send the rest of him in?"

"I believe I accept your credentials," Jeremy Lippincott admitted in a gulping voice. He unlocked the door, retreating to the stolid safety of his desk.

The door pushed open and the man stepped in.

"Please shut the door," Jeremy said quickly. "I do not like the help overhearing what is not their business."

The man obliged. That was a good sign. He shut the door, kicking Rawlings's flapping arm out just ahead of the closing panel. He was possessed of a wiry musculature that made the freakish thickness of his wrists all the more arresting, yet had the deadest-looking eyes Jeremy had ever seen. They held a positively merciless light.

Jeremy Lippincott drew himself up to his full imposing height as the man crossed the room. A pink-lined ear drooped, slapping his nose lightly. He flung it back with a jaunty toss of his fuzzy head, and squared his lantern jaw.

"I am Jeremy Lippincott, president of Lippincott Savings Bank. How many I help you?"

"You can start by telling me why you're wearing a pink bunny suit."

"Because they do not come in blue. And I consider that an extremely impertinent question, coming as it does from a man in a T-shirt and jeans."

"These are chinos."

"I stand corrected. Will you sit?"

"I'm just here for some answers."

"Then I will sit as I entertain your questions."

"A week back twelve million bucks was wire transferred into the Folcroft Sanitarium account. Who did it?"

"I have no idea. The funds simply appeared in the computers one morning."

"You tell the IRS that?"

"Of course not."

"Why not?"

"They would not believe so unlikely a tale, however true."

"How do you know till you try?"

"Because to admit to these facts is to incur the wrath of various meddlesome governmental agencies."

"As opposed to whose wrath?"

"I beg your pardon?"

"I told you I was worse than the IRS."

"I do not believe that is possible."

"All the IRS come after is your money and property. I usually don't stop at anything. Ask Rawlings."

Jeremy swallowed hard, absently wiping his moist brow with a convenient ear.

"No need. Actually you should be speaking to Rawlings. Commercial accounts are his responsibility."

"I'm speaking to you." And the man reached over and took Jeremy Lippincott's long fuzzy pink ears and used them to drag him unceremoniously across his own desk. Pens, papers and other items tumbled and spilled over the imported rug.

"Oof!" said Jeremy, crushing the nap with his spun-glass whiskers. He rolled over, throwing up his poufy pink paws.

"What do you mean to do?" he demanded of the looming brute.

"You look to me like the ticklish sort."

"I am nothing of the sort."

"I have an eye for these things." And the man planted a foot that had actually touched dirty sidewalk on Jeremy's fuzzy pink stomach. The air whoosed out of his lungs. Then the toe of the shoe began to insinuate itself into some of the most sensitive portions of Jeremy Lippincott's anatomy. Such as the inner arms, the belly button and that gooshy spot under the floating rib.

"Hah hah hah haha . . . Stop it! This instant!"

"Not till you promise to call the IRS."

"What . . . hah! . . . do I call them?"

"Place the call and repeat after me."

"Never. I will . . . hah! . . . not . . . hah! . . . incriminate myself. Heeee."

"People have been known to die laughing."

"Hah hah. You would not dare."

"There's nothing I wouldn't dare do to a snotty banker in a rabbit suit."

After five minutes of unbridled hilarity, the tears streaming out of his eyes, Jeremy Lippincott saw the supreme expediency of calling the IRS about the Folcroft account.

At first they would not take him seriously because he was tittering so, but eventually Jeremy calmed down and was connected to the proper person.

"That is correct," he told the official on the other end of the line. "The auditor was misinformed. No currency-transaction report was filed because we were completely unaware of the transfer. We thought it was a computer twitch and were awaiting the customer's response to the unexpected twelve-million-dollar credit on his next statement. Well, yes, we *did* invest the money. Purely as a good-faith gesture. Just in case the transfer was legitimate. No, we do not normally conduct our interbank transactions in so loose a manner. And I must say, I take exception to the term *loose*. It is inappropriate. The Lippincott family has been in the banking business since before there was such an entity as the Infernal Revenue Service—"

Jeremy winced painfully.

"I stand corrected. Internal. Yes, it was a slip of the tongue. No, I was not making light of the agency that is solely responsible for keeping the wheels of our great nation greased, as you so aptly put it. Yes, I will remember that in the future. Yes, I will expect your auditors to come round next week." Jeremy's voice turned wheedling. "Please, don't hurt us. We're only a savings bank, trying to make our way through these very trying times."

The line went click in Jeremy Lippincott's ear, and the receiver was taken from his hand and replaced on its cradle.

"That wasn't so bad, was it?" the thin brute with the thick wrists asked airily.

"We are to be audited, and that means the Federal Banking Commission will be poking their nasty little noses into our books. Not to mention the State Banking Commission."

"They'll stand up to scrutiny, won't they?" the intruder asked with entirely appropriate solicitousness.

"How am I to know? I only come in three days a week and leave the fine details to my incompetent staff. I never wanted to be a banker, but I only managed Cs at Yale. Although they were excellent Cs. Poppy positively beamed when he saw them. Oh, what shall I do?"

"If I were you," said Remo Williams, exiting the office, "I'd find a cleaner suit to wear."

Jeremy Lippincott put his head down on the desk and sobbed into it. Twenty minutes passed before he came up snuffling and noticed the door to his office had been left open and he had been exposed in all his poufy glory for the underlings to behold.

Mustering his strength, he got up and slammed the door shut. But not before calling out his righteous indignation, "I will have you all know that I am correctly attired for morning. My evening ensemble is an elegant sable, with silver accents on the paw pads and ear linings!"

EVEN AFTER the miracle, Basil Hume wasn't taking any chances.

Barely a week ago, he'd spent his days cowering in fear for his life. That had been a new experience for Basil Hume, director of the Grand Cayman Trust, situated in the colonial city of Georgetown on the balmy Caribbean island of Grand Cayman.

It was true that he did business with the scum of the earth. Drug barons, mafiosi and even lower forms of life such as U.S. senators. It was true also that these people were dangerous in the extreme. They were even more dangerous in the extreme where their money was concerned, and Basil Hume's bank had undertaken the very grave responsiblity of safeguarding their money. That was why it was called the Grand Cayman Trust.

In reality, its sole function was to be the bank of last resort for ill-gotten gains. There was no dollar or franc or kroner too soiled to be shoveled into the Grand Cayman Trust's bulging vaults.

In fact, most of the money that came to Grand Cayman Trust arrived by telephone, not delivered in satchels by armored car. That was the old-fashioned way. In the computer age, money moved as electrical impulses through the sophisticated medium of the international wire transfer of funds.

It was a very elegant way of shuffling large blocks of currencies of all nations. If francs were sent, they arrived as dollars. If yen, dollars also. Credited as dollars in the computer system of the Grand Cayman Trust. No client need ever set foot on Grand Cayman Island. He needn't leave a paper trail of any kind. His money was as good as the next rogue's. And when he had need of it, whether it be drachmas, lira or pounds sterling, it was wired back to him in the currency of his preference.

It was a wonderful system for those who wished to evade the snooping of their native governments into their personal finances.

But it had a downside. Oh, what a downside.

Basil Hume never believed there would be a downside—just as he long comforted himself with the belief that he would never ever have to concern himself with the actual clients who seldom came to his bank. Just their currencies, thank you very much.

Then came the banking crisis.

Now, more than a week after the near catastrophe, Basil Hume still had not quite grasped the matter. One morning he'd arrived to find the books in utter disarray. By books, of course, computer data bases were meant. All banking was a system of balances and bottom lines, debits and credits. It had simply moved from black-bound ledgers to computer workstations. The principle was exactly the same, except safer, smarter, more efficient, and as Basil Hume discovered to his unending horror, subject to electronic tampering.

The computers had lost the electronic digital packets—the bits and the bytes that quite literally represented hard currency—virtually overnight. There was no explaining it. It was simply impossible.

Not lost, actually. Transferred to a New York City bank that claimed not to have received the funds. Overnight, Grand Cayman Trust had become electronically insolvent—a first as far as Basil Hume knew.

It would have been embarrassing even under ordinary circumstances, if the clients were not extraordinary people.

With no funds available to be transferred out of Grand Cayman Trust, the phones had begun ringing at once. It was a nightmare. The D'Ambrosia crime syndicate. The Cali drug cartel. The survivors of the late and very much missed Pablo Escobar. And others too hideous to contemplate.

They all wanted to know where their money was.

In the midst of this, a U.S. Treasury agent named Smith had put in an appearance. He had had no jurisdiction, of course. Basil Hume very nearly threw him out, despite his claim to represent a depositor whose twelve million dollars was also missing. Some obscure federal agency, FEMUR or some such. The U.S. government was the least of Basil Hume's worries. They did not put out hits on those who misplaced their money. Often they simply gave them more. The U.S. government was a very curious business entity.

Smith had claimed knowledge of computers, and since he was grasping at straws already, Basil Hume has allowed the man access to the computer room, where he very quickly determined that the mess was not the work of a Grand Cayman Trust employee. It was a very convincing bit of logic there. No employees were unaccounted for; therefore, none were guilty. The murderous and vindictive nature of the trust's depositors absolutely guaranteed that. No one guilty of siphoning off the bank's assets would dare have shown up for work if that knowledge were rattling around inside his skull, knowing that at any minute an irate depositor would send his emissaries in with Uzis blazing to butcher everyone.

For a full day Basil Hume had suffered the nervous tortures of one who knows there is no place to hide.

Then miraculously the computers were restored to their proper bank balances within a day.

They had been working far into the night with guards picketed around the bank three deep. There was no hint, no forewarning, but as they hunched over their terminals, amazingly the bank balances began righting themselves. Within a matter of a minute or two—no more—the balances were all restored to the proper integers.

All, that is—an audit soon determined—except for a missing twelve million dollars in one account.

When this information was brought to his office by a sweaty manager, Basil Hume had shot bolt upright out of his chair and said, "Very good!" Then he had realized that he could end up just as dead from one irate customer as several. He'd asked, "Which is the short account?"

"The FEMA account, sir."

"And they are?"

"An agency of the United States government."

Basil Hume had collapsed back into his Corinthian leather chair, leaking a whistling sigh of sheer relief.

"They have no jurisdiction here," he said in an unconcerned tone.

And that had seemed to be the end of that. Later Basil heard through his network of informants in the world banking arena that the U.S. banking system had been similarly affected at the same time. Somehow all had been put to rights. No one knew how any more than Basil Hume understood how his computers had been corrected. But since all banking-system computers talked to each other electronically, he just assumed some sort of vile virus had been the culprit and the U.S. Federal Reserve people had squashed that particular bug.

Once the money began flowing through the system again, the telephones had stopped ringing so irately. Nothing like cash to placate the agitated. The threats likewise abated. And not surprisingly not a single customer deserted the bank. Where else would they go? Switzerland? The climate was positively alpine.

Each day Basil Hume had allowed one layer of guards to stand down. Now, some two weeks later, only a slightly stronger than normal complement remained, certainly enough to deal with any lingering bitterness on the part of the depositors. And more than enough should the U.S. government send their representatives where they were not welcome.

After all, they had no jurisdiction in the Grand Caymans, and without jurisdiction, they were just another depositor. One of the smaller ones, at that. Smaller and without teeth.

THE MASTER OF SINANJU saw the guards with their holstered pistols and their machine guns slung across their shoulders by straps. They wore tropical khaki, which made them look more like soldiers than guards. But they were guards. The way they formed a ring around the glass building in the sun-drenched city called Georgetown told him that. Professional soldiers would know enough not to present themselves like so many khaki ducks in a row.

"This is my destination," he told the taxi driver who had ferried him from the airport.

"Grand Cayman Trust?"

"Yes."

"Odd choice. They don't see much walk-in trade."

"They are a bank, are they not?"

"If you're looking for a place to cash a check," the driver suggested in his accent that blended a Caribbean lilt into a Scottish brogue, "I can take you to a nice neighborhood bank. You don't want to be going in there, sir. It's what they call a B-license bank. Strictly offshore trade—if you take my meaning."

"This is my destination. What is the fare?"

"Thirteen dollars American or ten dollars CI."

"Robber!"

"It is as the meter says, sir."

"The meter lies. I will pay half."

"And if I accept half, I must make up the balance."

"Better half than none."

"If you don't pay, I must call a constable."

"I see many strong and brave police standing before that bank," said Chiun, indicating the guards in khaki.

"You give me no choice, sir."

The cabbie whistled through the gap in his front teeth and waved toward the guards. Three broke ranks to approach. The space in the ring of khaki closed up like a wound healing.

"This old fellow, he won't pay his fare," the driver complained, jerking his thumb at the rear seat.

The three guards in khaki looked back and asked, "What fare?"

The driver craned his head around and saw not even a depression in the seat cushions to show that he had had a recent fare.

"Didn't you see him leave my cab?" he sputtered.

"No."

"But he was just there. A tiny bloke, dressed in an Oriental costume. It was black and gold, rather like the markings of a monarch butterfly."

The guards looked at the driver and opened the rear door.

"He is not hiding on the floorboards?"

"And the back is empty."

"Feel the cushions," the driver implored. "You will certainly feel the heat of his body."

A guard did so. He reported no warmth.

"The cushions are cold," another added.

The immediate vicinity was searched. Despite the fact that the cab had been in full view of the ring of guards at all times and the flamboyance of the missing fare, no one had seen a thing.

The driver was sent on his way, his face a knot of unhappiness, his pockets lighter by the amount displayed on the meter.

THUS did the Master of Sinanju breach the ring of guards that surrounded the stone building he had been sent to penetrate. No one had seen him approach. No hand was raised to stay him. For all eyes were on the frantic, greedy taxi driver and the three guards he was attempting to convince with his stumbling lies.

No one looked up when the Master of Sinanju entered the back lobby. There were minions seated at desks, their faces bathed in the emeralds and the ambers of their computer oracles. They were too intent upon their unimportant toil to notice him.

There was only one teller and one teller's cage. And no customers. Truly it was a bank unlike any other.

The Master of Sinanju glided through the aisles, his silken kimono sleeves fluttering like the wings of the butterfly whose markings they bore. He was a figure calculated to be noticed, yet no one noticed him.

That is, until he came to the door marked Basil Hume, Director.

A tanned young woman sat at a desk beside the door. A secretary. She looked up at the Master of Sinanju only when his shadow deliberately intercepted the overhead lights.

"May I help you, sir?" she inquired, smiling with her teeth but not her heart.

Chiun indicated the door with a long-nailed finger. "I seek audience with this man."

"Mr. Hume has no appointments today."

"Then he has no excuse not to treat with me," replied the Master of Sinanju, grasping the doorknob. It resisted his thin fingers. Locked. The Master of Sinanju increased the pressure, and the knob squealed, coming off in his hand. He handed it to the secretary, who reached out for it by reflex.

The Master of Sinanju left her juggling the friction-heated brass doorknob from hand to hand, squealing, "Whoo whoo whoo. My goodness, it's hot!"

BASIL HUME LOOKED UP from his desk and saw the tiny Asian in the riotous costume. His hand snaked to the guard buzzer, then froze momentarily in indecision. The figure confronting him, while dramatically gaudy, was impossibly old and frail, and therefore no conceivable threat to him.

"Yes?" he said.

"No," said the tiny Asian, who cleared the considerable length of the office with a graceful leap in which his wide-flung arms resembled the outspread wings of the monarch butterfly. His hand smacked down on the buzzer and the buzzer should have gone off from the impact. It did not. When the yellowed claw of a hand lifted, instead of a brass bump on the desktop, the buzzer button was now a crater.

Blinking, Basil Hume looked down. He could see the black button deep in the pit of the tiny brass-lined crater.

It seemed impossible for a sturdy buzzer housing to go from dome to crater under the force of one light smack, but there it was. So Basil dismissed the problem with a casual, "And how may I assist you, my good fellow?"

"You may die and save me the trouble," the old man squeaked.

"The trouble of what?"

"Dispatching you."

Basil Hume blinked. "Do I take that to mean what I believe it means?"

"Your death warrant has been signed."

Now Basil Hume's blood presure was rising. Trying to keep the man occupied, he let his finger creep toward the buzzer crater. Perhaps the electronic connection still functioned.

"By whom—if I may ask?"

"The emperor of America has called for your extinction. For you have lost funds entrusted to you."

"America has no emperor," Basil Hume pointed out.

"He is a well-known secret."

Basil Hume said, "Ah, I see," and his fingers touched the brass lip of the buzzer. "Well, my good man, if you are here to dispatch me—" he lifted his other hand airily "—then dispatch me by all means. I am guilty as charged." And he laughed self-consciously while his finger found the black enamel button deep in his desktop.

A fingernail nearly as long as the finger it grew from circled upward before his eyes to lash out like a slim asp.

When it withdrew, it did so with such speed that Basil Hume at first did not comprehend that he had been struck and if so where. He examined the front of his coat. His tie was intact. There was nothing unsightly fouling his pearl white shirt. His coat buttons were still in place.

It was only when he looked toward the buzzer crater that he noticed the blood. It was filling the depression like an inkwell. He wondered where the blood had come from and examined himself again.

When Basil Hume brought up his left hand, the one that had slipped into the buzzer, he felt the blood rilling down his sleeve. He examined his left wrist, and it was a wash of red. His wrist veins had been severed so quickly and cleanly he had felt nothing.

"My word," he said.

"Your last word," said the old Asian. "To ensure your silence."

And the fingernail that had cut with sure purity inserted itself into his Adam's apple, disconnecting his voice box.

Basil Hume knew this for a fact when he tried to speak and managed but an inarticulate gurgle.

Rising from his chair, he began thrashing about him in annoyance. Whereupon his right wrist suddenly opened up. It fountained blood. The hand that had done this was less than a blur in motion.

Dimly he heard a squeaky voice cry out, "Come quickly! Come quickly! This man had gone mad!"

Basil Hume's secretary thrust her head in and saw all the blood. Surprisingly she didn't faint. She turned guppy green and walked unsteadily to the ladies' room, not leaving until many hours later.

"What's going on here?" a man asked indignantly.

"I only asked him where my money was and he slashed his wrists," explained the cunning old Oriental, stroking his wispy beard in feigned agitation.

"Mr. Hume, is this true?"

Basil Hume thrashed around his desk, spattering blood everywhere. He tried to speak but could not. He tried to point an accusing finger at the old Asian, but he moved about so cleverly Hume's shaking finger could not indicate him with any accuracy.

"My God. It *is* true!"

The cry went out. "Call an ambulance."

The ambulance arrived inside of ten minutes. By that time the guards had all swarmed in to lay Basil Hume on the fine nap of his imported rug and tried to administer first aid. All of them at once.

Basil Hume was trampled, kicked and spent the last futile bits of his life giving new vibrancy to the maroon of his office rug and realizing he had underestimated the anger of the United States government. And its mighty secret emperor, whoever the cold uncaring bastard was.

No one saw the Master of Sinanju leave the Grand Cayman Trust, just as they failed to see him arrive.

Not long after, a taxi driver pulled over the main street of Georgetown upon being hailed.

"Convey me to the airport," a familiar squeaky voice insisted.

The driver stuck his head out. "Not you again!"

"I have never seen you before in my life," said Chiun in an injured tone.

"Pay me for the last fare, or I take you nowhere."

"How much?"

"Thirteen dollars American."

"Too much."

"Then you can enjoy the stink of my exhaust, you can."

The driver took off. He never heard the sound of his rear door open and close, nor did he notice that he had acquired a passenger. Not until he stopped at a traffic light near the clock monument to King George V and the door opened.

The driver looked back. To his astonishment, the tiny Asian had stepped over to an adjoining cab—which was also stopped at the light—and entered.

"Airport, O fortunate one," he cried. "And bear in mind I tip heavily for haste."

The light changed. The other cabbie took off before the first driver could warn him of the deadbeat fare.

The first driver buried his head in his steering wheel and sobbed until a traffic constable ticketed him for blocking the right of way.

12

Remo Williams kept looking at his inner watch.

Some people had an inner child. Remo had an inner watch. No matter what time it was, Remo always knew it to the nanosecond just by looking into his mind. He also had an inner compass, an inner alarm clock and inner thermometer.

The inner watch wasn't like his inner compass, which was the natural magnetic crystals in his brain recently discovered by biologists. Or his inner alarm clock, which was his biological clock. Or his inner thermometer, which biologists hadn't discovered yet because it was hidden in the left earlobe. The inner watch worked off whatever time zone Remo happened to be in. It was a function of his Sinanju training, just as all the unusual abilities Remo had come to take for granted were. But watches, as Chiun was fond of saying, were a Swiss confidence trick. It was not possible to have an inner watch any more than it was possible to have an inner can opener, Chiun had once insisted to Remo.

"So what time is it?" Remo had asked back on that long-ago day.

"Three hours before sunset."

"Four of five by my inner watch."

"There is no such technique," Chiun had scoffed. "Next you will be claiming you have an inner can opener."

"Not so far," Remo had retorted lightly. In time, he figured it out. He didn't have an inner watch. He had a perfect time sense—the same as Chiun. But where Chiun's sense of time was Eastern, and expressed in terms of hours past dawn or before sunset or moonrise, Remo's was calibrated into hours, minutes and seconds. In other words, Western style.

He figured that whenever he saw a clock, his brain simply and silently ticked off the seconds, minutes and hours after that, resetting itself whenever he came upon another clock.

It even compensated for daylight saving time. Provided Remo didn't forget twice a year.

It was exactly 3:48:09 by Remo's inner watch when the door to the Folcroft basement opened, sending a slowly elongating triangle of light down the concrete steps and falling on the body of the dead IRS agent Chiun had left there.

Remo was dreading this. All day long he had dreaded this moment. He had hurried back to Folcroft after paying a visit to the Lippincott Savings Bank, and relieved Chiun, who then left for Grand Cayman Island. Even with good connections and no hitch on the ground, it was bound to take the Master of Sinanju all day to complete his assignment.

That left Remo to baby-sit the all-important gold while Folcroft was being turned upside down by IRS agents.

Eventually he knew someone would come looking for the dead guy. And Remo was right.

"Anybody down there?" a voice from the top of the stairs called down.

Remo stood motionless in the dark. There were no windows in the Folcroft basement, so no betraying light beyond the spear of illumination coming from the stairs. He said nothing.

With luck the guy would go away. Of course, it was only a matter of time before someone ventured down. No one had gotten around to searching the basement yet, so the gold was safe.

The man at the top of the stairs started down. His hands brushed the rough concrete walls audibly, feeling for a light switch. When he found one, it went click. That was all.

"Damn!"

The man snapped the switch again rapidly. He was wasting his time. Remo had pulled the fuse on the basement lights.

The man came down anyway. He hadn't any flashlight—that much was sure. So when he tripped over the body at the foot of the stairs, he was surprised.

"Hey!" he said, getting up.

Remo could see perfectly in the near darkness, so he saw the man fumble on hands and knees until he encountered the inert body of the first IRS searcher.

"Jesus H. Christ!" he said, recognizing the touch of cool, dead human flesh.

The IRS man scrambled to his feet, stumbling back toward the stairs.

Remo had no choice then. The guy was going for help. He moved in.

His feet whisking silently over the concrete, Remo caught up with the man just as his hand got hold of the worn wood railing. Remo's hands went to the man's throat and squeezed hard.

The man went stiff, and Remo eased him off the stairs and laid him out beside the other stiff. Remo knelt down and whispered into the man's ear. "You'll be all right, pal. Consider this a caffeine-free coffee break."

Then he squeezed again, and the man went out like a TV.

Maybe, Remo thought as he crept to the top of the stairs and eased the door shut, the lid would stay on the basement until Chiun got back. Of course, that meant they still faced the problem of getting a ton of gold out of Folcroft under the noses of the IRS.

So he retreated to the triple-locked door and checked his inner watch again.

It was 4:01:28 and Remo hoped Chiun got here soon. Between the burned-plastic stink coming from Smith's computers and the disagreeable odor emanating from the dead IRS guy, this was no pleasure post.

13

It was damage-control time.

IRS Special Agent Jack Koldstad hated doing damage control.

It was the second day, and so far, they had found no sign of illegal activity in Folcroft Sanitarium. It was exactly what it appeared to be—a private hospital.

Except for the drumming. Everyone was reporting it now, but no one could find the source.

The birds still circled the building, too. Koldstad had put an agent on them around the clock. The man had reported the birds always vanished around sundown and were back in place at the crack of dawn.

"I told you to follow them to their roost."

"That's just it, sir. They don't appear to fly off."

"Are they roosting on the roof?"

"No, sir, it's just that when it gets dark, it's hard to see them. I lose sight of them in the darkness. But they're always back with the sun."

"Well, they have to go somewhere."

"If they do, sir, it's not clear where."

"Tonight I want you up on that roof with a high-intensity spotlight and that scoped rifle. I want those birds taken down."

"Yes, Mr. Koldstad."

And there was that damn phantom Chinaman. No one could find him, either.

Koldstad then put the call he dreaded in to his superior.

"What's the latest?" Dick Brull demanded.

"I'm sorry to report little progress, Mr. Brull."

"What do you mean by little?"

"We've uncovered no contraband, no illegal activity, no money laundering and no unauthorized operations such as plastic surgeries, abortions or other legal or quasi-legal sources of unreported income. The pharmaceutical department checks out. Their records are impeccable. No turkey drugs are flowing through this place in the guise of prescription drugs. No indication of a secret designer-drug factory, either."

"Well, the DEA must have had some good Intelligence. Otherwise, they wouldn't have seized the place, would they?"

"I know, Mr. Brull. But Folcroft checks out clean."

Brull's crushed-stone voice began to grind more harshly. "This is not satisfactory, Koldstad. Not satisfactory at all. The service seized this hospital at great cost to its morale and personnel."

"I know, sir."

"The service has a sacred mandate to seize people and businesses wherever justified. We have an excellent record in that respect. Over ninety percent of our seizures hold up in court, lawful or otherwise. The DEA can't say that. If our numbers ever go down, Congress could take away IRS power to do jeopardy seizures. If they start chipping away at the service's special powers, next thing you know they'll be hammering us on withholding rights. We have a great thing going here. And you don't want to screw it up like some candy-ass trainee.''

"What do I do? Just say it, I'll do it."

"Until we have chapter and verse on Folcroft, it's your campground. You stay there. You run it. You pare its operating costs to the bone. Fire whoever you have to, deinstitutionalize whoever you have to. Get to the bottom of that place, and then we'll sell it off brick by brick to satisfy its debt to Uncle Sam. You got that?''

"Yes, Mr. Brull."

Right then and there, Jack Koldstad knew his career with the IRS's CID was dead on the water unless he turned Folcroft Sanitarium into the most lucrative jeopardy seizure in the past twenty years.

He began calling in his troops, issuing marching orders.

"We're invoking the hundred percent rule here. That means Harold Smith's personal assets are forfeit. Seize his car and house and throw out into the street anyone you find living there."

"Yes, sir."

"Get the staff down to manageable levels. Every person we can cut from the payroll means more payroll for the service."

"Right away, Mr. Koldstad."

"I'll have our people in Martinsburg run a deep background check on Harold Smith. The master file will have his tax records going back to day one."

"I never heard of a filer who didn't fudge a return somewhere along the line."

"That's the beauty of the voluntary compliance system. The odds are long the taxpayer will hand us the pole we shove up his noncompliant ass, and the lubricant to boot."

"Understood, sir."

All morning long they came and went. One agent came in as the last was leaving. His face was pale. "Skinner is missing, sir."

Koldstad's small eyes got smaller. "I thought it was Reems who was missing."

"He still is, sir. Now Skinner has gone AWOL, too."

"No one goes AWOL from the service. There's no place to go AWOL to—unless you want to forfeit your citizenship. Where did you last see him?"

"I think he was sent to look into the basement."

"I thought the basement had been checked."

"That was Reems's job. It doesn't look like he completed it."

"Let me get this straight. Reems goes into the basement and doesn't come back?"

"That was yesterday, sir."

"And today Skinner goes in and isn't heard from?"

"That seems to be the size of it."

Jack Koldstad brightened. "Looks like the basement is where we hit the jackpot. Assemble the troops. We're going into that basement."

"Armed?"

"Of course armed. The IRS doesn't walk into situations where it doesn't have the upper hand going in. And if that damn Chinaman is hiding down there, he's going to pay for assaulting an IRS special agent. And I don't mean in interest and penalties."

REMO HEARD THEM coming from two floors up.

Even surrounded by the soundproof concrete foundation of Folcroft Sanitarium, it was impossible not to know that the IRS was closing in force and armed to the teeth.

They pounded down the stairs in the lead-footed tread typical of armed men. They jacked rounds into chambers and communicated by walkie-talkies.

A smaller contingent was circling around to the freight entrance, feet crunching grit.

That gave Remo plenty of time to step up to the two prone IRS agents, tuck one under each arm and stash them in the coal furnace. It was cold, fortunately. Not that it would matter to the first agent to have made the mistake of venturing into the Folcroft basement. But the guy who was still alive was probably relieved to be folded up and stuffed into the bed of cool brown ash, considering the other possibility. Even if a day-old dead guy was set on top of him.

"Try not to inhale too much," Remo whispered as he shut and dogged the fire door.

Remo looked around quickly. Chiun's sleeping mat and spare kimonos were out of sight. Remo had hammered the corrugated door shut with his bare hands, but a crack still showed. He had patched the rip from inside and locked the adjoining door.

The basement looked as ordinary as possible now.

So Remo went to the toolshed and pulled out a long-handled push broom.

When the IRS pounded down the inner steps, flashlights blazing, they found him coolly sweeping the dusty concrete floor, the happy-go-lucky strains of "Whistle While You Work" coming from between his pursed lips.

"Who they hell are you?" demanded a man with a long jaw and painfully pinched temples.

"Name's Remo. I'm the basement janitor."

"How the hell did you get in here?"

Remo pointed to the side door. "The usual way. Through the janitorial entrance."

"Didn't you see the IRS sign out front?"

"Nope. Can't read. Why do you think I'm pushing a broom in a basement?"

The IRS agent eyed Remo closely. "You a nonfiler, Remo? You look like a nonfiler to me. What's your Social Security number?"

From the side door came the pounding of fists on stubborn steel.

"Open up! IRS!"

"Open it up for them," the agent ordered Remo.

"Why not?" said Remo, setting the broom against the door to the computer room.

When the door opened, it really opened. Remo faded back only inches ahead of the inward surge of armed IRS agents.

"I thought you guys were from the IRS," he said as a fan of gun muzzles tracked him.

"We are." The agent with the pinched temples stepped up to flash his ID. "Jack Koldstad. With the IRS Criminal Investgation Division."

"You act like Paddy O'Toole with the IRA knee-capper squad."

"Shut up. I'll ask the questions around here. An agent came down earlier."

"Haven't seen him. And I've been here all day."

Koldstad eyed his agents. "Sweep this place."

"I think I beat you to it," said Remo.

"I meant sweep it for contraband."

"My job description covers dirt only," Remo said.

The agents moved through the basement with grim purpose. One of them found the fuse box and noticed a switch in the red position. He reset it. The overhead lights came on.

"Didn't you notice there was no light?" Koldstad asked Remo.

"I notice it now," Remo said.

An agent came upon the triple-locked door and called out, "Mr. Koldstad, I think I found something."

"What is it?"

"A door with a lot of locks."

Koldstad hurried over, saying, "Bring that smart-ass along."

"I'll go quietly," Remo offered as the gun muzzles closed in on him.

Koldstad was looking over the door.

"Where does this lead?" he asked Remo.

Remo shrugged. "To the other side."

"Don't get smart."

"If I knew, I'd say," Remo lied.

"Who has the keys?"

"Dr. Smith."

Koldstad grabbed an agent by the arm. "You go upstairs. Bring me every key from Smith's office."

While the agent was gone, Koldstad turned to Remo, "What's your name again?"

"Remo."

"Okay, Remo, we're the IRS. You know what that means?"

"I get a refund?"

"No!"

"Shucks."

Koldstad lowered his voice conspiratorially. "Work here long?"

"Too long."

"Good. You must know a lot of what goes on here."

"I know which end of a broom to hold." Remo swept the men around him with his deep-set eyes. "I also know not to point a weapon at a man unless I intend to use it."

"The IRS doesn't shoot compliant citizens," Koldstad assured him.

"I'll try to remember that."

"We've seized Folcroft."

"That explains all the guns."

"We suspect illegal activity is going on here."

"What kind?"

"You tell us."

"Got me. It's a hospital. The only thing out-of-bounds are the doctors' bills."

"You ever notice unusual activity here? Late-night deliveries? People coming and going after hours?"

"I'm the day-shift janitor."

"Ever been audited, Remo?"

"No."

"Keep acting stupid and we'll remedy that."

"Keep threating me and I might get mad."

"Don't mouth off. This is the IRS you're talking to."

"What about my constitutional rights?"

"IRS regulations supercede the Fourth Amendment protecting against search and seizure without due process."

"Since when?"

"Since the Civil War."

Just then the agent came back with a fistful of keys.

"This is everything I could find," he said.

Koldstad focused his too-small eyes on Remo. "Last chance to tell us what we need to know."

"I don't know what you want to know," Remo said.

"Okay, open that door."

They tried every key twice. None fit.

"Damn," Koldstad said. "Okay, get the ram. We're battering it down."

Remo tried to keep the worry off his face. The way they were going, it was just a matter of time. And

Chiun might be back at any minute, or not for hours yet.

Mouth thinning, Remo decided to let things play out a little while longer. There were only eight of them. Not too many to handle if it came down to that.

The ram was a solid slug of steel weighing maybe fifty pounds with two handles welded to each side. The nose looked as if ball-peen hammers had gone at it.

"Okay, let her rip."

Two of the beefiest agents took up the ram and swung it back and forth until it built up momentum. They sent it crashing into the door on a dead run.

The door was chilled steel painted gray to blend in with the gray-painted concrete wall. The first hit didn't even mark the paint. The second cracked a paint chip loose. The third hit bounced off.

"What's wrong with you milk balls! Hit it harder!"

This time they backed up a dozen yards, got a clumsy running start and slammed the door dead center. The door shuddered on its heavy hinges. The ram bounced back, taking the agents with it. They ended up on their asses on the dusty concrete, the ram cracking the concrete floor with a loud bang.

"There's something behind that door," Koldstad said, pacing like a caged tiger. "I know there is."

"We could shoot the locks off," an agent suggested.

"They only do that in movies," Remo said quickly.

"It's worth a try," said Koldstad.

"If there is something, then you could wreck it with bullets," Remo pointed out.

Koldstad whirled. "Then you do know something!" he crowed.

"Not me," Remo said grudgingly.

"Blow it open," Koldstad said, one eye on Remo.

Remo stood there, rotating his thick wrists anxiously. He wasn't worried about Smith's computers. They were a lost cause. But Chiun's gold was not bulletproof.

A man brought a MAC-11 up to the padlock, testing the angle of fire a couple of times, and fired once. The padlock combination became a smear. The hasp held.

"I'll try again, sir."

This time he fired a short burst. The hasp broke clean, and the padlock fell to the floor with a dusty clank.

"Great. Now the other locks."

Another agent came up with a .357 Magnum and put five shots into the remaining key lock. Each shot made a bigger dent.

Then they brought up the ram and finished the job.

Remo held his breath.

Koldstad turned to Remo. "By the way," he said smugly, "you're fired."

"You can't fire me. I work for Dr. Smith."

"And the IRS owns Smith's illegal ass. Now clear yours out."

Without waiting for Remo's reply, Jack Koldstad strode up to the battered steel door and used both hands to pull it open.

And his jaw dropped at the sight of stacks and stacks of gleaming yellow ingots that reached to the ceiling. They were packed together so tightly there was only one narrow walkway between the ingots. Even under the weak overhead lights, they shed a warm golden radiance that picked out yellowish details on every face turned toward them.

There was a collective intake of breath. In that crucial moment no eyes were upon Remo Williams. Everyone was gaping at the tall stacks of gleaming yellow ingots, realizing what they had to be.

"We hit the mother lode," someone whispered.

"Our careers are saved," another murmured.

And from the corrugated door came a fierce screech, followed by a burst of raw sunlight, and a voice boomed, "Stand back from the gold of Sinanju or face the wrath of its awesome protector!"

14

The voice of the Master of Sinanju was still echoing off the concrete walls when Remo faded back and took out the two IRS agents directly at his back with his elbows. He brought them back and up and nailed the agents on the point of their chins too fast for their dull senses to see him coming.

They dropped like wet oatmeal poured into off-the-rack suits.

From a standing position, Remo pivoted and took out a MAC-11 that was swiveling toward the corrugated door. The machine pistol lost its barrel, and the agent clutching the grip lost his weapon to the sudden fury of Remo's side kick. He was clutching his gun hand when something that felt like a ball-peen hammer knocked him flat.

Remo began weaving among the others, tapping them on their skulls with a steel-hard forefinger. Nobody got off a shot. Everybody went down hard.

"Take them out clean," Remo called.

"They have profaned my gold," Chiun squeaked.

"They only just found it. Now, do as I say."

The Master of Sinanju leaped into the basement like a great monarch butterfly taking wing. But he landed on Jack Koldstad with the ferocity of a pouncing tiger.

Koldstad threw up his arms to shield himself, but his arms were forced aside so that the raking fingernails scored vertical lines in his surprised face. His mouth opened in a frozen scream, and two thumbs found the indentations on either side of his narrow forehead.

Jack Koldstad never felt the long thumbnails plunge into his brain. He just rolled his eyes up and made a pile of clothes-covered meat on the floor where he had been standing.

Remo saw all this out of the corner of his eye as he finished his sweep of the IRS. He went for knees and, when collapsing legs brought agents' heads down, he slapped the consciousness out of them with the flat of his hands.

Smack smack smack.

The last agent collapsed onto the one just before him, and Remo turned toward the Master of Sinanju, who was shaking the dust from his wide kimono sleeves like a flustered black-and-orange bat.

"I said not to kill anyone," Remo complained.

"I did not."

"I saw you drive your nails into the head guy's skull."

"I drove them into the part of the brain he obviously did not use. He will live."

"I'll believe it when I see it," grumbled Remo, joining the Master of Sinanju at the open door to the computer room.

"Well, the cat's out of the bag now," said Remo, surveying the scattering of unconscious IRS agents.

"They must all die. It is Smith's edict that any who trespass upon his kingly preserves forefeit their lives."

"We'll check with Smith first."

"I will not leave my gold unattended, for obviously you are not equal to the task."

"So sue me. I didn't think they'd get the door broken down."

"You should have broken their empty skulls."

"Look, I'll take this up with Smith, I said."

"I do not trust you to return with the correct answer. We will both take this up with Smith."

"Fine with me."

HAROLD SMITH would have groaned had his body been his to command.

But the Master of Sinanju hadn't restored his bodily functions. It was a terrible feeling because it was the second day, and even though they had hooked up an IV tube and were feeding him intravenously, his bowels felt like sausages filled with cold, soggy bran meal. But his body refused to release the inert matter that made him feel as constipated as an elephant in tall sugarcane.

He forgot his inner distress as the Master of Sinanju tried to explain the situation. "The tax terrorists have breached your holy of holies, your *sanctum sanctorum*, O Smith."

"That means they found the gold," Remo added by way of explanation.

They hovered over his bed like anxious angels, Chiun's face a guarded mask, Remo's looking worried.

"But have no fear," continued Chiun. "We dispatched them all."

"Actually they're just down for the count. Except that guy Koldstad. Maybe he'll live, maybe he won't."

"They live or die at your pleasure, O Emperor. You have only to blink twice, and I will see that their body parts nourish the fish of the cold blue bay that is called the sound."

"It's up to you, Smitty. For my money, they were throwing their weight around like they were the KGB. They could use a lesson in manners."

Smith blinked furiously.

"He has decreed that they die!"

Smith blinked even more furiously.

Remo said, "Look again. He's blinking to beat the band. I think he wants to say something."

Remo reached out to Smith's forehead.

"No, I will do it." And Chiun's finger touched the spot.

"I instructed you to get rid of the gold first!" Smith said, sitting up. A strange expression crossed his face, and Remo pinched his nose shut with his right thumb and index finger.

The Master of Sinanju withdrew several paces with alacrity and continued the audience from a far corner of the room.

"I called for a moving van, Smitty. But the earliest they'd come is tomorrow. Besides, the grounds are crawling with IRS agents. So Chiun and I figured we'd take care of the other business first while we figured a way to work it out."

"You failed," Smith said bitterly.

"We screwed up," Remo admitted.

"*You* have screwed up." Chiun fairly spat out the words. "Emperor, Remo was on guard when the tax terrorists came to him. Only by my timely arrival was the day saved."

"Thanks for your moral support, Chiun," Remo said acidly. "Look, Smitty, we can still work this out. Do the IRS guys go or not?"

Smith's prim mouth thinned to a bloodless line. "Not."

Remo threw up his hands. "Great. So what's our next move?"

"The gold must be removed," Chiun said. "They must not take it."

"We can try to rent a truck, but I don't think they rent out semis."

"Do what you can, but do it soon," said Smith.

He started to climb out of bed, but Remo moved in and pushed him back into the bedclothes with a flat but firm hand. "You stay put until we pull this off," he said.

"I must change."

"Sorry."

Remo started to reach out toward Smith.

Smith threw up a pale hand. "Wait. There is something you must do for me."

Remo hesitated. "What's that?"

"I must attend to an important letter left on my desk in the confusion. Send Mrs. Mikulka in."

"They fired her."

"What!"

"It was the first thing they did when they took over. They fired me, too."

"You?"

"They mistook me for a janitor."

Smith gray eyes narrowed and turned to flint. "Then I must count on you."

"Shoot."

"On my desk is a sealed letter addressed to Winston Smith...."

"Wait a minute. This isn't one of your old security codes, is it? I remember your dippy Aunt Mildred. She didn't even exist, but I was always getting coded messages from her."

"I assure you that Winston Smith is a real person. Now I would like you to mail that letter."

"Promise me that it doesn't involve that dippy doomsday scheme of yours."

"I assure you that Winston Smith is no concern of yours."

"Okay," said Remo.

"See that it goes out express mail."

Remo blinked. "You running a fever?"

"No. Why do you ask?"

"Express mail costs, oh, a whole eight, nine dollars. I've never known you to spring for such serious bucks when the price of a first-class stamp will get the job done."

"We have lost a day, and the letter is very important to Winston Smith."

Remo asked, "What kind of name is Winston?"

"A family name," said Harold Smith before they sent him back into the oblivion of his numbed body.

15

It was a blow-and-go mission.

That was the first stupid thing. There were easier ways to inject a SEAL into North Nog than shooting him up out of the sail of a nuclear attack submarine in full combat gear. Why not a HALO night drop? Or Sea Stallion insertion?

Then there was the Fucking Ugly Gun.

His mission commander had come along for the ride. An hour before he was to go up the blow tube, the XO showed up in the cubicle where Winston Smith was fieldstripping his Heckler & Koch MP-5 machine gun.

"You won't be needing that, Smith."

Navy SEAL Winston Smith looked up. His eyes, brown as tree bark, frowned in his lean youthful face. "It's been scrubbed?"

"Fat chance. The mission is still a go. But you'll be using this."

The XO opened a deep ordnance box and exposed the weapon to the overhead lights. "Go ahead. Pick it up."

Winston Smith stood up and regarded the weapon, his face tiger striped with camo paint.

It was a machine pistol. No mistaking that. Not with a banana clip shoved into the oversize grip, and a clear Lucite ammo drum mounted in front of the trigger guard. There were Lucite clips radiating from the breech at equally spaced angles, like spokes on a wagon wheel. At a glance Smith estimated over 250 visible rounds.

"Looks like the mother of all Pez dispensers," he said.

"Pick it up."

Smith lifted the weapon from its crushed-velvet tray. It was a slab of some kind of ceramic material, plated with as much chrome as a '57 Chevy. The barrel was unusually long. There was a chrome laser sighter slung under it, and a side-mounted AN/PVS-4 night scope. Where the rear sight should have been was an attachment Smith didn't recognize but reminded him of a combination LED display and minishotgun microphone.

"Throw away half the crap on your combat vest, Smith. This baby has almost everything you need for the mission. She fires 4.7 mm hollowpoint Hydra-Shok subsonic rounds, fifty-five to a clip. Flick a switch, and the caseless Black Talon drum ammo is at your disposal. Also included for your dining pleasure are the spring-loaded bayonet, folding tripod, night scope and optional laser-targeting system. In addition, there's a built-in LED compass, distance reader, transponder and two-way SATCOM satellite uplink."

"What's this dohickey?" Smith asked, thumbing a button beside the clip release.

The XO smiled grimly. "Press it."

Smith did. A lip of blue flame curled out of the silencer-flash-hider muzzle.

"Butane cigarette lighter," the XO explained. "Never know when you're going to need a light." The XO's smile widened. "Ain't she a kick in the teeth?"

"Yeah," Smith growled, trying to shake the flame out, "if you like mirror-finish hardware. Why don't I just suck on the muzzle and pull the trigger? With this thing strapped to me, the warlord will see me coming two oceans away."

The XO looked wounded. "It's a CIA prototype. It came this way. It's called a BEM. Stands for Bullet Ejecting Mechanism."

"Looks more like a FUG—Fucking Ugly Gun." Smith dropped it back into its case. "Send it back. My H&K will do me just fine."

"This is part of the mission. Now, shut your dumb face and listen for once."

Winston Smith made a grim mouth. His eyes seemed to retreat into his skull. Folding his arms, he listened. He did not look happy.

"Aside from the features just described, this BEM weapon can be personalized to the end user."

"The what?"

"That's what the manual calls you. The end user. It's some kind of technical jargon. Forget it, Smith. Just listen."

The BEM came out of its case again, and the XO pressed something and tiny varicolored lights strung along the barrel began blinking like a pinball machine. Smith rolled his eyes, and the dull gold loop in his left ear began dancing in the bad light.

"Now," the XO continued, "I've engaged the voice-rec function. Just say a few words into the gun."

"Fuck you, gun."

The gun said, "Fuck you, gun." It sounded like a bad imitation of Winston Smith's own voice.

"A few more words. I don't think it got it."

"It's a stupid gun, then."

"It's a stupid gun, then," said the gun in a much clearer tone. This voice sounded almost exactly like Smith's voice this time. The LED display came on. It said "Rec."

The XO smiled. "Okay, it should be configured to your voice pattern. Here, try to shoot a hole in the bunk."

"We're on a submarine. We'll get our boots wet."

The XO smiled. "Trust me on this."

"Okay," Smith said, smiling the cool smile that made him instantly recognizable despite his war paint to other members of the Navy's elite counterterrorist unit, SEAL Team Six. "I will."

He took the weapon and leveled it at the bunk. His thumb did the natural thing and found nothing.

"Where's the safety?"

"There's no conventional safety. Test fire a round."

Smith squeezed the trigger. The weapon didn't so much as click. It might have been a very heavy super-soaker.

"Broken," he said.

"Now tell the gun to arm itself."

"You tell it to arm itself. I don't talk to ordnance."

"No, it won't recognize my voice. Watch—arm one."

The gun lights continued blinking merrily.

"Try firing it."

Smith squeezed the trigger. Nothing happened.

"Now, you say it."

"Arm one," said Smith.

The gun beeped. The barrel lights winked out.

"I think I killed it," Smith said.

"Try squeezing off the round now."

Smith dropped the barrel until the muzzle came in line with his dented pillow. He squeezed once. To his surprise, the gun convulsed. A hot round went into the pillow, and a smoking shell dropped clinking onto the steel deck floor.

When the submarine didn't start taking on water, Winston Smith threw the heavy pistol back at his XO and said, "So what?"

"You don't get it, you dumb SOB, do you?"

"No, I don't."

"This baby has a little chip in it. You know, like the one on your stupid shoulder, only ten times smarter. It recognized your voice. You say 'arm one,' and for five minutes, you can fire it all you want. Then it cuts out. If you're caught or disarmed, the gun is useless to the enemy. You can't be shot at with your own weapon. What do you say to that, smart mouth?"

"If you like talking to your gun, it's wonderful. If you get lonely on night drops, it's reassuring. I don't like either, so take the thing and shove it up the ass of the fool who designed it.''

"Stow the attitude. This weapon is part of the mission. I'm ordering you to carry it."

"Can I take my H&K along, too?"

"Absolutely. Not."

"Fuck."

"Fuck," echoed the gun.

"Is it going to repeat everything I say, too?" Winston demanded unhappily.

The XO frowned. "No. It shouldn't have done that. Give it a whack."

"You crazy? It's a firearm. You don't whack a loaded firearm."

"Well, wait until the five-minute firing window closes and then whack it."

Winston Smith lifted the gun to his forehead and said, "Blowing my brains out makes more sense."

"Look, I gotta check in with the Pentagon. There's a chronometer somewhere on that thing. It'll tell you when the firing window is closed. You just be ready. And I don't want to see any excess hardware hanging off your sorry ass when I come back."

The door shut, leaving Winston Smith holding the BEM gun to his forehead.

"What the hell. If you mission goes sour, I can always make blood pudding with my brains."

Lowering the gun, he said into it, "You suck."

"You suck," replied the BEM gun.

"But you suck worse," Winston Smith said amiably.

The BEM gun said nothing to that. Smith smiled. He was starting to get the hang of this hunk of steel. It reminded him of his Uncle Harold.

16

When they returned to the basement, the IRS agents were still where Remo and Chiun had left them.

"You know," Remo said, "when they wake up, they're going to remember the gold."

"That is why they should not wake up," Chiun said.

"Maybe if they wake up on the roof, they wouldn't be so sure about what they saw."

"It is a good idea. Go ahead. Carry them to the roof."

"You could pitch in."

"The gold has been left unguarded long enough. I must remain here."

Remo lifted an eyebrow. "That mean you're going to help move the gold?"

"Possibly."

"Then you help out with these guards."

"You may take the first."

"I got the first two," said Remo, hefting two agents under his arms. He ran them up to the top of the stairs and deposited both inside the door where they wouldn't be seen. Chiun brought one, dragging him by the tie and taking pains that his face hit every stair riser on the way up.

When they had a sloppy pile, Remo slipped across the hall and brought the elevator down. He held the doors open while the Master of Sinanju flung IRS agents like sacks of laundry into the car.

"One at a time!" Remo urged.

Three IRS agents came whizzing across the lobby like pillows shot from a repeating cannon.

Remo scrambled to catch them all. The last one went splat against the rear of the car despite his best efforts. Remo, noticing it was the dead guy, just shrugged.

"Is that all?" he called across the corridor.

"Yes."

Remo ran the cage up to the third floor and jammed the doors open while he tried to figure out the best way of getting them to the roof trap undetected. Their ties seemed of good material, so he grabbed the thick ends in two handfuls and dragged the agents around a corner to the trap.

They didn't go up the trap ladder as smoothly as they had down the polished corridor linoleum, but nobody lost any teeth in the process, so Remo considered it a successful transfer.

He happened to look up. The three circling birds were still up there. Remo angled around, shielding his eyes from the sun, but they remained as indistinct as ever. From the roof they looked less like birds than bats. Except bats never grew that big.

He noticed they cast no shadows on the roof. But the angle of the sun would explain that.

"The hell with them," he said. "I got more important things to do."

On his way down to the third floor, Remo heard a voice and went back up again.

"I do not know what to do," a voice was saying. "These IRS have ordered me to begin deinstitutionalizing patients. How can I do this? It is not humane."

Another voice said, "Dr. Smith will have a fit if he ever wakes up."

"This I know. But my hands are tied."

"Who is the first?"

"The deluded patient who calls himself Beasley. I cannot find any certification papers on him, so I dare not keep him, dangerous as he is. And there is no record of next of kin, and thus I do not know who to release him to."

"It is very strange that the paperwork is not in order. Dr. Smith is quite fastidious about such things."

The voices passed around a corner and faded away.

Remo came down, saw the elevator had been sent back to the first floor and made for a fire door.

A drumming sound penetrated from the other side. He hesitated. It continued, a doleful noise like a tireless but bored child beating a toy drum.

Doom doom doom doom . . .

Remo hit the door with his hand, and the sound retreated down the stairs. He flashed down to the next landing, but there was nothing there.

The sound continued somewhere down the concrete stairwell. This time Remo went over the rail, hands flat to his sides, and landed on the first floor.

The sound was suddenly above him now. Reversing, he took the steps five at a time, and while the sound was unhurried, what was making it was not. It beat him back to the third-floor landing.

He thought he saw something that looked like a pink powder puff melt into the shut fire door. Remo blinked. The blotch of pink was gone. He went to the door and looked through the vertical slit window above the latch. The corridor was empty except for a passing physician.

"Ah, the hell with whatever you are, too," said Remo.

Returning to the basement, he told the Master of Sinanju, "Bad news, Little Father."

"What?"

"The IRS has told the staff to begin releasing patients."

"The wicked Dutchman, too!"

"He's still there. But they're about to let Beasley go."

"This must not happen."

"Yeah, the only way to head this off is to put Smith back behind his desk. But I don't think we can trust him."

"We have no choice." The Master of Sinanju looked from Remo to the gold and back again. His face tightened like a spiderweb. "I will attend to Smith. You fetch a vehicle suitable for conveying the gold of Sinanju away from this place."

"Gotcha," said Remo. He slipped out the side door.

17

When Jack Koldstad awoke, he thought he was dead.

It was a reasonable conclusion to jump to under the circumstances. He lay out under the open sun, a trio of shadowy vultures circling over him on lazy wings, and he could taste blood in his mouth. His front teeth wobbled when he touched them with his tongue.

He tried to remember how he had gotten here. The last thing he could recall was the monarch butterfly. It was huge. Bigger than the birds circing overhead. It was the fiercest, most venomous-looking butterfly Jack Koldstad could ever remember seeing. Even as the memory returned, its hideous shriek reverberated in his skull.

"Oh, God," Koldstad groaned.

A voice said, "He's awake."

"Who is it? Who's there?" Koldstad demanded.

"It's me, Mr. Koldstad. Agent Phelps."

"Phelps! You're here, too. What happened?"

A head came into view somewhere between the circling birds and Koldstad's recumbent head. It was Phelps. His broad face was very concerned. "Don't you recall, sir? We were in the basement. We had just broken down that big door."

"Yes, I remember seeing gold."

"You saw it, too?"

"Of course. What's wrong? How did we get here? And where is here? All I see is sky."

"The hospital roof. We all woke up looking at the sky."

"The last thing I remember was the basement."

"What else do you remember?" Phelps asked solicitously.

Koldstad winced. "The black-and-orange...thing."

"Sir?"

"It was a giant. I'd never seen one that big."

"Seen what, sir?"

"Don't you remember?"

"We've just swapped impressions, sir. And for most of us, the lights went out when that janitor, Remo, turned on us."

"I remember him, too."

"Did he get you, too, sir?"

"No, it was the other...thing."

"Thing?"

"It clawed my face."

"We've sent for a doctor, sir. Your face is pretty badly lacerated. Did you see what did it?"

"Yes."

"So you can describe it for us?"

"It was a butterfly."

Silence greeted Jack Koldstad's admission. Other heads came into view. Koldstad's eyes tried to focus on their faces, but the overhead sun threw them all into shadow. But they blocked out those damn tireless vultures, so that was a good thing.

"A butterfly. Did you say butterfly?"

"A giant of a butterfly. With monarch markings and a face."

"You mean a butterfly face?"

"No, it was the face of that damn phantom Chinaman."

Silence greeted that admission, too.

"Do you think you can stand, sir?"

Koldstad lifted a wavering arm. "Help me up."

Hands reached down to grasp Jack Koldstad's hands and elbows and shoulders. He felt no pain as he was hauled to his feet. No pain at all. Oh, there was some stiffness about his face, but no bones complained. And he could see fine.

He saw a man lying on the gravel roof, his skin, hair and clothes a powdery gray.

"Who's that?"

"Agent Reems, Mr. Koldstad. He was with us when we woke up. I'm afraid he's dead, sir."

"What about Skinner?"

"Here, sir."

A man stepped into view. He was the same powdery gray mummy color as Reems. But he was alive. His sheepish smile broke through the gray like a whalebone corset emerging from the ashes of a banked fire.

"Skinner. What happened to you?"

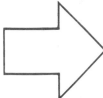

NO COST! NO OBLIGATION TO BUY!
NO PURCHASE NECESSARY!

PLAY "LUCKY 7"
AND GET FIVE FREE GIFTS!
HOW TO PLAY:

1. Get a coin, carefully scratch off the silver box. Then check the claim chart to see what we have for you—FREE BOOKS and a gift—ALL YOURS! ALL FREE!

2. Send back this card and you'll get hot-off-the-press Gold Eagle books, never before published. These books have a total cover price of $15.49. But THEY ARE TOTALLY FREE; even the shipping will be at our expense!

3. There's no catch. You're under no obligation to buy anything. We charge nothing—ZERO—for your first shipment. And you don't have to make any minimum number of purchases—not even one!

4. The fact is thousands of readers enjoy receiving books by mail from the Gold Eagle Reader Service. They like the convenience of home delivery . . . they like getting the best new novels before they're available in stores . . . and they love our discount prices!

5. We hope that after receiving your free books you'll want to remain a subscriber. But the choice is yours—to continue or cancel, anytime at all! So why not take us up on our invitation, with no risk of any kind. You'll be glad you did!

SURPRISE MYSTERY GIFT
IT COULD BE YOURS <u>FREE</u> WHEN
YOU PLAY "LUCKY 7".

PLAY "LUCKY 7"

Just scratch off the silver box with a coin.
Then check below to see the gifts you get.

YES! I have scratched off the silver area above. Please send me the free books and gift for which I qualify. I understand I am under no obligation to purchase any books, as explained on the back and on the opposite page.

164 CIM AQXW
(U-DL-09/94)

NAME

ADDRESS   APT.

CITY   STATE   ZIP

7 7 7	WORTH FOUR FREE BOOKS AND FREE SURPRISE GIFT
🍒 🍒 🍒	WORTH FOUR FREE BOOKS
● ● ●	WORTH FOUR FREE BOOKS
🔔 🔔 🍒	WORTH TWO FREE BOOKS

Offer limited to one per household and not valid to present subscribers. All orders subject to approval.

PRINTED IN U.S.A.   © 1991 GOLD EAGLE

THE GOLD EAGLE READER SERVICE: HERE'S HOW IT WORKS

Accepting free books puts you under no obligation to buy anything. You may keep the books and gift and return the shipping statement marked "cancel". If you do not cancel, about a month later we will send you four additional novels, and bill you just $14.80*—that's a saving of over 12% off the cover price of all four books! And there's no extra charge for shipping! You may cancel at any time, but if you choose to continue, every other month we'll send you four more books, which you may either purchase at the discount price . . . or return at our expense and cancel your subscription.

*Terms and prices subject to change without notice. Sales tax applicable in N.Y.

If offer card is missing, write to: Gold Eagle Reader Service, 3010 Walden Ave., P.O. Box 1867, Buffalo, NY 14269-1867

NO POSTAGE
NECESSARY
IF MAILED
IN THE
UNITED STATES

BUSINESS REPLY MAIL
FIRST CLASS MAIL   PERMIT NO. 717   BUFFALO, NY

POSTAGE WILL BE PAID BY ADDRESSEE

GOLD EAGLE READER SERVICE
3010 WALDEN AVE
PO BOX 1867
BUFFALO NY 14240-9952

"I don't know, sir. I woke up with the rest of you. But a skinny guy with thick wrists ambushed me and threw me into the coal furnace with Reems."

"Was his name Remo?"

"He didn't say."

Phelps spoke up. "It must have been that janitor, sir. It's the only explanation."

"Okay," Koldstad said. "We don't know how we got here. That's fine. We know what we saw and who we saw."

Phelps nodded. "The janitor."

"And the Chinaman who attacked me," Koldstad snapped.

"I thought you said it was a butterfly, Mr. Kold-stad."

"It was either a Chinaman dressed as a butterfly or a butterfly wearing a Chinaman's mask. Either way we're going to audit his ass to the conclusion of life on earth and back again to the dawn of time. Now, let's get off this stupid roof."

Jack Koldstad led the way, or tried to. He started to turn in place and kept on turning. Around and around he went, like a slow top. He couldn't seem to stop. The expression on his long face reflected that like a mirror.

The other agents watched in growing confusion. Then concern. Then horror as Jack Koldstad seemed unable to orient himself toward the open roof trap that was plainly in sight.

Finally an agent reached out both hands to steady his superior.

"Thanks," Koldstad said shakily. "I must be more dizzy than I thought."

He started for the roof trap and stepped over it. He kept on going. Right to the edge of the roof. The tips of his shoes bumped the low parapet. Koldstad didn't seem to understand why he couldn't keep going forward.

The agents were right behind him. It was a good thing. They saw that Jack Koldstad was about to step off the roof to his death.

A half-dozen hands plucked at his coat and sleeves and piloted him back the way he came.

"Sir, are you all right?" Phelps asked.

"Let go! Let me go! I can make it. I'm just woozy, that's all."

Just to be sure, the agents held his elbows as others stood by the trap to assist him down.

Jack Koldstad got on the ladder all right. Relief came over the IRS agents' faces. He was climbing down fine. A man started after him. Then another.

When they reached the bottom of the ladder, they found Jack Koldstad on his knees, still clutching the sides of the ladder. He might have been praying. Except he was banging his knees in alternation on the floor.

"Sir, what is it?" asked Phelps in a nervous voice.

"I'm okay. I'm just climbing down. Can't you see? Damn, this is a long ladder."

"Sir, you're on the floor."

Other agents dropped onto the floor as Jack Koldstad looked down and saw that his feet were no longer
on the rungs but folded under him.

He looked down, then up, then blank. Then very,
very worried.

"What's happening to me?" he asked in a tiny,
frightened voice.

"PARTIAL frontal lobotomy," pronounced Dr. Aldace Gerling.

"Yes," agreed Dr. Donald Bex, one of the resident
physicians.

"Unquestionably," concurred Dr. Murray Simon.

"But how?" IRS Special Agent Philip Phelps
asked, looking down at the Folcroft hospital bed
where Jack Koldstad lay sedated.

"You can see the marks here and here," said Dr.
Bex, indicating the natural indentations on either side
of Koldstad's squeezed-in temples. "A very thin instrument was employed to sever the frontal lobes with
absolute precision."

Agent Phelps saw no wounds. Only the rustlike
patches of dried blood on either side of Koldstad's
temples.

"Who could do that?"

"A brain surgeon," said Dr. Bex.

"Yes, one with consummate skill," added Dr. Simon.

"He claimed it was a butterfly," Phelps said, dull
voiced.

Three pair of concerned eyebrows quirked upward. "Yes?"

"A butterfly. One with the face of that Chinaman named Chiun."

"Korean. Chiun is a Korean," said Dr. Gerling.

"You know him?"

"I know of him. He suffers from Pseudologica Fantastica."

"What's that?"

"A severe character disorder whose chief manifestation is the telling of improbably outrageous stories. He comes around from time to time. A former patient, as I understand it. And very friendly with Dr. Smith."

"Well, when we find him, he's going to do federal time. Assaulting a Treasury agent is very serious."

"I do not believe Mr. Chiun could be capable of such violence," said Dr. Gerling.

"Or such skill," added Dr. Bex.

"Who's on staff with that kind of surgical expertise?" Phelps demanded.

"Why, no one. We do not do brain surgery at Folcroft."

Frowning, Phelps indicated Koldstad with his square jaw. "Will he get better?"

"No," answered Dr. Gerling. "But he will not get any worse, I do not think."

"He couldn't seem to control himself. He almost walked off the roof. And when he tried to climb down the ladder, he couldn't stop himself."

"A partial frontal lobotomy often produces such behaviors," said Dr. Gerling. "You see, his impulse-control centers have been damaged, resulting in a condition we refer to as disinhibition. This simply means that he will act upon any impulse that comes to mind without regard for the consequences. When his brain recovers from the trauma, he will have to be re-trained, but he will have limitations. He may also re-peat physical or mental actions. He may be unable to stop impulsive behaviors once begun. If asked to add a column of figures, he may add them ad infinitum, until someone forcibly restrains him. This is called perseveration."

"That means his career is over."

"Not necessarily, but probably. And he claimed a butterfly did this to him, you say?"

"That's what he said. But no one else saw the but-terfly."

"Has this man demonstrated delusions prior to this incident?" Dr. Simon asked.

"Not that I know."

The doctors crowded around, faces growing very interested now. "Can you tell us if you observed any other abnormal behavior prior to this attack?" asked Dr. Simon.

"No."

"And yourself? You said you were attacked, as well. By whom?"

"It was the basement janitor. He took us all bare-handed. I never saw hands move that fast. Bruce Lee's ghost couldn't have touched him."

Dr. Bex furrowed his brow. "Basement janitor?"

"His name was Remo."

The doctors exchanged puzzled glances. "I know of no basement janitor by that or any other name," Dr. Gerling said ponderously. "And you say he defeated eight armed men with only his bare hands?"

"He was faster than light. We never got off a shot."

The doctors crowded closer. They had surrounded him now.

Agent Phelps didn't like the way they were looking at him, so he backed out of the hospital room saying, "I have to report this to Special Agent Koldstad's superior. If you'll excuse me . . ."

The Folcroft doctors followed him out into the green antiseptic-scented corridor.

"If you would like to talk more about these things you claim to have seen, we will be happy to listen."

Walking backward, Phelps retreated to the elevator. "Yeah, right. Thanks. Appreciate the offer. Bye."

"If not you, one of your fellows."

"I'll tell them. Thanks again."

AGENT PHELPS broke the bad news to the others.

"You all know what this means?" he finished in a grave voice. They had gathered together in Dr. Smith's drafty office.

"Yeah. Big Dick is coming."

"Big Dick for sure."

"Yep, this is a Big Dick situation, without a doubt."

No one looked happy at the prospect. They just looked at the office phone and swallowed hard.

"Well, someone has to make the call."

"We'll flip for it."

They flipped two out of three, then three out of five, in rotation until a shoving match broke out between the last two agents left in the running.

Finally they drew straws. Agent Phelps pulled the short straw and went to the black glass desk and sank his rear end into the chair heavily.

He picked up the phone and began dialing. It took three tries. His trembling fingers kept hitting the wrong keys.

RICHARD BUCKLEY BRULL had come up the hard way, from a lowly IRS transcriber to the assistant commissioner of the service's New York City regional branch of the CID. It was a long climb. He had started in the Examination Division, slid over to Collection and from there worked his way up to Criminal Investigation. By his own estimate, that was twenty-eight million returns personally eyeballed, 2.4 million audits conducted, and over fifty thousand criminal investigations prosecuted during the varied stages of his career. A lot of paper.

Through it all Richard Buckley Brull never met a taxpayer he liked. Or trusted. Or who was audit-proof.

If Richard Buckley Brull had his way, the Internal Revenue Service would be renamed the Internal Revenue Force. Every agent down to the secretaries would be armed. There would be none of this witholding crap. It only made citizens scheme and bend their returns to get as much of it back as possible.

The way Richard Buckley Brull saw it, the only program to bring the nation into total compliance with the Internal Revenue Code would be to have employers pay all salaries directly to the IRS, which would disburse it to the taxpayers upon receipt of a weekly voucher.

Why, just the bank interest alone would make the IRS a fortune and lower taxes in the final analysis.

His superiors, however, did not see the wisdom of his vision.

"Why not?" he once argued. "It's our money. Why should the filers have it even temporarily?"

"Because there would be a taxpayer revolt. The government would be overthrown, the nation would fall into bankruptcy, and most importantly we'd all be out of work."

"Nobody objects to withholding," Brull had said stubbornly. "Hell, the filers are technically paying taxes on a portion of their salaries they never even touch. Yet our polling shows that most citizens' opinion of the force—I mean service—goes up twenty-six percent when they get their refund checks. Not that it ever lasts."

"Look, Brull. Don't rock the boat. Shuffle your papers. Make your quotas. Exceed them if you feel ambitious. But don't rock the boat that tows the ship of fucking state. Okay?"

But Richard Buckley Brull was an ambitious bureaucrat. He didn't want to shuffle papers, make or exceed quotas or do any of those safe bureaucratic things. He wanted to shoot to the top, no matter how many filers he had to gouge.

In an agency where little mercy was shown to transgressors, Dick Brull was ruthless, heartless and a bully. He browbeat his staff into spying on one another. Once he struck the fear of the Almighty into them, he set them on the filers. And got results. When assets were seized, not even the bank accounts of dependent children were spared.

Given his winning personality, it was probably only a matter of time before the nickname "Big Dick" was hung on him.

No one ever called Richard Buckley Brull "Big Dick" to his face. Now one even called him Big Dick within the confines of the IRS New York offices. No one dared. They knew that Big Dick Brull would tear them entirely new biologically unnecessary orifices.

For Big Dick Brull did not earn his nickname because he was big or stood tall.

Big Dick had come to the IRS straight out of the Marine Corps. He had never worked for anyone other than the corps. Not even a paper route blemished his employment record. But when the military began to downsize, there was no longer a need for tough drill instructors like Dick Brull. He took early retirement and went in search of a civilian equivalent to the corps.

A job-hunting specialist had pointed him in a natural direction—the Internal Revenue Service.

"You're nuts!" Brull had told the man. "I wouldn't fit in with those paper shufflers."

"You don't know the IRS. It's run by master sergeants. You'd fit in perfectly. Just give it a shot."

Amazingly it turned out to be true.

Brull had come to the IRS for one simple reason, security. But he stayed for an entirely different one: power.

There was no field on earth in which Big Dick Brull could wield such absolute power. Hell, even the President of the United States had checks and balances on him.

The only person Big Dick Brull was answerable to was what he called the Almighty. In this case, he didn't mean the Lord. He meant the commissioner of the Internal Revenue Service, who in these strange days was a woman.

Right now he was fearlessly chewing a new orifice for the local supervisor of the Drug Enforcement Administration.

"You *will* pull your people out of the Folcroft perimeter. Today. That means I want those flashy boats of yours pulled back beyond the three-mile fucking limit. IRS won't stand for being spied on by DEA."

"You have no jurisdiction over us."

"The IRS has total jurisdiction *everywhere*. What was your Social Security number again?"

"I didn't give it," the DEA man said flatly.

"Let me see," Brull said slowly, tapping the keys to his desktop Zilog computer. "I have 034-28-4462. From Massachusetts originally. Isn't that right? You know, compliance up there in Mass has always been a problem. We did a sociological study of the citizens in that area, and do you know what we concluded?''

"No, I do not."

"We concluded that New Englanders in general and Massachusetts taxpayers in particular have an independent streak. They think the rules apply to everyone except them. They actually think they're above the rules. Do *you* think you're above the rules?''

"I play by the rules, same as you."

"I see by your last year's return you made 1,567 dollars in charitable deductions. That's well above the statistical norm, did you know that? Discriminant function formula is the term we use around here. Your numbers slip above the DIF line, and the service's computers kick out your return, red-flagged for an audit. I guess the computer hasn't gotten around to you yet."

"My charitable contributions are my own business."

Brull pounded his desk. Behind him a wall sign reading Seizure Fever—Catch It! shook.

"Wrong! Your charitable contributions are exactly IRS business, and if you want the service to stay out of your back returns, you stay out of the service's seizures.''

"We have a legal claim to Folcroft assets."

"Right behind *us.*"

"You vultures will pick that place clean and leave nothing for DEA."

"And you jerks like nothing better than to seize a property and pick it up at government auction three months later. We know your game. We've audited you DEA cowboy types before.''

"I'll take your recommendations under advisement," said the DEA supervisor begrudgingly.

"I know you will," Big Dick Brull said in a suddenly unctuous voice. "I know you will."

Big Dick Brull hung up the telephone and just because he was the kind of guy he was, he red-flagged the DEA official's most recent return for a field audit. It would take three to four months for the notification to go out. Let him kick about it then. Not a damn thing he could do about it. And the agents were sure to find something really fishy. That was an ironclad guarantee. The tax code was over ten thousand pages long and so confusing that even the service couldn't make heads or tails of it.

That made it the perfect bureaucratic bludgeon to pound loose cash out of even the most stubborn taxpayer.

As Big Dick Brull finished issuing the electronic instructions, his desk phone rang.

"Who is it?" he asked his secretary via intercom.

"An Agent Philip Phelps."

"There's no Agent Phelps authorized to report directly to me."

"He says he's reporting from a seizure site called Folcroft Sanitarium on behalf of Special Agent Jack Koldstad."

"What's wrong with Koldstad? Scratch that. Put Phelps on. I'll ask him myself."

The trembling voice of Agent Phelps came on the line. "I have bad news, Mr. Brull."

"I hate bad news."

"Jack Koldstad has been injured in the line of duty."

"That careless bastard! He knows we have an insurance problem. Did he die?"

"No, sir."

"His mistake. One he'll rue, I promise you. What happened?"

"We found a hidden room in the basement of the place, Mr. Brull. It was the jackpot."

"What kind of jackpot?"

"Gold bullion."

Brull perked up. "How much gold?"

"We don't know."

"Didn't you count it?"

"We were, er, forcibly ejected before we could take inventory."

"What the hell's the matter with you! No one throws out IRS agents!"

"A man attacked us. When we woke up, we had ended up on the roof. Koldstad was with us. It seems someone performed a partial frontal lobotomy on him, Mr. Brull. He's a basket case."

"Christ! You know what this means? Long-term rehab. That screwup will be a burden to the service to the day they dump his worthless ass into the cold ground, and there's fuck-all we can do about it."

"I know, sir."

"You secure that gold?"

"No, sir, we're afraid to go back in."

"Afraid of what?"

"Well, there's the guy with the thick wrists and the, um, giant butterfly."

"What giant butterfly?"

"The one Mr. Koldstad claimed lobotomized him." Agent Phelps cleared his throat quickly. "Sir, I know how this sounds—"

"It sounds," Big Dick Brull said in a grinding voice, "as if you had better seal off that basement until I get there and have your résumés in order for your next careers. Because it won't be with the Internal Fucking Revenue Service."

Big Dick Brull slammed down the telephone. It was time to blow the Folcroft file wide open, and there was only one way to do that. Take charge personally.

18

It was mission creep at its worst.

Winston Smith had no problem with the primary mission. He just wondered what took the Pentagon so long to get around to authorizing it.

Warlord Mahout Feroze Anin was a penny-ante clan leader and arms merchant in the divided Horn of Africa nation of Stomique until the UN relief mission blew into North Nog—as the Stomique regional capital of Nogongog was called—to set up what started as a people-feeding operation and mission-crept its way to a nation-building debacle.

When the UN tanks rolled ashore, Warlord Anin dug out his one Western suit and welcomed them with open arms. It was good PR. It got his beaming face on CNN and made him instantly the most recognizable Stomique citizen in human history.

But when the UN command didn't annoint Warlord Anin as the natural unifier of Stomique, he ordered hit-and-run attacks on UN peacekeeping forces. Anin made the mistake of not keeping the chain of deniability intact, and the next thing Anin knew he was wanted by UNOSOM for ambushing a French UN contingent.

That was when the U.S. Rangers rolled in. And speedily got their tails shot up.

Navy SEAL Winston Smith had a ringside seat to it all. SEAL Team Six had been sent in, disguised as Army grunts to reconnoiter the situation. In the rabbit warren of North Nog, there was no finding Warlord Anin.

Smith personally witnessed the multimillion-dollar Blackhawk helicopter brought down by a two-hundred-dollar Soviet-remaindered RPG while riding shotgun on a Humvee down Mission Support Road Tiger. His team was among the first on the scene. They got their tails shot up, too. But they fought their way through the sea of Stomique civilians and pulled the dead and wounded to safety, except for the one guy they missed.

When his face hit the covers of *Time* and *Newsweek,* the ball game changed. The public gasped. The President choked. And the Pentagon went into severe reverse mission creep.

Even a year later Winston Smith had a hard time believing how chicken-shit Washington had turned.

Anin was small potatoes. A grinning thug. One lucky shot, and he was dubbed The Strongman Who Made The U.S. Back Down.

The U.S. had never backed down. Just the wusses in Washington. Word came down from on high. A deal was struck, and the hostage was freed. The wanted posters on Anin came down, too. Within months the relief-mission-turned-nation-building operation fizzled out, and Mahout Feroze Anin, labeled victorious over the rest of civilization, became de facto ruler of Stomique, which promptly reverted to anarchy.

Winston Smith's blood boiled every day for a month as it all played out.

After that he suggested the UN motto become You Lose Some And You Don't Win Others.

His XO told him to shut up. "Six's time will come."

A year later it did.

"Winner, you're the man for this job."

He didn't know the job. But he was twenty and full of confidence so he said, "I'm the man for every job."

"Maybe. But you're really the man for this job. Word from on high is to take out Anin."

"I'm definitely the man for this job. How many men involved?"

"Just one. You."

"Hey, Six is a team. You can't send me on a lone-wolf mission."

"Those are the orders. As far as the team goes, you're on leave. And they'd better not hear different."

Even when they airlifted him aboard the USS *Darter,* contrary to any mission logic, he was pumped. SEAL Team Six was set up to take out the bad guys. They trained and trained and trained, and never got used except for training missions or to run war-game scenarios.

This time it was different.

The Fucking Ugly Gun shouldn't have been part of the bargain, but Smith had no choice. In his cubicle, he ditched his gear and strapped it on. It hung off his shoulder rig like a water main.

After he'd spent five minutes breathing pure oxygen, they shot him out of the blow tube under pressure. He exhaled all the way up to the surface so his lungs didn't rupture and his bloodstream carbonate from excess nitrogen.

His Draeger bubbleless underwater breathing apparatus got him to shore undetected.

After that things got hairy. His plastic foldout map didn't exactly jibe with the terrain. And then there was the manual that came with the gun. It wasn't as thick as the Yellow Pages, but it came damn close. Since the pages were waterproof plastic, it weighed more than the BEM itself.

After a futile twenty minutes of wandering, Smith growled, "Where the fuck am I?"

A very near voice said, "Thirty klicks south-southeast of North Nogongog."

Smith dragged his gun out of its nylon holster and hissed, "Who's there?"

The thing in his hand hissed, "Who's there?"

"Damn. That was you."

"Damn. That was you."

"Shut up."

"Shut up," said the Fucking Ugly Gun.

Smith gave the thing a hard whack, and the gun shut up.

He went back to his map and saw that according to the BEM gun's telemetry readout, he was a solid mile north of the landing zone.

"No wonder I'm fucking lost."

This time the gun didn't say anything.

Smith pressed on. Okay, it was a fuck-nuts mission. He could accept that. Just so long as at the end of it Warlord Mahout Feroze Anin ended up in a shallow grave.

19

It was the best news DEA Agent Wayne Tardo had had in a day.

A full thirty-five hours had passed since the IRS had booted him and his team off the Folcroft grounds. It was humiliating. IRS even made them carry their wounded off in stretchers.

"But this is a hospital," Tardo had protested.

"This is *our* hospital," Special Agent Jack Koldstad had told him. "And this is IRS property. Until we secure it, it's off-limits to DEA personnel."

"You can't do this."

"It's done. Unless you want to shoot more IRS agents in the line of duty," he added sarcastically.

Tardo had consulted with his superior by cellular phone.

"We can't let this get out to the press," the DEA honcho had told him. "Pull back."

"But the IRS stands to lose as much face as we do."

"The IRS is essential to the smooth working of government and the national defense. We're fighting a war on drugs everyone knows is a holding action at best. They have the high ground. Pull back. But keep that building staked out, just in case I can work something on this end."

"Roger," Wayne Tardo had said, and ordered the most humiliating retreat in the history of the Drug Enforcement Administration.

They took the boats out into the sound and dropped anchor. From there it had been a dull routine of close surveillance and stale fast-food cheeseburgers.

It was the strangest thing. Cars came and went from Folcroft—mostly they went. Staff being sent home, according to the license plates they read by binoculars. Not much activity otherwise except for the damn buzzards that kept circling like a film loop.

Then came the word by secure cellular phone.

"I just got a call from a Richard Brull over at IRS," the DEA commander said.

"Yeah?"

"He threatened to audit me if DEA doesn't stand down on the Folcroft matter."

"The bastard."

"I can stand up to an audit. How about you?"

"My returns are clean."

"Poll your men. Anyone with an audit problem, send them away. The rest of you go in."

"They claimed the place is clean of turkey drugs," Tardo pointed out.

"They can claim that all they want. You're seizing Folcroft. Every damn brick of it."

"What if they resist?"

"What are they going to do, shoot you dead?"

"Understood, sir. I'll report back when the operation is over."

"You do that."

Wayne Tardo snicked shut the antenna to his secure cellular phone and said to his men, "Word from on high is we seize Folcroft."

A cheer went up. Half-eaten cheeseburgers went over the side.

"Only those of you who are audit-proof can go along."

Two agents groaned and cursed under their breaths.

"Get word to the other boats. All who aren't clean, assemble in the relief boat. The rest of you, lock and fucking load."

In the end only three agents had to transfer to the backup boat. Tardo himself was surprised. He was sure he was going to lose half his team.

When everyone was organized, they donned their assault hoods and readied their weapons, and Wayne Tardo gave the order.

"Hit the beach!"

The engines kicked into life, and they hunched low to the decks just in case the IRS decided to defend their seizure.

"I don't think this has ever been done before," a grinning agent muttered.

"We're making interagency history here," Tardo said. "And guess who's going to lose?"

HAROLD SMITH did not believe his eyes or his ears.

The Master of Sinanju had returned to his hospital

bed. "I bring tidings both glad and dire," intoned Chiun.

Smith blinked his gray eyes rapidly.

"I have come to release you from this unhappy state. But only if you promise to me that you will refrain from causing harm to yourself. Blink your kingly eyes twice if you agree to this, and you will be set free."

Smith blinked his eyes twice.

And a fingernail whose touch was as light as a moth's feelers grazed his forehead.

Smith felt life return to his limbs. He sat up. Immediately he felt the heavy load in the seat of his pants.

"I must change clothes," he said weakly.

"There is no time. For the taxidermists of terror have given the order to break the chains of certain evil ones who are held in your thrall."

Smith had to think about that a moment before it made sense. "Beasley?"

Chiun nodded grimly. "And the terrible Dutchman, as well."

"Summon Dr. Gerling. I will countermand the order."

Chiun bowed once. "It will be done as you say." And he flashed from the room like a fluttering black-and-orange comet.

Smith pulled himself out of the bed and stumbled toward the bathroom. He had not been so embarrassed since that time in the third grade when he stubbornly refused to ask to go to the bathroom in the middle of an important English test and had soiled his pants where he sat.

He hoped there were enough towels to clean himself with. If not, he would take this up with the supply staff, whichever of them remained.

DR. ALDACE GERLING hesitated before the steel door in the psychiatric wing of Folcroft Sanitarium.

He had his instructions, but he also had his duty to his patients.

To release the man calling himself Uncle Sam Beasley would be a grave injustice to the poor fellow. His delusions made him unfit for society. Utterly unfit. Moreover, the man was a menace to those around him with his threats of violence and retribution.

God alone knew what he would do if he ever got to California and the Beasley Corporation. He had vowed to lynch virtually every employee of the vast corporation, from the CEO to the lowly greeters in their Monongahela Mouse and Dingbat Duck costumes.

Still, the IRS had decreed this. And the IRS had seized Folcroft.

So Dr. Gerling undid the steel latch bar and inserted the brass key into the lock, giving it a hard twist. The lock squealed and grated.

"It is time," said Dr. Gerling, entering the room that was kept at a sultry 92 degrees because the pirate demanded it.

The man who thought he was Uncle Sam Beasley was as usual seated at his writing desk working on his art.

Beasley didn't bother looking up. "Time for what, you quack?"

"It is time to go."

"Go. Go where?"

"To go from this place. You are being released."

"My time is up?"

"The way I see it, your luck has run out."

Uncle Sam Beasley stood up and adjusted the pirate ruffles around his throat with his good left hand. He clumped toward the door on his artificial leg.

"It's about damn time you morons woke up to reality. Where's my hand?"

"You mean your hook?"

"No, my mechanical hand. I was brought here wearing a mechanical hand. Where is it?"

"I know only of a hook."

"They switched my hand for that idiot hook. Who wears a hook these days?"

"Someone who dresses as Blackbeard the pirate?" Dr. Gerling said.

"Don't be funny. Now, are you going to get my hand, or do I have to go get it myself?"

"I am afraid you are to be released in your present state. Do you have any relatives I should call?"

"If I had any relatives worth a damn, do you think they'd let me rot in this hellhole? Now, point me to my hand!"

"I will escort you to the front door, where a taxi will be waiting for you. In the meantime, you must wait here."

"Like hell," said Uncle Sam Beasley, taking Dr. Aldace Gerling by his plump throat and squeezing.

Dr. Gerling fought back as fiercely as a man of such soft muscles and extra poundage was able, which was to say not very hard at all. His round face turned red, then scarlet, and just as the purple was coming to the fore, his fat-fingered hands stopped slapping the ruffles at Uncle Sam Beasley's wattled throat and he slid to the floor.

Uncle Sam Beasley broke Dr. Gerling's glasses on his face with the heel of his solid silver foot as he stepped out into the corridor and freedom.

As he clumped down the corridor in search of his missing hand, he paused to open doors with a brass key he picked up off the linoleum beside Dr. Gerling's twitching body.

"Come out, come out, whatever you lunatics are," he sang as he flung open doors at random on either side of the corridor.

When he came to the door marked Purcell, the occupant of the room only turned his neon blue eyes in his direction and stared at him blankly and made no move to leave.

"Idiot," growled Uncle Sam, going on to the next door.

REMO WILLIAMS had no sooner slipped out the side door of Folcroft's basement when the noisy roar of approaching speedboats came from the direction of Long Island Sound. He ducked around a corner and saw them tearing toward the rickety dock, throwing up dirty waves of foam.

Even from this distance his sharp eyes could make out the white stencil letters DEA on their black battle suits.

"Dammit," Remo said. "Don't I get a break once today?"

Fading back to the freight door, Remo hesitated. No time to move the gold now. And the minute Chiun got wind of this, he was sure to fly into a killing rage. In fact, he was probably halfway there by now.

Remo knew he'd have to head the Master of Sinanju off before Chiun started taking down DEA agents left and right. But if he abandoned the gold, the DEA would pounce on it.

Remo stood in the shadow of Folcroft, rotating his thick wrists, his face warped with confusion.

If only there were some way to make all that gold disappear...

THE MASTER OF SINANJU found Dr. Aldace Gerling unconscious outside an unlocked door.

He flashed into the room and saw no sign of the man Beasley. This was a calamity, but there was a worse calamity at hand.

Up and down the corridors other doors lay ajar. The Master of Sinanju flew from open door to open door, his heart pounding.

Jeremiah Purcell had been sealed behind one of these doors. Jeremiah Purcell, who was also called "the Dutchman." He'd been a disciple of Chiun's first pupil, Nuihc the Renegade. The Dutchman was the only white other than Remo to be shown the secrets of the sun source that was Sinanju. He had learned well. But he was as evil as his Master, who had been Chiun's nephew.

Thrice before they had battled the wicked Dutchman. In their last encounter, he had slain the maiden Mah-Li, whom Remo had intended to marry. Remo had tracked the Dutchman to his lair and exacted a terrible vengeance. When it was over, the Dutchman had been rendered helpless, his mind shattered. With no mind he had no memory of Sinanju, and thus was no threat.

The Dutchman had other powers, as well, subtle hypnotic ones that made him a menace beyond the skills he had learned from Nuihc the Renegade. The shattering of his mind had banished that threat, as well.

Still, Chiun thought wildly as he raced from room to room, there was a legend of Sinanju that linked the Dutchman to the dead white night tiger, who was Remo. If one died, so said the legend, the other would perish.

If the Dutchman should come to harm wandering Folcroft in his infantile state, Remo would suffer the same fate.

And if the evil one and Remo should cross paths once more, surely both would perish. For Remo might well finish exacting the vengeance of so many years ago.

So Chiun leaped from room to room, his parchment face twisted in concern. It softened when he came to the door to the Dutchman's room. It lay open but Purcell sat within, unconcerned. He was watching television, his eyes fixed on the screen, his arms helplessly wrapped about himself.

The Master of Sinanju stood there, regarding him in silence. Some intuition or remnant of the Dutchman's old Sinanju training must have come to the fore, because slowly Jeremiah Purcell turned his wan face toward the open door.

The awful radiance of his neon blue eyes fixed on the Master of Sinanju. The Dutchman smiled a crooked smile and stuck out a too-pink tongue in vague derision.

He tittered, the sound as unpleasant as it was mad.

The Master of Sinanju threw the door closed and, because there was no key about, he drew back a tight fist and sent it into the area of the lock. The door groaned under the sudden impact, the tiny glass window shattering.

When the hand came away, the door was as fixed to its frame as if it had been welded at lock and hinges.

Turning, the Master of Sinanju glided down the corridor. One threat had been averted. There was still Beasley, a much lesser problem. He would not be difficult to find and conquer.

Then, from beyond the thick walls of Fortress Folcroft came the concerted roar of motorboats and the beginning of gunfire.

"What is this!" Chiun squeaked. "What is this?"

Going to a window, he looked out with shocked eyes. He saw the boats converging as before, and the men in black with their loud weapons jump off to land in the mud of the bay.

"The gold!" he shrieked, and flung himself toward the stairwell like a moth on fire.

This time he would show no mercy to those who vexed him so.

20

Warlord Mahout Feroze Anin was a crafty man. Everyone knew that. During the days before the UN had come to Stomique, he had scammed his way up from simple gunrunning to control of lower Stomique. When UN relief supplies began pouring in, his ragtag militia hijacked the food, stockpiling some and selling the rest back to various relief agencies.

The hungrier the Stomique people became, the more free food poured in. The more food that came ashore, the richer Warlord Anin became.

It was amazing how long it went on before the international community noticed that Warlord Mahout Feroze Anin had managed to become the indirect recipient of one fifth of all charitable contributions to the various United Nations relief funds.

Anin showed his craft by playing the U.S. off the UNOSOM and both off the international press until everybody lost and only Mahout Feroze Anin really won.

In the days after the UN-U.S. pullout, he consolidated his control over the countryside, enforcing his will by political assassination and starving those who didn't support him.

He deserved to die. Winston Smith was happy as a pig in shit to be the one to blast him to the boneyard.

If the guy would just stop bobbing and weaving.

Once he'd gotten his bearings, Smith had found his way to Anin's French colonial villa. Or his mistress's villa, according to Intelligence reports.

Anin did have a wife. She lived in Canada, where Anin had supposedly sent her to be safe from his political enemies. In truth, she was fat and over forty and lived off the largess of the Canadian dole while Anin happily porked a vast array of mistresses who opened themselves to him because he filled their bellies with pilfered UN-supplied relief food.

When Winston Smith got up into a sniper position in the crown of a banyan tree, he sighted Anin through the lighted window. The LED distance reader called it less than one hundred meters. It looked as if it was going to be a piece of cake.

Anin's head appeared almost immediately.

Smith brought the BEM weapon up and whispered, "Arm one."

"Louder," requested the gun.

"Arm one," Smith barked into the sight microphone.

"Arm one," the weapon replied.

That gave him five minutes. Plenty of time for a clean head shot.

Except Anin kept bobbing in and out of view.

At first Smith thought he might be doing push-ups. But as Anin kept going at it, his face darkened and the sweat crawled off his balding brown forehead. Then he started going faster.

Smith got it then.

"Damn."

Winston Smith debated the ethics of shooting a man when he was doing the wild thing. Should he wait? Or should he nail Anin while the nailing was good?

While he was giving it thought, the gun disarmed itself.

"Damn you," he said.

"Damn you," said the BEM gun.

Smith said, "Arm one."

"Arm one" came the reply.

He lined up on the window and used the night scope again. The laser would give him away. What kind of moron put a laser targeter and a night scope on the same piece of equipment anyway?

Warlord Anin seemed to be coming to the end of his exercise. He stopped, arms trembling, face flushed, eyes closing.

A woman's shriek of pleasure pierced the damp African night air.

It was a perfect head shot. So Winston Smith took it.

The trigger came back smoothly. He heard a click, and the gun said, "Congratulations. You have executed a perfect kill. Mission over. Return to pickup zone, please."

"What the fuck," Smith blurted.

"What the fuck," the BEM gun dutifully repeated.

Smith fired again.

The gun told him, "Twelve-point demotion for unnecessary fire. Return to pickup zone, please."

"Why don't you fire?"

"Antifiring interlock is armed," said the gun.

"Well, tell me how to disarm it!"

"See manual."

"My ass is hanging out a fucking tree! I don't have time for any goat-fuck manual!"

The gun said nothing, so Winston whacked it with his hand.

"Arm one."

"Arm one."

He fired a test shot at the low-hanging moon. Nothing happened.

Dragging the clips out one by one, he thumbed out rounds, holding them up to the moonlight. "Nothing wrong with these rounds. What the fuck!"

His shout was heard by Warlord Mahout Feroze Anin, who came to the window, buck naked except for a Dragunov sniper rifle.

Anin used it to methodically chop the branches surrounding Smith's perch to pieces.

Smith dropped to the ground and ran for his life, swearing softly but often.

The unwieldy gun swore back with amiable vehemence.

21

Wayne Tardo had point. He was ready for armed IRS agents, heavily armed drug traffickers—ready for anything.

Except for what he did encounter.

It flew across the landscaped grounds of Folcroft Sanitarium like a vampiric butterfly. Face fierce, shrieking in fury or agony or God knew what, it tore directly at him on billowing black-and-orange wings.

It was not armed, so Wayne Tardo hesitated. The hesitation was brief and fatal.

The DEA agents bringing up the rear saw it all. So did the IRS agents who had flocked to the Folcroft windows, alerted by the roar of the speedboats and the battle cries of the DEA agents.

Everyone saw the same thing, and no one believed their staring eyes.

A monarch butterfly flew screaming at Wayne Tardo. Its shriek of fury froze the DEA agent in mid-stride. He had his Uzi up. He started to drop it into line. He looked as if he were moving in slow motion. Or perhaps it was only an illusion created by the headlong fury of the butterfly creature with the bald human head.

Its great wings suddenly spread, and from the tips great yellow bird claws seemed to sprout. It left the ground with a flutter of fabric like a boat sail cracking in a high wind.

The butterfly seemed to pass over Wayne Tardo's head. Its shadow fell across the paralyzed DEA agent's body. Its great wings obscured him only a moment, no more.

But when it passed beyond him, Wayne Tardo was gone.

That was what their slow eyes and brains told them when the onlookers saw the spot where Wayne Tardo had stood. The butterfly alighted a short distance beyond the spot and threw up his winged arms in the faces of the other agents of the DEA. One arm swept back, like a stage magician indicating a feat of legerdemain.

On the spot where the butterfly with the human head pointed, Wayne Tardo began to reappear. One limb at a time. A leg fell first. Then his head. It bounced and bounded toward the water.

By far the loudest sound came when Tardo's barrel-chested trunk went splat on the grass, ejecting fountains of blood from all five stumps.

The butterfly let out another shriek, this one articulate. "Behold the fate of those who defile this fortress!"

At first the DEA agents didn't quite know what to make of this. They stood wide-eyed and riveted in their heavy mud-caked boots.

Two of them shook off the shock and, shiny steel pistols elevating, issued a warning.

"DEA! Freeze."

The human butterfly lunged at them. He should have died right there. The DEA agents had plenty of time to riddle him. In fact, two had already begun to squeeze their triggers in unison.

This became very apparent when yellow claws caught them at the elbow and forced their arms around so their weapons faced one another. The shiny muzzles came together with a clank that welded them nose to nose.

The agents stood blinking, obviously slow to comprehend how they had come into this awkward position. They tried to withdraw their weapons, but they refused to separate, like Chinese handcuffs holding two facing fingers together.

The weapons had hair triggers. The exertion of trying to separate the muzzles caused them to fire. Both weapons exploded in their gun hands, sending gun metal flying into soft organs and fragile skulls.

"Who will challenge the Master of Sinanju now?" shrieked the butterfly with the voice of a man.

As it turned out, no one. The remaining DEA agents beat a hasty retreat to their boats and pushed them off.

For their part, the gawking IRS agents decided discretion was the better part of valor. They shut the windows they had been leaning out of, not wanting to attract the fury of the butterfly that they now realized was no figment of Jack Koldstad's lobotomized brain, but a very real creature with the power to wreak incredible damage.

"Big Dick will have to handle this," one said, voice shaking.

"Yeah, this is a job for Big Dick."

"I pity the butterfly when Big Dick gets here."

"I pity us if that butterfly comes searching the building for more government agents to maim."

"Someone should look out the window to see where it is."

No one cared for that particular duty, it turned out. So they drew straws.

The agent who pulled the short straw made the sign of the cross and crawled to the nearest window. They had all laid themselves flat on the office floor because who knew but the butterfly might flap by on a search of more victims. He poked his head up to the sill like a frightened periscope.

"See it?"

"No."

"See anything?"

"I see the DEA out on the water."

"What are they doing?"

"I think they're trying to rescue some guys from a sinking boat."

"Did the butterfly sink a boat?"

"Can't tell."

"See anything else?"

"Yeah," the agent said in a suddenly disheartened voice. "I think I see Big Dick coming through the gate, hell-bent for audit."

From the open door, a lemony voice demanded, "Who is Big Dick?"

REMO WILLIAMS MET the Master of Sinanju at the loading dock to the basement of Folcroft Sanitarium.

"Did you have to do it that way?" Remo demanded.

Chiun's wise face gathered its wrinkles like a fist clenching. "The gold is inviolate. They must not find it. And why are you not with the gold?"

"I moved it."

"Impossible! There was no time."

"See for yourself."

The Master of Sinanju flew past his pupil and into the dank basement, his feet whisked along the concrete flooring until he came to the vault door. It lay open to any white eye that happened along.

The mute and inert computers of Emperor Smith stood at the rear of the space. Of the gold of Sinanju, there was no sign. Not even a grain of gold lay on the floor, knocked off by careless movers.

Chiun whirled on his pupil. "Where is the gold?"

"I told you, I moved it."

"Then why are you not with the moved gold, guarding it with your life?"

"Because it's safe."

"Safe! Where safe? Where is safe in this land of madness and lunatics with boom sticks and loud voices and taxidermists! There is no safe except in the House of the Masters in the village of my ancestors—who are now calling down curses on my aged head because I entrusted the future to a dull round-eyed white!''

"Trust me," said Remo.

"Trust! You have lost the gold. My gold."

"Not true. Some of it was mine. Some Smith's."

"Most of it belonged to Sinanju. I demanded to know where it is."

"On one condition."

"Blackmailer!"

"The pot is calling the kettle black, seems to me."

Chiun stamped a sandaled foot. A portion of concrete floor cracked under his tiny toes. "Speak!"

"Promise?"

"Never!"

"Okay, you're just going to have to trust me."

"Where gold is concerned, trust is impossible."

"It's gone, it's safe, and we can get it back at any time," Remo was saying as the Master of Sinanju fluttered about the basement, looking for nooks or crannies that might conceal single ingots.

"It is in the walls!" he shouted triumphantly.

Remo folded his lean arms. "Nope. Not in the walls."

"It is buried under this floor."

"Not even warm," said Remo.

"It is on the roof, then."

"There was no time to carry it all to the elevator. Even if there was, the cable would have snapped under all that weight."

"Then it has vanished."

Remo shook his head. "Safe as soap," he said.

Chiun's brow knit together. "How is soap safe?"

"Search me. I just made that up."

Chiun padded up to his pupil and looked up at him with chill hazel eyes.

"Do not trifle with me, rootless one."

"Hey, if I'm to be Reigning Master some day, shouldn't I be trustworthy enough to handle the village gold? Besides, if only one person knows, the IRS can't torture it out of you."

"Wild yaks could not wrench this secret from me— if I only knew it."

Remo shook his head firmly. "Can't take that chance. Sorry."

"But Remo," Chiun said plaintively, "if harm befalls you, the secret of the gold goes to your grave."

"I guess you'd better see that no harm befalls me," said Remo, smiling thinly. "That reminds me. Where's Beasley?"

"I do not know. He was escaped. But the Dutchman is secured. The drooling idiot did not possess wits enough to leave his cell when it was open."

"Well, that's one break today. What about Smith?"

"I have released him."

"Then I guess it's up to Smith to try to put a lid on things," said Remo.

"Then we will remain here until these matters are resolved," said Chiun, his eyes questing about the basement suspiciously.

"You're only saying that because you think if you keep sniffing around, you'll stumble across your gold."

"It is somewhere."

"It is safe. That's all you need to know," said Remo, trying to suppress a grin. It was rare that he put one over on the old Korean.

22

Big Dick Brull sent his onyx black Cadillac Eldorado tearing through the Folcroft gates like a hearse trying to catch up to a funeral procession. It swept up the road and stopped at the main entrance.

The door opened. A black brogan came out and struck the asphalt like a jackhammer punch.

Dick Brull stepped out and strode into the lobby. There was no guard, no one to stop him. Not that anyone would dare. The look of intensity in Dick Brull's hard eyes usually stopped an ordinary man in his tracks. Brull clomped through the lobby, his feet making distinct reports that bounced off the walls. Where Dick Brull walked, people took notice. Wherever Dick Brull entered, it became his domain.

The lobby was spacious and empty, but the striding feet of Big Dick Brull filled it as if he stood forty feet tall.

His pumping legs took him to the elevator. He gave the button a punch. The elevator, as if intimidated, responded without hesitation. The steel doors parted. Brull stepped aboard. He stabbed the second-floor button. The door closed.

The elevator whisked him up, and he stepped out, pausing. The corridor was empty. His icy black eyes swept left and right. They came to rest on the plain door marked Dr. Harold W. Smith, Director.

Shooting his cuffs, Dick Brull stormed toward that door. The hard tapping of his shoe heels warned anyone who knew that dreaded sound that Big Dick Brull had arrived, Big Dick Brull was on-site. Big Dick Brull was taking charge.

And the devil take the man who saw it otherwise.

AGENT PHILIP PHELPS was literally shivering before the sound of footsteps outside the office door.

"Now you're in for it," he muttered to Harold W. Smith, who stood pale faced and grim.

"What do you mean?"

"Don't you hear that sound? That's Dick Brull."

"Who?"

"Big Dick Brull. The guy you just asked about. He's the most feared assistant commissioner in the service. Better straighten that tie of yours before he sees it."

"I do not work for the IRS," Smith said.

"You do now."

"Is Brull responsible for this outrage?"

"He's the man."

"Then I'll have words with him."

"It's your ass," said Agent Phelps as the door flew open.

Harold Smith's eyes went to the door, which was reverberating against the wall where it slammed.

A man stood in the doorway. The first thing a person noticed about him was the shock of virile black hair over a face like a thundercloud. It was not a face made for smiling. The lines of the man's face went all the wrong ways. Possibly he had never smiled in his entire adult life. His brow was a scowl, his mouth a frown, his eyes hard and black and uncaring.

Big Dick Brull stood in the open door, and his head turned in one direction then another like a deliberate radar dish, his black eyes tracking every face.

"Report!" he thundered, his voice as big as all outdoors.

Heels clicked. "Agent Phelps, sir."

"Where's Koldstad?"

"In rehab. Third floor, sir."

"What was that commotion I heard on my way in?"

"DEA agents, sir."

"What happened to them?"

"They stormed ashore without warning."

"You deal with them?"

"No, sir. We did not."

"Too bad. DEA owes IRS a few scalps. Who did?"

Agent Phelps hesitated. He swallowed. "It was—"

"Out with it."

"It was the butterfly, Mr. Brull."

"We all saw it, Mr. Brull," another agent blurted out.

"It was real. Honest," added a third.

"It killed those three DEA agents, and the rest took off," Phelps finished.

Dick Brull's head swept from side to side, his icy black eyes boring into those of each man. One shuddered and turned away. Another sobbed.

Then his eyes fell on the colorless orbs of Harold W. Smith.

"Who the fuck are you?"

Smith strode over and stopped toe-to-toe with Dick Brull. Their eyes met and locked, Brull's looking up, Smith's glaring down.

Harold Smith stood exactly six feet tall, but looked taller because of his elongated Ichabod Crane frame.

Dick Brull's brush-cut black hair came up to Harold Smith's lower ribs. Brull had to step back two paces in order to hold Smith's cold gaze.

"You responsible for what happened here?" Brull demanded.

"No," Smith said coldly. "You are."

Hearing this, the IRS agents gasped.

"You can't talk back to him like that. He's Dick Brull."

"I don't care if he is the President of the United States," Smith said, not looking away. "This outrage is his responsibility."

"Kiss my ass," Dick Brull yelled.

"I won't dignify that with an answer."

"Then answer this. Where is the gold?"

An agent piped up. "In the basement, sir."

"Shut the fuck up! I wasn't talking to you. I was talking to this lying sack of shit."

Harold Smith's patrician face turned a smoldering crimson. His prim mouth thinned to a bloodless line until he looked like a reverse color negative of an unhappy clown.

"Why don't you see for yourself?" he said bitingly.

"Let's all do that." Brull looked at Smith's trembling-with-rage hands. "Why isn't this man in irons?"

"We thought he was paralyzed."

"Bring him with us. I want to see the look on his sad-sack face when we shove his lying nose into the gold."

Strong hands took Harold Smith by the arms. Smith shook them off, saying, "I can walk under my own power."

"That's what we're afraid of. That you'll try walking out of IRS jurisdiction. Let's go, Smith."

Harold Smith allowed himself to be escorted to the waiting elevator. He and the other agents crowded aboard. The door closed. The elevator began to descend.

Smith looked around, frowning. "Where is Brull?"

"Here, beside you," a voice growled from somewhere in the pack of brown and gray suits.

Smith looked down. Dick Brull's bristly hair floated in the vicinity of his elbow like a hairy jellyfish.

"I see," he said.

The elevator ride was a one of the longest in Harold Smith's memory. He wondered how he would explain what was in the basement. Then, remembering that the Master of Sinanju was lurking somewhere on the premises, he wondered if he would have to.

"HARK," the Master of Sinanju cried. "Smith comes!"

Remo listened to the elephant stampede of feet over the hum of opening elevator doors one floor above and said, "Smith? How can you tell?"

"The creaking of his knee."

Remo focused his own hearing. Harold Smith had an arthritic knee that creaked when he walked. It was a sound Remo had come to associate with the CURE director.

The familiar creaking was audible over the stamping of many feet, but only because Remo's sensitive Sinanju-trained hearing enabled him to pick it out of the din.

"It's Smith, all right," he muttered.

"He walks under duress. Let us free him."

"Let's fade into the woodwork. We'll take our cue from Smith."

They retreated into the deep shadows far to the rear of the basement and waited, immobile and attentive.

HAROLD SMITH was holding his breath as he was marched into the dimly lit basement. They marched him down the stairs as the lights came on and across the sloping floor to the white-painted concrete vault that was CURE's most inviolate secret.

As Smith approached, he saw the door was ajar. Even though he was prepared, his heart leaped like a game fish and a splash of stomach acid seared his esophagus.

Other than that, Smith felt calm. This surprised him. Perhaps he was still numb from the shock of these lightning-fast events.

Big Dick Brull marched up to the door and took hold of it with one musclar hand. "How," he asked, "do you explain this?"

The door swung open.

"Explain what?" Smith said.

The agents gasped. Brull pivoted on his lifts. He found himself looking into the weakly lit interior of the concrete vault.

At the rear stood a line of mainframes, their tape reels still. On either side stood the smaller WORM array server systems.

But there was no gold. Not a single ingot.

Big Dick Brull whirled on Harold Smith. "Where's the damn gold I was told about?" he roared.

Smith met Brull's glare with a frosty one of his own and said nothing.

Brull turned on his agents. They flinched. "Where's the gold you jerks promised me? I was promised gold. Stacks of bullion. Where's the damn gold?"

Agent Phelps mustered up an answer. "We don't know, Mr. Brull. It was here less than an hour ago."

"You promised me a mountain of motherfucking gold."

"That's what we found. It was stacked to the ceiling. There must have been a ton of gold."

"Two tons," another agent chimed in helpfully.

"You don't move a ton of fucking gold with a fucking forklift," Brull howled. "You move it with a crane and a crew of men and a truck to load it on. A big truck. Who took my fucking gold?''

"Obviously there is no gold," said Harold W. Smith calmly.

Fists clenched, Big Dick Brull strode up to Harold Smith and tried to tower over him. He came up in his tiptoes, stretched his neck out of his starched shirt collar, and the veins in his face and throat bulged big and blue while the whites of his eyes seemed to detonate with bursting blood vessels. He looked like a boil about to pop under pressure.

"Don't lie to me, you smug tight-ass!" he screamed.

"As you can plainly see, there was no gold in this vault."

"Say that again, I dare you."

"I said," insisted Harold Smith in a brittle but restrained tone of voice, "there is no gold in this vault. Not today, not yesterday, not ever. Folcroft is a private hospital. And I deeply resent the implication that it is a center for illegal activity."

The IRS agents watched with stunned expressions as Harold Smith stood his ground. A glint of admiration came into their eyes. They had never seen anyone stand up to their boss and hold his own. Most people were reduced to a heap of quivering jelly under the hard radiation of Big Dick Brull's personality.

"You're a damn liar." Not taking his eyes off Smith's stiff face, Brull spoke out of the side of his mouth. "How much gold would you say?"

"Easily a couple million dollars," Phelps said.

"Fine. Excellent. Assuming two million, stored here for a minimum of five years, no taxes reported or paid on it, we have 1.4 million dollars in taxes due, including interest and penalties."

"Your math is off," said Smith. "It would be 1.3 million."

"Then you admit to the gold?"

"No. And you have to produce gold in order to levy taxes on it."

"I'll have sworn depositions from these fine, upstanding IRS agents that they saw the gold."

"They also saw a giant butterfly dismember three DEA agents," Smith retorted.

"We won't mention that part," Brull said quickly.

"But I will be sure to bring it up in tax court," said Smith.

Big Dick Brull's ankles began to tremble with the strain of holding his bantam body off the concrete. He heightened the fury of his glare to its maximum intensity. Harold Smith met it with a cool confidence that would have chilled a polar bear to the bone.

It was a standoff, pure and simple. Gradually Big Dick Brull lowered himself back to his normal height.

"Explain these computers."

"Folcroft used to be a sociological research center. The computers are left over from those days."

"Bullshit! Those are IDC mainframes. You don't mothball expensive equipment like that! You use it or you sell it."

"You have your answer."

"No, I don't have my fucking answer. I don't have anything near an answer. You're dirty, Smith. This place is dirty." Brull shook a blunt finger into Smith's unflinching face. "I don't know what kind of dirt, but I'm going to find it, sweep it up and make you eat it. That's a promise."

"Good luck," said Smith without emotion.

"You know what I can do to you?"

"You have already done it," Smith said bitterly. "You barged in to my place of work, disrupted my staff, threatened some, fired others and you are preparing to deinstitutionalize patients you know nothing about."

"Folcroft belongs to the service. And your ass belongs to the service. Until we get to the bottom of this, you're confined to this building under administrative detention."

"I don't believe you have the legal authority to do that."

"I have the power to toss your scrawny ass in the federal pen at Danbury if you dare set foot off these grounds."

"Then I remain under house arrest?"

"You're goddamn right. You're going to run this place under my direct supervision. Let's see how long it takes for Folcroft's true nature to reveal itself."

"I accept your challenge," said Harold W. Smith thinly.

As they marched him up the stairs, they heard a distant drumming.

Doom doom doom doom . . .

"What's that?" Big Dick Brull demanded.

"We don't know," said Agent Phelps. "But we've been hearing it off and on since we took over."

"You. Smith. What's that sound?"

"I have no idea," said Harold W. Smith truthfully, wondering what on earth could be making the noise. It struck his ears as vaguely familiar, but he could not for the life of him place it.

"YOU HEARD that drumming, too?" Remo asked Chiun after the IRS agents and Harold Smith had finished clumping up the basement steps.

"Yes."

"Sound familiar to you?"

Chiun's eyes became knife-blade creases in the wizened dough of his face. "Yes, but I cannot recall where I have heard this strange sound."

They continued listening. Soon the sounds faded away as if whatever was beating on the drum—if it was a drum—was going down a very long corridor.

They stepped from the shadows. "This isn't getting any better for Smith," said Remo.

"He is equal to that loud cockroach."

"Maybe one on one, but that little red-faced jerk represents the IRS. And they've definitely got a mad on for Smith."

Chiun sniffed derisively. "They do not suspect who they are dealing with. Emperor Smith controls mighty armies, spies beyond number and vast wealth greater than that of the pharaohs."

"None of which he can touch right now. Look, his computers are down for good, he can't reach the President, and the IRS is riding him hard. Let's face it. CURE is finished."

"It is finished when Smith informs me that it is finished. Until then, we fight on."

"Fine. You fight on. I have an errand to run."

"What erand?"

Remo lifted his T-shirt and tapped a letter tucked into his waistband. "I slipped this out of Smith's office when no one was looking. It's that dippy letter he thought was so important. I gotta mail it."

"Hold," said Chiun, lifting a long fingernail.

Remo's eyes flicked to the fingernail and too late back to his waistband. He never felt the letter leave, so expertly did Chiun remove it.

"You are not the only one who can make things disappear," Chiun said aridly.

"What manner of address is this—FPO and a number?"

"Means Fleet Post Office. Guy's probably in the Navy."

The Master of Sinanju lifted the letter to the weak 25-watt bulbs and frowned unhappily.

"Bad manners to read someone else's mail," Remo pointed out.

"It is stupid to mail a letter whose contents one does not know in case it bears tidings that could harm the mailer."

And the Master of Sinanju blew on the flap once, then slipped a fingernail in. The flap snapped open without tearing. He withdrew the letter. Remo crowded around to read it, too.

Dear Nephew,
Congratulations. This is the year you reach your twenty-first birthday. You are now ready to take your place in the world and no longer require or are due any further assistance from me, whether financial or spiritual. Please accept my sincere good wishes on your future, and under no circumstances return to visit the place where you were raised.

Dutifully,
Uncle Harold

"Nice guy," said Remo. "He just told his nephew to kiss off forever."

"It is his right," said Chiun.

"Well," said Remo. "This doesn't concern us. It's family stuff. I'll mail the letter and we can forget it."

Chiun handed the letter and envelope back and said with a disdainful sniff, "Whites have no appreciation of family ties."

Remo took the letter, stared at it and said, "Aren't you going to reseal it?"

"You are the postman. That is your task."

"What are you going to do?"

"Find Beasley."

Frowning, Remo resealed the letter with his tongue. It tasted so bitter he spit his mouth dry. And when he remembered who must have licked the flap in the first place, he spit twice more for good measure.

Remo slipped from the basement and made his way to the brick wall that enclosed the Folcroft grounds on three sides. He went over the fence in one leap, landed on the other side and went in search of his car.

He found it down the road with an IRS seizure sign clipped under a window wiper with a yellow Denver boot immobilizing the right front tire.

Kneeling, Remo took hold of the gripping mechanism and began wrenching odd pieces away. They snapped under his powerful fingers until the tire was freed. Then he drove off, whistling.

When he reached town, Remo stood in line for twenty minutes at the Rye post office waiting to mail the letter to Harold Smith's nephew, Winston.

The mail clerk said, "You'll need an express envelope and an air bill. You can fill them out at the counter over there."

"I just stood in line twenty freaking minutes," Remo protested.

"You're supposed to fill out the air bill *before* you get in line."

"Where does it say that?"

"Nowhere. You're supposed to know these things."

Grumbling, Remo got out of line, dropped the envelope in a cardboard mailer, sealed it and filled out the air bill. After another ten minutes in line, the same clerk took the cardboard mailer, weighed it and said, "Eight seventy-five, please."

Remo dug into his pockets and found only a crumpled-up five-dollar bill and an old buffalo-head nickel.

"Take a credit card?" he asked.

"No."

"Damn."

Stepping out, Remo noticed a Western Union office across the street and went in. "You accept major credit cards?" he asked the clerk.

"Even minor ones."

"I want to send a telegram."

The clerk handed over a blank, and Remo was allowed to transfer the text of Harold Smith's letter to the blank without having to get out of line. When he was done, the clerk processed the telegram, ran his credit card through the charge machine and handed the card back with a receipt and a friendly "Thank you."

"A pleasure doing business with private enterprise," said Remo, stepping out into the light.

23

They were waiting for Winston Smith at the escape zone. Three members of SEAL Team Six, loaded for bear, hunkered down over two beached Boston whalers.

A dark hand waved at him. "Hey, Winner!"

"Fuck you," snarled Smith.

The gun echoed his sentiments.

Six gathered around him. "Hey, we heard you nailed the guy."

"He isn't dead," Smith snapped.

"Maybe next time they'll give you live ammo. Hah."

"Fuck you," he said a beat ahead of the gun.

"Where's the XO?" Smith asked.

"Back at the sub."

"You guys were aboard for the ride?"

Beaming grins pierced the dark. "All the time. We watched the mission unfold from the gun camera."

"What gun camera?"

"The laser, numb-nuts. It wasn't a laser. You shoulda known that. What kind of moron sticks a laser on ordnance already rigged with a night scope?"

"Fuck."

"That's another thing. You gotta watch your language. All manner of clean-minded admirals are gonna be watching your footage. Don't want to embarrass them in front of the spooks."

"Hey, Winston, how do you feel about nailing a target when he's porking his best girl?"

"Conscience bothering you yet?"

"Just shut up everybody," Smith barked. "Shut up."

"Man appears a mite out of sorts," a voice drawled.

They returned to the *Darter* in the whalers.

The XO was there to greet him as Winston Smith climbed down the sail into control.

"Sir, I—"

"Not a word, Smith. Not in front of the crew."

They were escorted to a tiny debriefing room. The rest of Team Six were made to wait outside.

"You did a great job," the XO began. "You proved the mission is doable and the BEM gun performs to expectations."

"Begging your pardon, sir, but performing the mission for real would have proved the identical thing. And much more satisfactoraily, sir."

"That wasn't in the mission profile. Not this time, anyway."

"Sir, Six is getting tired of all these dry-fire missions. We're the best the Navy has to offer. We can do the job. Why aren't we sent after the bad guys for real?"

"This is how the JCS wanted it to go down."

"Permission to speak frankly, sir?"

"No. Now take your BEM back to quarters and familiarize yourself with it thoroughly. Next time may be for real."

Winston Smith saluted and stormed back to his cubicle. He ignored the back slapping of his teammates as they followed him down the cramped sub passageways. He shut the door in their laughing faces.

"The Navy sucks," he said bitterly in the confines of his cubicle.

Two hours later someone knocked on the door and said, "Got a sea gram for you, Smith."

"Shove it up the ass of somebody who cares."

"It'll be out here if you want it."

Winston Smith rolled over in his bunk and, when sleep would not come, he got up and fetched the sea gram.

He unfolded it and read the text.

Dear Nephew,

Congratulations. This is the year you reach your twenty-first birthday. You are now ready to take your place in the world and no longer require or are due any further assistance from me, whether financial or spiritual. Please accept my sincere good wishes on your future, and under no circumstances return to visit the place where you were raised.

Dutifully,
Uncle Harold

Winston Smith's eyes grew wide, then shocked, then hot.

His fingers shook and the cable trembled between them.

"Fuck," he said softly. "Fuck fuck fuck."

This time the gun said nothing. There was nothing to say. He was all alone in the world now.

As he lay back in his bed and stared at nothing, Winston Smith wondered why he had been abandoned by his only living relative.

24

On the ride up to the third floor, Big Dick Brull began barking out orders.

"I want a lid clamped down on this place. No press, no outsiders coming in, no personal leave. We're all staying here until someone cracks, and it won't be me."

"I would like to call my wife," said Harold Smith without a trace of the concern he felt.

"Don't bother."

"She must expect me home by now."

"If she didn't miss you yesterday, she won't miss you today."

"I protest this treatment."

"Protest all you want, deadbeat. There isn't fuck-all you can do about it." Brull paused. "Unless you'd like to confess to tax fraud here and now."

"I am guilty of no tax fraud."

"Suit yourself. I'm denying you calling privileges."

The elevator doors hummed apart, and Harold Smith exited, the lenses of his rimless glasses starting to fog up. No one noticed this as they strode down the corridor in a tight knot, the feet of the IRS agents tattooing in unison.

"By the way," Big Dick Brull added, "we've invoked the one-hundred percent rule in your case."

Smith halted, turned. "I beg your pardon?"

"We're seizing your personal assets, as well as your place of business. That means your car, your house and everything in it. The operation should be getting under way—" he looked at his watch "—right about now."

"You cannot do this."

"I can overrule it if you have something to say to me."

Smith compressed his lips until they all but disappeared. His glasses were completely fogged up now. Still, Smith's cold gray eyes seemed to bore through the condensation like hateful agates.

Big Dick Brull happened to notice the Timex on Smith's thin wrist and said, "Nice watch you have there."

"Thank you," Smith said thinly.

"Looks expensive, too."

"It is not. Merely of excellent quality."

Brull put out his hand saying, "Hand it over."

"You cannot be serious."

"I said, 'Hand it over.' The tie and clasp, too."

"This is a school tie."

"When I said we're seizing your possessions, I meant it. Don't stop with the watch and tie. Take off your coat and shoes."

"This is outrageous. I am a lawful taxpayer."

"No, you are what we like to call the 'screwee.' I am the 'screwer.' Is that your wedding ring?"

"Of course it is."

"Gold?"

Smith said nothing.

Big Dick Brull smiled grimly and said, "Fork it over."

Harold Smith was trembling now. He looked like a man in the autumn of life, gray with age, thin from the spare appetite of his years. His eyes disappeared behind the steam coming from every pore to cloud up his lenses. He made no move to doff his coat, watch or wedding ring.

"You will take my wedding ring over my dead body," he said in a voice as thin as his lank frame.

What Big Dick Brull would have said to that was never known. A drumbeat sounded somewhere close.

Doom doom doom doom . . .

"There it goes again," Agent Phelps moaned.

"Who's making that?" Brull demanded of Smith.

"If I knew, I would put a stop to it this instant."

The sound seemed to come from around the corner, so Dick Brull said, "Follow me."

They followed the drumming by sound and not sight. Nothing up and down the corridor seemed to be the source of the sound.

The drumbeat led them to a hospital-room door. Two agents pulled out Delta Elite pistols and rammed rounds into the chambers. They took up positions on either side of the door. At a nod from Brull, one flipped open the door while the other went in, pistol held before him in a two-handed grip. The other swept in right behind him.

"Freeze!" they shouted a beat apart.

"Oh, God," one said.

The other began retching.

Dick Brull shouted, "What is it? Did you corner it?"

A voice wavered, "Mr. Brull, you'd better see this yourself."

Brull hesitated. So Harold Smith broke free and barged into the room. Brull mustered up his courage and followed a pace behind him.

A low, strangled sound came from Harold W. Smith.

Behind him Big Dick Brull bounced on his heels trying to see over Smith's tall, lanky frame. "What is it? I can't see. Stand aside so I can see."

Harold Smith obliged.

Big Dick Brull got a good look at the room. His eyes were drawn to the quivering steel Delta Elites in the two IRS agents' hands. They were pointing to a hospital bed. On the bed lay IRS Special Agent Jack Koldstad.

Koldstad was scratching himself. It looked as if he had been scratching himself for over an hour. The tips of his fingers were bloodied, and the side of his face that itched was a raw wound. It leaked blood like a sponge. Nevertheless, he kept scratching at the itch that his fingernails must have long ago conquered.

"What's wrong with him?" Brull croaked.

"Disinhibition combined with perseveration," said Harold Smith. "I recognize the symptoms."

"Make him stop, dammit! Somebody make him stop. It's making me sick just to look at him."

Harold Smith moved in and took Jack Koldstad's restlessly scratching right hand by the wrist. He had to use both hands because that was the only way to get the man to stop scratching his face. When the fingers came away, they could see what looked like a pulsing blister in the bloody rawness of the cheek. It moved, questing like a red slug. After a moment they realized they were looking at Jack Koldstad's tongue, visible through the wound he had excavated in his own face.

Big Dick Brull plunged out of the hospital room holding his hand to his mouth. A spray of watery vomit came out from between his fingers, and the chunks of his lunch began bouncing off his polished shoes.

When the doctor came, Big Dick Brull demanded in a hot voice, "Why wasn't this man under constant watch?"

"Because someone fired half the orderlies," he was told.

"What moron did that?" Brull roared.

From his hospital bed, Jack Koldstad lifted a weak hand.

The doctor quickly strapped it down along with the other so the patient wouldn't injure himself further.

MRS. HAROLD W. SMITH wondered if she should call Folcroft Sanitarium.

Normally she would not have hesitated. Normally she called dutifully if her increasingly absentminded husband failed to call her. Usually Harold was very good about calling if he was going to be late. Sometimes he slept over at work. Lately he'd fallen into that habit quite a bit. She had begun to wonder if Harold had taken an unprofessional interest in his secretary.

As a consequence, Mrs. Smith, who answered to Maude but was affectionately called Irma by her husband, had begun to feel neglected.

So when her Harold—he was never Harry or Hal—once again forgot to call her, she decided to let him get around to it in his own good time.

But it was a day later, and there had been no call. This was too much. Not that it hadn't happened before. It had. But Mrs. Smith was starting to feel taken for granted. And another carefully prepared meat loaf was congealing in the refrigerator, untasted.

Mrs. Smith was pacing the living room eyeing the beige AT&T desk telephone, wondering if she should call Harold or hold her ground until he remembered to call her, when a very loud knock came at the door.

Mrs. Smith went to answer it. The door was no sooner unlatched than several white-shouldered men in neat suits and drab ties began pouring in.

"Mrs. Harold W. Smith?" one demanded in a gruff voice.

"Yes. What is it?"

"Internal Revenue agents. We are seizing this property in settlement of outstanding federal taxes." He handed over an official-looking document.

Mrs. Smith tried to reason with the men. "I'm afraid you have the wrong house. My Harold has always paid his taxes."

"You have five minutes to gather up any belongings you can carry in two hands and go."

"Go? Go where?"

"Anywhere. This is a free country."

"But this is my home."

"This dwelling is government property, and you have four and one half minutes left."

Shocked to the bone, Mrs. Smith watched as the unfeeling IRS agents began rifling through cabinets and drawers. She grabbed her purse off the end table and bolted from the house, sobbing.

What was the world coming to?

HIS FACE TURNING PURPLE, Big Dick Brull swung on Harold W. Smith and roared, "Confine this man to the brig!"

"You are mad," said Smith.

"And clap him in irons if you can find any!" Brull added.

"You are overstepping your lawful authority," Smith warned.

"I am IRS. IRS is the supreme authority. We have more manpower than the CIA, FBI and the Pentagon put together. We have an Intelligence-gathering capability that makes Red Chinese Intelligence look like Canadian Intelligence. Our annual budget is 6.5 billion dollars—the largest in human fucking history. We can do anything we want in the taxpayer's name. And we answer to no one."

"Wrong. There is one agency more powerful than yours. And you *will* answer to it, I promise you that."

"This is no such entity."

Harold Smith compressed his lips. He had already said too much.

"Big talker," Brull said contemptuously.

Two IRS agents grabbed Harold Smith by his elbows and pulled him down the corridor as much for his own safety as in response to the direct order.

"This way, Dr. Smith," one said.

Smith obeyed, walking stiff spined, his face the color and texture of the New England rock from which he sprang.

Dick Brull's voice roared after him. "By close of business today, Smith, I'm going to have the goods on you. IRS has the goods on every citizen. It's only a matter of digging up the dirt. You'll see, you noncompliant bastard."

Harold Smith said nothing. But his glasses had begun to steam up again.

They escorted him to the psychiatric wing. Smith groaned aloud when he saw the doors ajar up and down the main corridor.

"Where are my patients?" he demanded.

"Deinstitutionalized," said an agent unconcernedly.

As they escorted him along, Smith mentally tallied the missing patients. He saw with relief that the door to Jeremiah Purcell's padded cell was firmly shut. The sound of a television was coming from the other side. But when he saw the Beasley door ajar, Smith repressed another aggrieved groan.

Yet not all the patients had been released. In fact, they seemed to have been let go in an unprofessionally haphazard fashion. Smith made a mental note to upbraid Dr. Gerling for this. The man knew better.

The IRS agents brought Smith to the last door on the left. It was not locked. One held the door open for him while the other gave his back a firm shove. Smith entered without complaint and turned as the door was slammed in his face.

"When you're ready to talk, we'll let you out," one agent said as the other threw a restraining bar across the door, locking it from the outside.

Smith said nothing. The agents' faces left the field of the small glass window that was honeycombed with chickenwire. The sound of their shoes echoing along the corridor began receding.

Then it stopped, stopped abruptly, and another sound came. It was a gurgling. A hoarse curse came in its wake.

Smith rushed to the window, trying to see what was happening.

"Let him go, damn you." It was the voice of one of the agents.

The gurgling stopped amid a sound like bones grating together. Smith thought he recognized it.

"Don't hurt them!" Smith shouted suddenly. "Master Chiun, do not harm those men! That is an order!"

The other agent cried out. "I know you! You're—"

A second gurgling started.

"Release that man at once!" Smith howled.

The fracturing of bone squelched the ugly death gurgle.

Grinding his teeth in frustration, Harold Smith could only crane his neck in a futile effort to see down the corridor.

Then a face appeared in the window. It was a wrinkled mask of hate. A single eye rolled at him while dry lips peeled back off peglike teeth under a frosty white mustache.

"Avast me hearty," a voice cackled. "The tables be turned."

Then a hydraulic steel hand came up into view and began expanding and contracting like an articulated vise.

25

The Master of Sinanju walked the lonely corridors of Folcroft Sanitarium.

There was no reason to remain any longer in the dank basement where the gold had lain. It was time to patrol the fortress that had for the first time since he had set foot in it fallen to enemies.

That these enemies were representatives of the Eagle Throne of America was of small comfort. Harold Smith had ordered them not to be slain, and so they would not be felled by the implacable hand of Sinanju. So long as their grubby hands did not despoil the gold of Sinanju—wherever it was.

Chiun's smooth forehead gathered in wrinkles as he considered the missing gold. It was miraculous, what Remo had done. It smacked of magic. The white had learned well. Perhaps too well, for not even the one who had taught Remo all he knew could fathom its fate.

Perhaps, Chiun ruminated, he would chance upon the secret hiding place of the missing gold in his search for Uncle Sam Beasley.

His wanderings took him past prowling IRS taxers of wealth, who—although their eyes were open wide and their ears unplugged by wax—saw and heard only a fraction of what they should. He passed them undetected and unsuspected while his eyes and ears caught all. His fingers relieved them of their wallets in passing. If they later complained, he would call it the Sinanju tax.

Coming to the great gymnasium where long ago he had first been introduced to his pupil, Chiun stopped and let the memories roll over him.

It was here that Remo's training had begun. First the Master of Sinanju had been content to offer his unworthy white pupil simple arts suitable to his lack of promise. Karate. Aikido. Judo. The castoffs of the purity that was Sinanju. Chiun had even presented him with a white karate *gi* and, because the simpleminded white seemed to think it was a mark of distinction, a pretty-colored sash to wear around his overfed waist.

It seemed hopeless. The white drank fermented barley, smoked foul-smelling weeds and virtually lived on the fire-scorched meat of dead cows. Years of being a hamburger fiend had filled his essence with all manner of poisons.

The first week he had made Remo eat kimchi to leach the poisons from his system. The second, water was allowed. And on the third he got cold rice. After the fiery kimchi, Remo had been thankful for the water. By the time he had his first bowl of rice, Remo was grateful simply because it was not kimchi.

"When do I get warm rice?" Remo had asked, shoveling the sticky grains into his mouth with his fingers because, typically, the chopsticks were beyond his comprehension.

"When you have mastered the most rudimentary steps."

"How long is that in dog years?"

"I do not know, but certainly within the first five years of your training."

The look on the hamburger fiend's face had stayed with Chiun all these years.

So when Remo was allowed warm rice in the first six months, the white had been exceedingly pleased with himself.

What had been asked of Chiun was simple but odious. To train a white man in the assassin's art so that the white could move among his own kind, undetected and unsuspected.

It was not only an impossibility, but an insult. Chiun, retired because his own pupil, Nuihc, had gone renegade, had all but balked at the requested service.

"The Masters of Sinanju, my ancestors, have served thrones going back before the days of Herod the Just," he had told Smith. "Point to me your enemies, and I will slay them. You need no white to do the work which is properly done by a Korean."

"We require an assassin who will if necesary do our bidding for the next decade. If not two," Harold the Grim had said.

"It is too late," Chiun had countered. "One begins at birth. Remo is fat and sloppy. On the other hand, I am prepared to perform such service if the gold is plentiful."

"You are very old," had said the thoughtless and insulting white.

"I have seen but eighty summers and will see another forty before I am considered old by the measure of my ancestors."

"What we want is much different," Smith had said. "Please, Master Chiun. Train Remo as best you can."

And so Remo was trained in the foolish arts that had nothing to do with Sinanju except that they were pilfered from the sun source by Chinese and Japanese thieves who copied the moves but not the soul.

Over time Remo showed promise. Over time he took to the breathing and the grace as if of Korean blood. In time, Chiun had begun to supect that somewhere in Remo's mongrel past, Korean blood flowed. Not just the blood of any Korean, but the blood of the heirs to his village traditions, his own ancestors.

It was ridiculous, but to think otherwise was to accept that Sinanju could be taught to anyone—even a white—with satisfactory results. This was impossible, Chiun knew. For even some of the village men had proven incapable of mastering such basics as the fundamentals of correct breathing.

No, Remo was Korean. But the Master of Sinanju did not come to this understanding until many months had passed and he had made Remo throw away his karate *gi* and started him on the true path to Masterhood.

In this gym of so many memories, Chiun reflected how Remo had become like a son to him, and how he had happily fallen into the role of adopted father.

Many happy years had come and gone since those days.

Now, because of one enemy—a mind that was not human but a fragment of the white machines that plagued the very society that worshiped them—all was being sundered.

The organization for which they worked was no more. Emperor Smith was a willing prisoner of his own government, and Remo was determined more than ever to find his past.

This last worried the Master of Sinanju more than any of these other events, significant as they were. This time Remo would not give up. This time he was driven by the spirit of his own mother. This time he would not rest until he knew all.

And if he succeeded, if he should be reunited with the man from whose loins he originally sprang, would there be any room in his new life for the old man whom he called Little Father?

The Master of Sinanju hung his aged head and prayed to his ancestors that Remo's father be struck down before that would happen.

Then, his heart hardening, he turned silently on his heel and went in search of his emperor.

BIG DICK BRULL sat at the black glass-topped desk making telephone calls.

"His name is Harold W. Smith. Taxpayer ID number 008-16-9314. I want everything the master file has on him and I want it tonight."

"Fax number?"

Brull looked around the office. There were two phones, a multiline ROLM office phone and a blue AT&T desk model, but no faxphone. Brull blinked. Why would the director of a hospital need two telephones?

"Get back to me personally with the raw data. I don't see a faxphone anywhere."

"Yes, Mr. Brull."

Brull hit the intercom. Agent Phelps poked his head in.

"Sir?"

"Find out where these phone lines go."

"Yes, sir."

Twenty minutes later Phelps returned and said, "The ROLM phone line goes out on poles. We don't find any trace of a terminal for the blue instrument."

Brull picked up the blue receiver. The dial tone came loud and steady. "It works. It must go somewhere. Find it."

"Yes, sir."

Brull got up and started going through file cabinets. There were two kinds, green metal ones that looked old and oak ones that seemed ancient. Except for the futuristic desk, every stick of office furniture looked like a Salvation Army castoff.

The files contained administration and purchasing records. Nothing out of the ordinary.

"You'd think the noncompliant asshole would have computerized his own office," Brull muttered.

He found the worn briefcase tucked between two of the filing cabinets. It was locked. It looked so worn and frayed at the edges that at first Brull thought it was simply being stored there. But when he picked it up, he found it quite heavy.

Bringing it over to the desk, Brull set it down. The catches were shut. There was a combination lock. Idly Big Dick Brull played with the numbers, but the briefcase refused to surrender to him. He set the thing aside.

It was growing cool, and an offshore breeze was coming through the break in the big picture window.

Brull tried to ignore it, but it grew stronger.

Getting out of the chair, he tried to move it so he was out of the way of the cold. But no matter where he placed the chair, the back of his head was in the draft.

Dick Brull next tried to move the desk. It was too heavy. Three or four men would be needed to relocate it.

It was while testing the desk's weight that he found the button under the edge of the desktop.

"What have we here?" he muttered, peering under the desk and pressing the button.

Nothing happened. No secret drawer rolled open, and no hidden panel popped.

Pressing it several times brought no response.

Grumbling, Dick Brull sat down just as the telephone rang.

"Brull."

"This is Schwoegler from Martinsburg."

"Go."

"We pulled the tape record, Mr. Brull."

"What have you got for me?"

"Nothing. The space where the Harold W. Smith record should have been stored magnetically was blank."

"Blank?"

"It seemed to have been accidentally erased."

"Get off it. Nobody erases master-file taxpayer records, accidentally or otherwise."

"We have no record of Harold W. Smith with that Social Security number."

"Then go find the original paper returns. Get me every damn one."

"Mr. Brull, that could take weeks—months."

"Damn. Then get me his most recent returns."

"We don't have those in the master file."

"Then call the people who do and have them call me. I have no time for this horseshit!" And Brull slammed down the phone.

He began going through drawers. In the bottom drawer he came upon another telephone. It was as red as a fire engine. He grabbed it by receiver and cradle and set it on the desktop.

"I'll be damned."

The phone had no dial, no buttons, no nothing. Just a flat red shelf where the dial should be.

"What the hell kind of telephone is this?" he muttered. The phone was disconnected. The plastic cord with its modular jack was held in loops by a knotted string.

"What kind of phone is this?" he repeated.

The main phone rang again. He snapped the receiver to his bulldog face.

"Brull."

"Ballard from the New York office here, Mr. Brull. I was the Folcroft auditor."

"Go ahead."

"We have Harold W. Smith's last three years' 1040s here."

"How do they look to you?"

"Average."

"Do better than that."

"Well, they're absolutely average."

"What do you mean?"

"Everything falls within the statistical average. Deductions. Charitable contributions. Investments."

"Perfectly?"

"Yes."

"So perfect it could be designed not to trip a red flag?"

"Well, yes."

"I knew it. He's dirty."

"Sir?"

"Use your head. Nobody's returns come up perfectly average, year after year. It's statisically impossible. Smith has been filing stealth returns configured to foil IRS radar."

"I never heard of stealth returns."

"That's why you're a fucking G-12 and I'm an assistant commissioner. Now, messenger those returns to Folcroft. I want to eyeball them myself."

"Yes, Mr. Brull."

Brull hung up and found himself staring at the blank red telephone again. What the hell could it mean? He looked around for a wall jack, found none and shoved the red telephone aside.

That's when he saw the amber line.

At first it looked like a reflection on the black glass desktop, except it wasn't a reflection. There was no amber light source in the office. Only the overhead fluorescents.

The vertical amber line floated under the black glass of the desktop like a smoldering wire.

Reaching out to touch the slick surface, Big Dick Brull froze. Ghostly lines of white symbols sprang into life under his hovering fingers. A keyboard. But there were no keys. Only the letters glowing in rows just under the black glass like metal shavings in ice.

Brull touched one experimentally. The letter *A*. It flashed white-hot under his touch.

Nothing happened. Just the flash. When he withdrew his hands, the keyboard symbols darkened into obscurity.

It was a touch-sensitive keyboard. No question. Capacity type. The keyboard had activated when his hand disturbed the magnetic field surrounding it. And the amber line could only be generated by a hidden computer screen. You got a line just like that if you turned on your monitor without booting up the system.

But who had turned on the screen?

"That damn black button!"

Brull reached under the desk and hit the hidden button. The amber line went away. He hit it again. It returned.

"Folcroft is not what it's supposed to be," Big Dick Brull chortled in a low, gleeful voice. Then his face contracted into a muscular knot. "But what the fuck is it?"

26

Remo Williams pulled his sedan off into the woods well short of the Folcroft gate and let it coast, engine off, down to the lapping waters of Long Island Sound.

He got out, opened up the hood and pulled the spark plugs, hiding them in the hollow of a tree.

Let the IRS try and seize it now, he thought as he went down to the water and let it take his body.

Remo swam through the darkness, wide of land and low to the silty ocean floor where no one could possibly spot him. Air bubbles seeped from his parted mouth in ones and twos so tiny that when they reached the surface they would be mistaken for fish exhalations.

Using his inner compass as a guide, Remo veered toward shore again, exactly where his senses told him Folcroft would be.

A beer can floated down from above, and the faint pressure waves riding ahead of it made Remo bob out of the way.

He looked up. Against the moonlight, four wedge shapes bobbed. DEA Cigarette boats.

Remo continued on.

Another beer can blooped into the water and tumbled slowly into his field of vision. That decided Remo.

Twisting like a porpoise, he redirected his momentum upward, zeroing in on the boat directly above. One hand took hold of the propeller, steadying the boat and himself. With his right index finger, Remo peppered the sleek fiberglass hull with neat round holes.

The boat began taking on water.

Remo went on to the next.

He sank all four DEA boats in as much time as it would take to pop open a six-pack of Coors and returned to the water.

The hoarse cursing of the DEA stakeout team came through the cold water. The burbling of the boats going down drowned out the the shouting.

While their feet were kicking in an attempt to tread water, Remo slipped up on them and began nipping at their heels with his hard fingers.

The frantic cries of "Shark!" cut through the water, and a mad splashing began. The DEA agents must have read somewhere that a shark can be frightened off by splashing.

Remo tugged at two more sets of heels.

The DEA responded with a rain of bullets that veered crazily in all directions once they struck water, their force dissipating. Moving fast, Remo batted them back with just enough force to sting but not injure.

The firing stopped.

Grinning in the dark silence of the sound, Remo resumed his swim.

If the DEA wanted to stake out Folcroft, they'd need a whole new team, he thought. These guys were not coming back.

IT WAS like something out of a nightmare.

Except that Harold W. Smith was rarely visited by night terrors. He lacked the imagination to conjure up fantasies, even in the deepest sleep. It was one of the reasons he had been chosen to head CURE. A man with imagination might see the possiblities in the near-absolute power the secret office gave one.

Yet Smith now confronted a nightmare beyond his deepest fears.

Framed in the square glass window was the mugging face of Uncle Sam Beasley, world-renowned illustrator, animator, and motion-picture studio executive, founder of the most popular and universally known theme parks in the world. And as far as the world knew, dead for nearly thirty years.

Harold W. Smith had thought him dead, too. Until an invasion of Cuba launched from American soil was traced back to Sam Beasley World in Florida, and Remo and Chiun had uncovered the truth: Uncle Sam Beasley, rumored cryogenically frozen since his death in 1965, had been brought back from the dead outfitted with an animatronic heart and artificial limbs to replace those that suffered cell damage during his long icy sleep.

Seeing the fall of Cuba near, Beasley had mounted a secret invasion force with the intention of toppling the Castro government and turning the lush Caribbean isle into the ultimate theme park—not to mention a tax-free haven from which to run his global entertainment empire.

It was mad, it was insane, and it had very nearly succeeded. Only the intervention of CURE had stopped the invasion of Cuba by one of America's most famous and beloved corporations—and averted the embarrassing international incident that would have resulted.

In the end neither Remo nor Chiun, both of whom revered the legendary animator, could bring himself to kill Beasley. Neither could Smith in the final analysis. So he had had the man rendered harmless by the removal of his deadly hydraulic hand and institutionalized in Folcroft, where his cracked claims to be a resurrected Uncle Sam would fall on deaf ears.

"Look what I found," Beasley said with a satisfied cackle, making his steel fist whine open and closed. There was blood on it. And a fleck of froth bubbled in the corner of Beasley's grinning mouth.

Smith shuddered. The man was now a caricature of his folksy former self. And he was loose in Folcroft, with Smith himself trapped in one of his own padded cells.

If ever there was a nightmare for Harold Smith, this was it.

"You are not well," Smith said in a calm voice. It was best to speak calmly to the deranged. And Uncle Sam Beasley was definitely deranged.

"Belay the bedside crap," Beasley snapped. "Whose necks did I just snap?"

"Innocent IRS agents."

"No such thing. And that'll teach the bastards to nickel-and-dime me into early heart failure."

Smith changed tactics. "You have no place to go."

"What are you talking about? I'm Uncle Sam Beasley, beloved father-figure storyteller. Hell, there isn't a city, town or hamlet in the world where I wouldn't be welcome. France aside, that is."

"The world knows you're dead."

"You know I'm not. In fact, with my new ticker, I'm good until the Mouse's centennial."

"Perhaps. But you are instantly recognizable. If you set foot off these grounds, you will attract attention and have to explain youself."

"Good point."

"So you see you must remain here."

Beasley fingered his frosty mustache with a gnarled finger.

"So I must, so I must."

"I am glad you see the true nature of your position," said Smith through the glass.

"I do, I do. And I appreciate your pointing these things out to me."

"Return to your room please," said Smith, relaxing.

A chilly eyebrow crawled up from under the black eye patch in slow surprise. "Don't you want to be let out?"

"Not at the moment."

"Why not?"

"I don't care to discuss it," said Harold Smith.

"Suit yourself. Ta-ta."

Harold Smith heard Uncle Sam Beasley clump away on his silver-filigreed artificial leg. He continued listening. The clumping echoed all the way down to the end of the corridor. It stopped. Smith listened for the closing of a steel door. No such sound came. Instead, the ding of the arriving elevator came distinctly.

"My God!"

The elevator doors dinged shut again over a throaty chuckling, and Harold Smith knew that Uncle Sam Beasley had been let loose on the world.

And all because of the stupidity of the Internal Revenue Service.

Smith began banging on the door and shouting loud, inarticulate words.

It was a nightmare. And it was about to get worse. Much worse. If only someone would hear him.

THE MASTER OF SINANJU was picking the pocket of a prowling IRS agent when he heard the hoarse shouting from two floors above.

The IRS agent did not hear this shouting, of course, any more than he felt the delicate finger extract his leather wallet from his back pocket.

The agent was bent over a water bubbler, refreshing himself. The Master of Sinanju had slipped up on him like a phantom, as he had on two others, each time relieving them off their fat wallets.

So far, he had collected less than three hundred dollars, but it was at least partial repayment for all the trouble the taxidermists had caused.

The hoarse shouting caused the Master of Sinanju to retreat before the agent straightened, wiping his mouth of water.

Chiun took the stairs, floating up them like a wraith. His feet brought him to the door behind which Emperor Smith pounded and shouted like a madman.

"Never fear, Emperor," Chiun squeaked, straining on tiptoe so his eyes could see through the high square window. "For I have come to succor you."

Chiun laid fingers on the metal bar.

Smith cried, "No! Don't let me out!"

"Why not?"

"I need an alibi."

"For what?"

"For the two dead agents down the hall," said Smith.

Chiun turned his head. "One moment," he said, floating down the hall. He returned moments later with the wallets of the two dead agents stuffed up the wide sleeves of his kimono.

"Yes, they are dead. Their necks have been crushed."

"It was Beasley. He just escaped by the elevator. He must be stopped."

"Why? He is slaying your enemies for you. And you have a perfect alibi, being a prisoner of these very same enemies."

"I don't want him to slay the IRS. It will only bring more grief down on our heads."

Chiun frowned. "I do not understand whites."

"Please, Master Chiun, stop Beasley. Do it quietly. Kill him if you have to."

"Slay the brilliant inventor of Mongo Mouse and Screwball Squirrel? My ancestors would rain imprecations down on my head until the end of all time. No, I could never do this."

Smith squeezed his eyes shut. "Just capture him, please."

"As you wish, Emperor."

And the Master of Sinanju padded off to do the bidding of his crazed emperor. Oh, but if only he had lived in the days of the pharaohs. Now, they were rulers. Or the Romans. Czarist Russia would have been acceptable. The barbarian Britons under Henry VIII might have been tolerable.

Surely Chiun worked for the maddest emperor since Caligula. For who hired the finest assassins in the modern world and asked that they refrain from killing?

27

Big Dick Brull knew he was on to something now.

Folcroft was not what it seemed, all right. It was a cover of some kind. But what kind? What could it be?

One thing was certain—the DEA had been barking up the wrong elm with that crap about turkey drugs. Folcroft was no drug factory. Money was being laundered, sure. That was the only way to explain the twelve million that had appeared in the Folcroft bank acount. And the gold—assuming it really existed and wasn't some fantasy concocted by his own agents.

But who stockpiled illegal gold? In all his years with the service, the only people Dick Brull ever heard of stockpiling gold was the Feds.

The moment the thought crossed his mind, the ROLM phone rang.

"Brull here."

"This is Schwoegler down at Martinsburg. We located the backup paper on Harold W. Smith, and analyzed his 1040s going back as far as we could."

"About damn time."

"They're clean. In fact, they all conform to the DIF, year after year, without exception."

Brull banged his fist on the desk. "I knew it!"

"It's very strange, sir."

"No, it's not. It's very calculated. Tell me this, when did Smith first list director of Folcroft as his occupation on his 1040s?"

"That was in, um, 1963. Before that he was an analyst with the Company."

Brull blinked. "What company?"

"Central Intelligence Agency, sir."

"The CIA!" Brull roared. "Harold W. Smith worked for the CIA?"

"Yes, sir. He came to Folcroft in April of 1963. Oddly enough, these records indicated Folcroft was some kind of sociological think tank or something in those days."

"The damn computers! That's what he said they were for."

"Sir?"

"Never mind. Express those papers to Folcroft. I want to eyeball them personally." And Brull slammed down the phone.

He leaned back in the high-backed leather chair that Harold W. Smith had occupied for over thirty years according to his tax records, his face screwing up like a gnarled root.

Smith was ex-CIA. Maybe he was *still* with the Company. Maybe this wasn't an illegal operation after all. Maybe it was CIA all the way.

Brull picked up the telephone and called CIA headquarters in Langley, Virginia. He asked to speak with the director of personnel.

A maze of bureaucratic referrals later, Brull had his man.

"Dick Brull, IRS CID here. I want a background check on one of your current employees. Harold W. Smith."

"We don't do background checks on Agency employees here. You'll have to take it up at a higher echelon."

"I'm taking it up with *you*. This is the Internal Revenue Service calling. *We* are the ultimate echelon. And no one, not even the damn CIA, better have anything to hide from IRS. Now, his name is Harold W. Smith. Do I give his Social Security number to you—or the guy above you who is going to be just thrilled that you bounced me in his direction?"

"Give me the number," the CIA man said wearily.

A full five minutes later the answer came back in the form of a return call. "We have no record of a Harold W. Smith with that Social Security number on our payroll."

"How about in the past?"

"I did a deep computer search. No Harold W. Smith ever worked for Central Intelligence."

"He claimed on his 1040s to have been an analyst out of Langley."

"His claim is false," the CIA man said flatly.

"You telling me the truth or is this the usual deniability runaround?"

"Is there anything else I can do for you?"

"Yeah. You can hang up, dink," said Big Dick Brull, hanging up.

Brull leaned back again. Okay, he thought. There were only two scenarios here. Maybe three. Smith was lying. Or Central Intelligence was lying. Maybe both were lying. But somebody was lying.

That still pointed Dick Brull in one direction—Folcroft Sanitarium was a CIA outpost or was manned by an ex-CIA operative. Guys like that, once they were cut loose, were always running weird spook operations on their own initiative.

Big Dick Brull looked at the strange red telephone, the superfluous blue telephone that didn't go out on NYNEX lines and the desk with its hidden computer setup.

Maybe Folcroft was dirty. Maybe it was just off the books. Either way, it didn't matter to the IRS or Dick Brull. If it was a conduit for black budget money, the IRS was going to get its share, deserved or not. That was going to be the price for all those dead IRS and DEA agents. Dick Brull would either bring home the bacon or blow the whistle on Folcroft.

After all, in the scheme of things, the CIA was hardly forty years old. IRS went back to Abraham Lincoln.

And CID still had its quarterly quotas to meet.

Big Dick Brull got out of his chair. It was time to rub Harold Smith's nose in the very disagreeable political reality.

HAROLD SMITH HEARD the unmistakable hard heels sound coming down the corridor.

When Big Dick Brull's black brush cut appeared in the square window, Smith was prepared. But not for Brull's first words.

"The bull is off the nickel."

"I beg your pardon?" said Smith.

Brull hoisted himself up on his feet so his grinning face, like a boiled apple peeling, showed. "I know what Folcroft Sanitarium really is."

"You do," Smith said in a blank voice, his heart racing.

"Damn right I do."

"Then you know everything."

"I know enough. You're running a covert installation for the CIA here. I found your trick computer terminal and funny phones. So much for that thin story of yours about those basement mainframes."

"You are very clever," said Smith, his voice cool as brook water.

"What I'm not clear on is exactly what kind of operation this is. Domestic Intelligence gathering. Illegal radiation experiments. Safehouse. What?"

"I have no comment on that."

"That damn drumming is part of it, isn't it?"

"No comment."

"The gold that disappeared faster than reasonably possible. Those stupid vultures circling the building day and night. That killer butterfly. The bank account. They all hook up together."

"I know nothing whatever of these things," said Smith, wondering himself what Brull meant by circling birds.

"Don't bullshit me, Smith! I haven't forgotten how you threatened me with a government agency bigger that IRS. Hah! Like I'm scared. Those CIA spooks suck at the service's teats the same as anyone."

Smith said nothing.

Brull snapped his fingers. "I know! You're doing genetic experiments here. Breeding mutants. Am I right?"

"No comment."

Brull's face came close to the glass. Smith met his icy black eyes with his own cool gray stare.

"Whatever it is, you're not off the hook until you square accounts with IRS."

"I fail to follow."

"This damn place is off the books. Way off the books. I understand that. I'm not stupid. I know how things work. You're moving big blocks of cash if not gold to support it. All of it tax free."

Smith said nothing.

"Technically tax free. But if you want the lid to stay on Folcroft, you're going to have to kick through thirty percent to IRS coffers."

"Are you talking about a bribe?"

"Don't use that word with me!" Brull exploded. "I take nothing. But IRS takes thirty percent. In return, Folcroft goes back to you, just like we left it."

Harold Smith's glasses began to steam again.

"It is a shambles," he said, bitter voiced. "There are two dead IRS agents just down the hall. How are you going to explain them away?"

Brull looked. "I don't see anything."

"They are around the corner."

Brull left. He came back, his face the color of a sheet.

"Jesus, what killed them?"

"I did not see. I was locked in here. But I heard them being strangled."

Brull wiped his suddenly moist brow with a hand-kerchief. "Their necks are squeezed to the diameter of fucking pencils," he said.

"A dangerous lunatic was deinstitutionalized on IRS orders. He is obviously running amok."

"I can cover up a few more dead agents. Hell, they should be proud to have gone out in defense of the Revenue Code."

"They did no such thing," Smith said hotly. "And you know it!"

Brull waved a finger in Smith's face. "You think about what I said while I look into this, Smith. This could only get uglier if the truth behind Folcroft becomes public. Whoever it is you report to would chew your ass to rags if your cover is blown. You digest that while I have this floor policed of bodies."

Big Dick Brull turned smartly and, heels clicking, strode away.

In the solitude of his cell, Harold Smith said, "You bastard. I have the power to crush you like a bug."

But even as he said this, he knew he could not have Brull slain and solve the essential problem the IRS agent represented. That would only bring in more agents and increase their exposure. Containing the situation was the only way, but if there was a way to engineer it, Smith lacked the imagination to initiate an ironclad coverup.

It was hopeless. Utterly hopeless.

Once again Harold Smith began to wish for his coffin-shaped poison pill. Barring a miracle, it was the only way out. His failures had cost America CURE, its last bulwark against lawlessness, and his wife the comfort and security of a safe home and good husband in her declining years.

His failure was absolute, his future bleak.

Smith returned to the narrow bunk and lay down to let his nerves shake his body like a gnarled branch in a gale.

28

Uncle Sam Beasley heard the drumming when he stepped off the elevator and into the dark and deserted Folcroft lobby. He hesitated, his hydraulic hand splayed to grasp any neck that came within reach. He wished he had the cybernetic laser eyeball the Beasley concepteers had designed for him, but the hospital bastards had hidden it too well. He had been lucky to find the hand.

The drumming seemed to be coming around a corner.

Doom doom doom doom . . .

It was impossible for a man with a silver peg leg to steal up on anyone, even under the cover of a monotonous drumming. But Uncle Sam Beasley tried anyway.

He turned the corner, and his tight face broke into fracturing lines of shock.

He could see the thing that was drumming. It was smaller than he expected and very, very pink.

The hot pink creature looked up at him with blank eyes and said, "Hello."

"Did I create you?" Beasley blurted out.

"No."

"Did Maus send you?"

"No."

"Then what are you doing?"

"Drumming."

Doom doom doom doom...

"I can see that, you little pink turd!"

"Language, language."

At that, Uncle Sam Beasley decided to strangle the pink creature, if only to stifle that idiot drumming. It was starting to drive him crazy.

But when he reached down for its spindly neck, the creature was no longer there.

Instead, Uncle Sam Beasley found himself looking into a mirror.

It was very strange. He hadn't noticed any mirror. But there he was, looking back at himself.

What was even more weird was that his mirror image was speaking while his own mouth hung slack in surprise.

The mirror Uncle Sam said, "I can help you escape."

"I don't need any help. Especially from a cheap imitation like you."

"They will be looking for you."

"Let them. I have friends on the outside. One phone call and I'm home free."

"I can fix it so they stop looking."

Uncle Sam Beasley blinked his single eye. His icy eyebrows crawled higher on his puckering forehead.

"It will buy you all the time you need," the mirror image said.

"What's in it for you?" Beasley asked, his voice growing warm with interest.

"Revenge."

"I think," Uncle Sam Beasley said, "you and I are starting to speak the same language."

THE MASTER OF SINANJU reached the Folcroft lobby by the fire stairs. The door was flung open ahead of him, and he leaped out, keen eyes going right and left.

He spotted Uncle Sam Beasley exiting through the main door.

Chiun's eyes narrowed in satisfaction. The man walked on a clumping leg. He would be easily apprehended.

The only problem would come if the illustrious Uncle Sam chose to fight.

He would be no match for the Master of Sinanju, true. But it would be unpleasant if Chiun had to injure him even slightly. What would the children of the world think of him if it ever got out?

REMO WILLIAMS was creeping around the Folcroft grounds when he heard the first muffled clump. He recognized the sound at once. The rubber cap on the end of Uncle Sam Beasley's silver leg made the identical sound.

"Damn! Hasn't Chiun grabbed him yet?"

Remo veered toward the sound, his face more annoyed than angry. It was, after all, a minor annoyance. How hard could it be to stop a man with an artificial leg?

THE MASTER OF SINANJU emerged into the clear night air.

Uncle Sam Beasley had moved with surprising quickness in the few moments when he had been out of the Master of Sinanju's sight. He had almost reached the parking lot, where many cars waited empty of drivers.

Chiun flew after him, saying "Stop!" in a voice that squeaked more than it carried.

Uncle Sam Beasley looked over his shoulder and continued his energetic progress. He was all but running in a lopsided gait that was painful to behold. His entire body convulsed with every step, sending the ruffles at his wrists and throat shaking manically.

Then he turned the corner.

Chiun cleared the intervening space with a flourish of skirts. He popped around the corner, and stopped, face aghast.

The scarlet figure of Uncle Sam Beasley was nowhere to be seen.

Frantic, the Master of Sinanju rushed among the parked cars. He began looking down the rows. Still, there was no sign of Uncle Sam Beasley. It was impossible. Pausing, Chiun peered under the chassis of the neatly ranked cars.

He did not see a prone Uncle Sam or the strange feet of a lurking Uncle Sam.

Straightening, the Master of Sinanju wore his wrinkles like a puzzled web in which his hazel eyes quivered like uncertain spiders.

"It is impossible!" he squeaked.

REMO WILLIAMS took the corner at a dead run and almost collided with the Master of Sinanju.

"Where'd he go?" Remo asked.

"Who?"

"Beasley. He just came this way."

Chiun stamped a frustrated foot. "He could not. I have chased him to this spot, and he has vanished."

"Well," said Remo, looking around, "he's somewhere around here."

"But where?" Chiun squeaked. "He could not elude us both."

"There," said Remo, pointing toward the gate.

The ridiculous buccaneer figure of Uncle Sam Beasley was trying to reach the Folcroft gate on foot. It was absurd. He could never do it, exposed as he was. On the other hand, he was making good time. Even if he was practically hopping like a ungainly red rabbit.

"Let's go," said Remo.

Together they raced after Uncle Sam Beasley, easily overtaking him.

"Give it up," called Remo.

"You cannot escape us," added Chiun, running alongside.

Beasley stopped. He whirled to confront them.

Uncle Sam Beasley smiled his wintry smile, and his skeletal steel hand clenched, fingers clicking as they made contact with his shiny palm.

"I do not wish to harm you, purveyor of cartoons," warned Chiun, his hands fluttering before him uncertainly.

"On the other hand," said Remo, "we don't have time to screw with you."

The hydraulic hand feinted toward Remo.

"Remo, do not hurt him!"

"Don't sweat it," Remo said as he met the steel appendage with a chopping blow that knocked the hand from its stump.

The hand fell to the grass with a surprisingly soft sound. It lay there, whirring, fingers clenching and unclenching like an upside-down steel tarantula trying to right itself.

Remo brought a hard heel down on it, there was a snap, and the whirring just stopped.

Uncle Sam Beasley lost his wintry smile. He said nothing.

"You coming without a fuss?" asked Remo.

Hanging his head, Beasley raised his mismatched arms in abject surrender.

"Guess without your robot hand, you're not very brave," grunted Remo.

Beasley said nothing to that, either. Remo took hold of his good arm and marched him back to Folcroft.

"Well," Remo told Chiun, "this is one thing that's gone well so far."

Headlights blazing, a car roared out of the parking lot and bore down on them.

"Watch out, Little Father!"

Whirling, Chiun broke left. Remo pushed Uncle Sam in the opposite direction, leaping after him.

The car swooshed by, sucking air, grit and dry dead leaves behind it. Its red parking lights vanished through the gate and down the road.

Remo pulled Beasley to his feet.

"Who the hell was that?" Remo demanded.

"I do not know. But he possessed but a single eye."

"You're thinking of Beasley," said Remo, giving the unresponsive Uncle Sam a hard shake.

"Yes, I am thinking of Beasley," said Chiun solemnly.

"But we've got Beasley right here."

"It must have been some other one-eyed pirate," said Chiun suspiciously, giving Uncle Sam a very hard look while stroking his wispy beard.

HAROLD SMITH came off his bunk when the rapping of knuckles on glass came.

Remo's face floated in the door window.

"Remo! Have you seen Chiun?"

"Better than that. Here's Beasley."

The hangdog face of Uncle Sam Beasley was brought into view, held steady by Remo's fingers at the back of his neck.

The Master of Sinanju's bald head came up into sight. "What should be done with this misguided one, O Emperor?"

"Lock him in a cell. He should keep overnight."

"No problem," said Remo. "What about you?"

"Brull was here. He suspects Folcroft of being a CIA front."

"So, let him."

"He's trying to extort money on behalf of the IRS."

"We can convince him of the error of that position," said Remo.

"No. It would not work."

"So what will?"

"I do not know," Smith admitted, his lemony voice dejected.

"Look," Remo said impatiently, "this running around can't go on forever. We gotta poop or get off the pot."

"Yes," chimed in Chiun. "Let us turn these taxidermists into poop, and all our troubles will fade like yesterday's fog."

"They've seized my home. I do not know where my wife is. She is my chief concern now."

"We can look into that. But what about you?"

Smith said listlessly, "I am not important."

"Smitty, stop talking like that. We have unfinished business. I want you to find my father for me."

"It is impossible."

"Like hell it is. My mother—I mean the woman who spoke to me—claimed I knew my father. Look, how many people can that be? You can do background checks on everyone I ever knew. Something will turn up. Until then, you stay in the game."

"I make no promises, Remo. For the life of me, I do not see how we can put the pieces of the organization back together."

"Sleep on it," said Remo, shaking the silent Uncle Sam Beasley. "Let's start with putting this loose end to bed for the night."

As they walked away, Harold Smith could hear Remo scolding Uncle Sam Beasley. "I can't believe you turned out to be such a pill. I was a big fan of yours when I was a kid, you know."

"Even in my humble village," Chiun was saying, "the name of Uncle Sam made childish eyes glow like candles."

If Uncle Sam had any reply to that, Smith did not hear it as he lowered himself onto the narrow bunk. He didn't close his eyes until he heard the clank of a cell door shutting. Then he turned over on his side and he fell instantly asleep.

29

In the hours before the sunless dawn of submarine life, Winston Smith awoke like a spark flaring. His hands fished under his pillow, and he turned on the light. He sat reading the sea gram over and over.

"The bastard," he said feelingly. "The cold, mother-loving bastard."

After a while he lit a cigarette and smoked it to a stub. Then he cracked open the door and stuck out his close-shaven head. A seaman was making his way along the corridor.

"Hey, sailor. When do we make port?"

"We're in it."

Smith blinked. Only then did he notice the absence of vibrations and other sounds of a submarine under way. "What port?"

"Search me. It's classified."

"Sounds like my kind of port," said Smith, shutting the door to smoke another Lucky.

This time he used the lit end to ignite the sea gram. It refused to burn until he blew on the smoldering edge. Then it caught, burning briefly in his fingers.

Winston Smith didn't bother to let go when the flames licked at his fingers. He just let the fire run its course and crushed the curled black paper in his unfeeling fist while it was still hot.

"Uncle Harold, you picked the wrongest damn day to do this this to your favorite nephew."

He picked up the BEM gun and laid the plastic manual on his knee. There must be something in the specs that would disarm the damn antifiring interlock.

30

In the deepest part of the night, Harold Smith heard a familiar voice. It snapped him from his dreamless sleep.

"Harold?"

"Maude?" Blinking, Smith rushed to the locked door.

There was Maude Smith in all her blue-haired matronly glory. Nevertheless, she was a welcome sight.

"Harold, what are you doing here?"

"I am under house arrest. Please do not enter. How did you get past the IRS?"

"That doesn't matter, Harold. I have come to tell you something important."

"What is it?"

"Harold, I have been keeping a dreadful secret from you all these years."

"Secret?"

"Yes. I have been too ashamed to reveal it to you until now. But with all that is happening, I think you should know."

"Go on," said Harold Smith, unable to comprehend what his wife could have on her mind. She seemed incredibly calm under the circumstances.

"You have always been a good husband. You know that."

Harold Smith cleared his throat. "Thank you."

"But you have not always been home. You were away a lot during your days with the CIA. After you came to Folcroft, I thought that would change, but if anything, your absences grew worse."

"I have my responsibilities," Smith said defensively.

"There was a time many years ago when you were away for nearly a year. Do you remember?"

"I remember. I was in the Philippines."

"During that time, Harold, I am afraid I was not entirely faithful to you."

Harold Smith reeled on his feet as if punched in the stomach.

"No," he said, shocked.

"His name doesn't matter. We were younger then. It was brief, passing, inconsequential. But I have suffered pangs of guilt to this very day."

"Why tell me now?"

"Because," Maude Smith said, lowering her voice and eyes, "during that time I had a baby. A son."

"Impossible."

"I know it sounds ludicrous, but it's true. He was a happy little boy with dark eyes and such a winning smile. I wanted to keep him but I knew it was impossible." Maude's faded blue eyes squeezed shut in the frumpy cushion of her face. "Harold, to this day I don't know if he was your son or the product of my... indiscretion. You see, I learned I was pregnant only six weeks after you had left. There was no way to tell by whom I had the boy, so the week he was born, I put him up for adoption."

"A son," Smith said dazedly. "By now he would be grown. An adult."

"Harold, you have no conception of how this has torn me apart all these long years."

Smith touched the glass before his wife's pained face. "Maude..."

"As time went on, I became more and more convinced that he was your son, Harold. I don't know how I knew that. But I feel certain of it. And every day I miss that little fellow more and more."

"I...I don't quite know what to say. What happened to this boy?"

"I put him up for adoption."

"He can be traced. Surely he can be traced."

"I left him on the steps of an orphanage in New Jersey one morning. And I never looked back. I don't know how he could be found now."

"Orphanages keep records."

"This one burned down long ago, Harold. It's a dead end."

Something caused Harold Smith's gray face to pale. "This orphanage, Maude. What was it called?"

"Saint something. A Catholic name. I chose it because no one would think to trace it to me."

Smith's voice grew low and urgent. "Maude. Think carefully. Did you leave a note? Perhaps identifying the baby by some name?"

"Yes. I gave him a made-up name. I guess I thought I might recognize him later by that name."

"And this name?"

"Williams. Remo Williams."

Harold W. Smith stared at his wife as if at a ghost. There was a sudden roaring in his ears.

"You named your son Remo Williams?" he croaked.

"I picked the name off a map of Italy. San Remo. It had such a nice sound. Williams was the name of the college my sister went to."

Harold Smith wore his face loose with shock. He had to swallow twice before he could speak again. Even then, his voice shook and quavered.

"Maude. We cannot speak of this here. Go to your sister's and wait for me. I promise that together you and I will find this boy and determine his paternity. I promise."

"Oh, Harold, you're so good to me. So understanding."

And Maude Smith pressed her pale lips to the glass of the window, leaving a colorless imprint there.

Then she was gone. Harold Smith stared at the faint imprint by the wan light of the corridor for a long time before he returned to his bunk.

He did not sleep the remainder of the night. His mind was working furiously.

And in his tired gray eyes was a new light and a new resolve.

DR. MURRAY SIMON was making his rounds.

He pushed the cart that contained the various generic prescription drugs for the remaining inhabitants of Folcroft's psychiatric wing ahead of him. Normally a nurse dispensed medications. But the nursing staff had been cut to the bone, and the remaining nurses were attending to patients' needs in the convalescent ward.

And normally the rounds Dr. Simon made were Dr. Gerling's responsibility. But Dr. Gerling was in the convalescent ward himself, where he had been taken after he had somehow been overpowered by one of the patients he was discharging from the psychiatric wing.

Dr. Gerling had not yet given a coherent story. And in the hectic aftermath of the IRS seizure, his situation did not warrant great concern. He would recover. Folcroft, on the other hand, might not. A great many patients had gotten loose from their rooms and had been rounded up and returned with difficulty. There were whispers of IRS agents having been taken to the hospital morgue. No one knew what had happened to them, and no one dared to inquire. After all, this was the IRS. They knew how to punish people with long noses.

So while IRS agents ran hither and yon, to God alone knew what purpose, Dr. Murray Simon took responsibility for dispensing psychiatric patients their medication.

It was fairly routine. Dr. Gerling had left very clear instructions. The routine brought Dr. Simon to the door marked Beasley.

He looked in. The patient sat at his writing desk, his scarlet pirate costume askew.

"Time for your daily dose, my good friend," Dr. Simon called as he unlocked the door.

The patient turned his head. His grin was cracked. His single exposed eye rolled up in his head.

Simon shivered. It was uncanny how much a resemblance to Uncle Sam Beasley the man bore. Of course, had Uncle Sam lived, he would be much much older than this poor wretch. In fact, the joke on the floor went, Uncle Sam was so old if he had lived he'd still be dead.

"Time for your meds," he said cheerily, handing over a single bright pink pill and a paper cup filled with water.

The patient accepted them. He frowned at the pill when he looked it over. "This is the wrong color. It should be purple."

"Nonsense. It's your usual. Now take it."

The patient obliged. He popped the pink pill into his mouth, chasing it down with water.

"Open, please."

The patient opened his mouth. When the questing tongue depressor showed that the pink pill hadn't been hidden under the tongue or secreted between teeth and cheek, Dr. Simon nodded and continued his rounds.

He was very surprised to find a familiar lemony face staring out of a padded cell a few doors down.

"Dr. *Smith?*"

"Bring Brull here," Smith said hoarsely. "Tell him I have something important to say to him."

"But what . . . Why?"

"Get Dick Brull!" Harold Smith thundered.

BRULL WASTED NO TIME getting to Dr. Smith's cell.

"Had enough, Smith?" he gloated, eyes straining to see over the lower edge of the door window.

"I am prepared to tell you what you want to know."

"Shoot."

"You are correct. Folcroft Sanitarium is a secret U.S. installation."

"Of course I'm correct." Brull's eyes narrowed. "But how correct am I?"

"This is not a CIA site."

"No?"

"When I came to Folcroft, it was a sociological research center. That much is true. Over the years it became a hospital for special long-term-care cases. But that is only a cover."

"Come on. Out with it. A cover for what?"

"The Federal Emergency Management Agency."

"FEMA?"

"FEMA," said Smith.

"FEMA," repeated Big Dick Brull in an uncertain voice. "What kind of FEMA operation?"

"You are aware of the mission of FEMA—the *true* mission?"

"Yeah, emergency preparedness in the event of nuclear war. IRS has a doomsday program just like it. If we ever got nuked, the service has emergency powers to levy a flat tax on everybody."

"The Federal Emergency Management Agency was set up to handle domestic disasters such as hurricanes, floods, earthquakes and other natural calamities. Ostensibly."

"And done a damn poor job of it until recently."

"Until the Cold War ended, you mean. Since then, the actual mission of FEMA has leaked out. The agency was set up to keep the U.S. government operating in a postnuclear environment. Among the assets are mobile communications vans designed to keep the fractured power centers in touch with one another. These centers are hardened safe sites scattered throughout the nation. The broad plan was very simple. Should there be a nuclear attack, the President, First Family and certain key members of the legislative and judicial branches will be whisked to these hardened sites. From these places, a skeleton government will operate until the emergency has passed."

Brull swallowed.

Smith went on. "I told you that I represented an agency more powerful than IRS. This is it. Folcroft is a FEMA site."

"What kind? I mean, we're a heck of a long way from Washington."

"If that information were to come into your possession," Smith said coldly, "I would be sanctioned to terminate your life on the spot."

"You can't do that," Brull barked. "I'm essential IRS personnel."

"And I am FEMA."

"This is crap. It's just words. I don't buy any of it. Not without hard, concrete proof."

"Proof could be dangerous to your health," Smith said grimly.

"Don't screw with me, Smith. We can't take people's words for things in the service. I gotta have solid, verifiable proof before I close the books on this seizure."

"Does that mean you are prepared to relinquish IRS control over Folcroft once its bona fides are established?"

Brull hesitated. "Maybe."

"You know that as powerful as you are, as important as IRS is, FEMA is essential to national security in the event of a catastrophe."

"Says fucking you," Brull snarled.

"Bear in mind that in order for IRS to continue operating in a postnuclear scenario, it must have a secret site. A FEMA site."

"Why didn't you tell me all this before?"

"I am sworn to keep these secrets. You have forced my hand through your gross incompetence. I only hope we can resolve this matter without having to resort to extreme measures to ensure your silence."

"Okay, okay, I'll play this out. But where's my proof?"

"Walk four doors down on the right and look through the glass port."

"All right."

A moment later Big Dick Brull was back, his face three shades paler than before.

"There's a guy in there dressed like a fucking pirate."

"Did he look familiar to you?"

"Yeah. He looked a lot like old Uncle Sam Beasley."

"The Uncle Sam Beasley who died nearly thirty years ago?" asked Smith.

"Yeah. Of course."

"The Uncle Sam Beasley who has been long rumored to be suspended in a state of cryogenic preservation until the day his heart disease can be cured by medical science?"

"That's a load of manure!" Brull exploded.

"Is it?"

"You're not saying..."

"In the postnuclear world, there will be a need for entertainment to keep a frightened populace pacified. What better choice than the most beloved animator and filmmaker of all time?"

Eyes enlarging, Brull croaked, "That's the *real* Beasley?"

"There are others here who are equally important," added Smith.

"Like whom?"

"The butterfly everyone has seen."

"What is he?"

"That is so highly classified I dare not entrust that information to you."

"This is crazy!" Brull blurted. "You can't expect me to swallow this cock-and-bullshit!"

"The computers in the basement are part of our postdisaster mission," Smith went on relentlessly. "The purpose of the gold is obvious. Cash will be worthless after the fall of our economy. As for the funds that through a clerical error came into the Folcroft bank account, it represents our budget for the coming fiscal year."

"You gotta explain that money to IRS! We can't just wish it away."

"The twelve million dollars came from the Grand Cayman Trust in the Cayman Islands."

"I *knew* it stank of offshore money!"

"But it originated at FEMA. A discreet inquiry will confirm that FEMA wired twelve million dollars to Grand Cayman Trust more than a week ago. There is no electronic or paper trail to the Folcroft bank for security reasons I cannot get into. But the bank officer there will verify the money appeared in their computer ledgers overnight, after hours and without explanation. It will leave the bank that way, once the way is cleared, going to its proper destination."

"I gotta check this out."

"Lippincott Savings Bank will confirm the movement of funds," said Smith. "Grand Cayman Trust will not, of course, without serving papers and a protracted legal struggle. You do not have the luxury of time. Whether or not you wish to trace the funds back to FEMA and embroil yourself in a high-security exposure, remains up to you. But let me urge you in the strongest terms possible to have your highest superior make the call."

Big Dick Brull licked his lips. "It's that sensitive, huh?"

"The true nature of Folcroft Sanitarium is of such cosmic importance to America's continued survival that in the past people have been killed to protect it."

Brull pushed the knot of his tie from side to side. "All right," he said. "I'll look into it. But no promises. Except this one—if anything you say doesn't pan out, you are in very big tax trouble. And that's the worst kind of trouble there is."

"And if it does, it may be you who are in trouble."

"We'll see about that," Brull said.

When he stormed off, the sound of his heels on the flooring was not very confident.

Harold Smith allowed himself a tight smile. It sat on his face like a lemon slice.

Perhaps the long-dead President who had chosen him to head CURE had been mistaken. When inspired, Harold W. Smith did possess something like an imagination.

BIG DICK BRULL WAS sweating bullets as he bowled down the corridor of Folcroft's psychiatric wing.

FEMA. Christ in a sarong! He never dreamed this was a FEMA operation. It was beyond the worst-case scenario. You could theoretically audit the President, or any member of Congress, and create less of a stink. He had unwittingly gotten the service tangled up in an interagency squabble that would make the fuss with the DEA look like a battle between the DAR and the PTA.

So Folcroft was a FEMA hardsite. God knows what really went on here. From the sound of it, they were going to be on the front lines in the reconstruction phase of the postnuke era. For all Dick Brull knew, Folcroft would be the headquarters for IRS itself after the fallout settled.

First he would have to take care of his own personal fallout.

On the way down to the elevator, Brull paused to take another look at the cell where Uncle Sam Beasley was warehoused. For the first time he noticed the door was actually marked Beasley.

Uncle Sam was slumped in his seat, staring at the cartoon-covered walls. His one good eye looked sleepy. As Brull watched, Beasley started. He had caught himself nodding off. Beasley shook his head as if to clear the cobwebs out of it. One hand lifted to his forehead and revealed a smooth, scarred stump.

"Damn," Big Dick Brull muttered to himself. "Sure hope that isn't his drawing hand."

Brull paused at the next cell door. The plate under the window read Purcell.

This was one of the padded rubber rooms. It was bare except for a low cot and the television set high in the wall where it couldn't be pulled down. The set was off.

On the cot lay what looked at first glance to be an anorexic woman. She was staring at the ceiling, her long corn-silk hair spilling over the pillow. Her arms were wrapped around her thin torso by the bound sleeves of a canvas straitjacket.

The figure lay so completely still and unmoving that Brull wondered if she were dead.

That was when he noticed she was a he. No breasts. No soft lines. And it looked like no brain, either.

Brull continued on, wearing the look of a man who had been handed a hot potato and no one to pass it on to.

31

The Master of Sinanju insisted on being let off by the main entrance to Folcroft Sanitarium.

"You're crazy," said Remo, pulling over to the side of the lone access road. "The IRS will land on us like a ton of bricks."

"And we will land back."

"They'll seize the car. They already tried it once."

"It is time you got a new car," Chiun sniffed.

"New? I trade this in every six months. You know that."

"I meant a vehicle of quality and worth. Not an American garbage can on wheels."

"Take it up with me if we're still employed at the end of all this."

"Next time buy Korean."

"I wouldn't drive a Korean car off a cliff," said Remo, opening the door. "Now, are you getting out or not?"

"Why must I walk?"

"Because you can't fly, and neither can I. Let's go. Not that I'm looking forward to telling Smith we came up empty trying to find his wife."

Chiun emerged from the passenger side. They began walking. "You will explain that to him, not I."

"You gonna back me up?"

"Yes. I will confirm your failure if that is your wish."

"You didn't find her, either."

"That is not my fault."

"Then it's not mine, either."

"That will be for Emperor Smith to judge. But you will explain all this to him because technically you are not employed by him. You can afford to incur his displeasure. As the sole support of the House of Sinanju, I cannot."

They came to the gate. Remo got up against one of the brick gateposts and peered around it cautiously.

"The coast looks clear," he said.

"What about Fortress Folcroft?" Chiun asked.

"That's what I meant."

"And I meant the cretins who sit in boats with their guns."

"The DEA? I took care of them."

They entered through the gateposts.

Remo's eyes went skyward. He noticed that the trio of circling birds were flying lower, their great wings rising and dipping in languorous waves. It seemed impossible that the air could support them. Their wings were barely moving.

"Looks like they're back," Remo muttered.

Chiun frowned. "They seem familiar to my eyes."

"I was just thinking the same thing."

"They are not sea gulls."

"Sure aren't vultures, either."

"They resemble vultures."

"Maybe they're condors."

"Perhaps they are not birds at all," said Chiun, frowning quizzically.

"They gotta be birds. What could they be except birds?"

"I do not know, but they are an ill omen."

"No argument there," said Remo. "Come on. Let's go in the assassin's entrance."

They reached the freight entrance unseen, and the moment they entered the basement the Master of Sinanju repeated a question that had seldom left his papery lips all night long.

"Where is my gold?"

"Safe as soap."

"That is no answer."

"If it were my gold, I'd say it was the best answer there is."

"Pah!"

They floated up the steps to the first floor and took a chance on the elevator. It was resting on the first floor, and their sharp hearing told them it was unoccupied.

The doors rolled open at the touch of the call button.

They rode it to the third floor, and Remo stuck his head out, looking both ways before he signaled for Chiun to follow.

The psychiatric wing was quiet. No doctors seemed to be on the floor.

As they passed Jeremiah Purcell's cell, Remo's face hardened.

"He remains a prisoner?" Chiun asked, noting Remo's stare.

Remo nodded. "I wish he were dead."

"Beware the wish that comes true."

"I don't believe that crap about our destinies being entwined."

Chiun sniffed derisively and said nothing.

Uncle Sam Beasley was still visible through his cell-door window when they passed him.

"I'm sure glad he's on ice again," said Remo.

Chiun nodded sagely. "Agreed."

"I'd wring Purcell's neck with pleasure, but I couldn't bring myself to take out Uncle Sam himself."

When they reached Harold Smith's cell, Remo knocked twice.

Smith had been lying on his cot, staring at the ceiling in a posture that was almost identical to Jeremiah Purcell's. At the sound of Remo's knock, he started and rolled off his cot, fumbling for his glasses.

"Remo!" said Smith when he came to the window.

"Bad news, Smitty."

"Remo," Smith repeated, his voice low and wondering. His eyes searched Remo's face.

"By the time we got to your house, the IRS had seized it," Remo explained. "It's locked up tight as a drum. None of the neighbors knew where your wife went."

"She was here," Smith said softly.

"Here?"

"Last night she came to me. I sent her to her sister's."

"That's a relief."

Smith's voice became low and forceful. "Remo, she told me something incredible."

"Yeah?"

"Why do you regard Remo so strangely, Emperor?" Chiun asked.

Smith's voice dropped to a hiss. "Remo, I know who your father is."

"Since when!" Remo exploded.

"Since last night."

Remo and Chiun looked at each other.

"Look, Smitty," Remo said. "This has been a strain on all of us. Why don't you just take a long nap and we'll come back?"

"No! Remo, I want you to open the door."

"What about your alibi?"

"I may not need one. Now, open the door. Please."

Harold Smith's eyes and voice were so beseeching that Remo felt he had no choice. He undid the latch.

When Smith stepped out, he threw out his long arms and gave Remo a stiff, awkward hug. He buried his gray head in Remo's hard shoulder.

Remo looked over Smith's trembling shoulder to the quizzical features of the Master of Sinanju. Chiun shrugged. Remo gave Smith a vaguely distasteful pat on the back.

"It's all right, Smitty," Remo said gently. "We're glad to see you, too. You can let go now. Okay?"

Smith stepped back, cleared his throat and looked Remo Williams dead in the eye. "When the woman you saw in the cemetery told you that you knew your father, she was exactly right. I have no idea who she really was or how she knew this, but she was correct."

"Yeah..."

"Your father *is* someone you have known for a very long time."

Remo blinked. His lean forearms trembled briefly. He willed them to be still.

"Someone very near to you for most of your adult life."

Remo's eyes flew wide. He turned.

"Little Father!" he said wonderingly. "You?"

"Never!" snapped Chiun. "I would sooner sire a monkey than one such as you."

"You don't mean that. You can't."

"You are not my son, Remo Williams," Chiun flared.

"He's right," said Smith. "Chiun is not related to you."

Chiun lifted his wispy chin defiantly. "I would not go that far. There may be some Korean blood in him. Possibly three drops. Small ones."

Remo's brow was furrowed up. "If it's not Chiun, that only leaves..."

Harold Smith adjusted his tie primly. Clearing his throat, he said, "Yes. That only leaves me, Remo. I am your father."

"Not a chance!" Remo said hotly. "I'd sooner have Richard Nixon for a dad."

"Remo. My wife explained it all to me."

Remo frowned sharply. "How would she know?"

"She's your mother."

"*My* mother? No way! I saw my mother in the cemetery the other day. She was young and beautiful—just like I always imagined her."

"I do not know who that woman was, but Maude explained everything. It happened while I was in the Philippines many years ago. She had a baby. That baby was you, Remo."

"No freaking way!" Remo shouted.

"Remo, will you calm down? You will call attention to us all. Maude explained everything to me. She placed you on the doorstep of Saint Theresa's Orphanage, along with a note naming you Remo Williams."

"Bull!"

"Stop it! Stop this instant! Maude knows nothing of you or your history. How could she relate the precise details of your foundling days if she was not speaking from experience?"

Remo took an uncertain step backward. His face went pale.

"But the woman in the cemetery looked like Freya," Remo said dully. "She said if I found her resting place, I would find my father. How do you explain that?"

"It is a fantasy, Remo. All your life you have wondered about your parents. You created fantasies about them. What you saw that night was just the manifestation of one such fantasy. This is reality. I am your father and Maude is your mother."

"If that's so," Remo said hotly, "why did she dump me on the doorstep?"

"Er, this is awkward," Smith began.

Remo grabbed Smith by his coat lapels and pressed him against the wall. "Talk, Smitty."

"Mrs. Smith had an affair during my absence. She thought the baby—you—had been fathered by this other man."

"What other man?"

"I do not know. She did not identify him."

Remo let go. "This is crazy!"

Smith straightened his coat front stiffly. "She could not face me with a baby of uncertain parentage," he said, "so she abandoned him. I only wish I knew then what I know now."

"I wish I didn't know any of this," Remo said, throwing up his hands. "It's crazy."

"Remo, I know this is hard...."

"This is stupid. I've met your wife. She's dumpy as an old sofa, a frump."

"Remo!" Chiun admonished. "Do not speak of the emperor's consort so!"

"No way that's my mother!"

"There is no escaping the truth, Remo," Smith said testily. "I wish you would take the blinders off your eyes."

"And you're not my father."

"There is the possibility of that. Mrs. Smith has grown convinced over the years that I am the father to the baby, but there is no proof. This other person remains a possibility."

"Him, I'll accept. You, never."

"But Mrs. Smith remains your mother."

"That will take a blood test, chromosome test and the word of God Almighty to convince me," Remo snapped. "And maybe not even then."

"We will have to deal with this later," Smith said quickly. "I believe I have set in motion events that will eject the Internal Revenue Service from the Folcroft picture."

"What'd you do, call for an exorcist?"

"No. I wove a web of truth and prevarication for Dick Brull's benefit. If it works, we should see results very soon."

"I'll believe that when I see it, too. The IRS are worse than leeches."

"Remo," Smith said, "there is something else you should know—"

A drumming came from the stairwell.

Doom doom doom doom...

Turning, Remo said, "I don't know what's making that racket, but I want a piece if it."

And he was off down the green corridor like an angry arrow.

32

Big Dick Brull had just assembled his agents in Dr. Smith's office when the muffled drumbeat returned to haunt him.

"There are still some patients running around loose," he was saying. "Get out the nets and get them back into their rooms. Other than that, until I get to the bottom of this, don't touch anything, don't seize anything and most of all don't *do* anything."

Doom doom doom doom . . .

"There's that sound again," Agent Phelps said unhappily.

"Damn! Everybody out into the corridors. Before I surrender this seizure, I gotta know what's making that racket."

Big Dick Brull followed his agents from the office.

"It's coming from the stairwell," an agent cried, pointing to the nearest fire door.

"Let's go get it!" Brull snapped. "Surround it! Don't let it get away, or it's your asses!"

A rushing knot, the agents raced to the fire door.

Two hands reached for the latch bar. The door exploded off its hinges in their faces.

Big Dick Brull stumbled back in the face of the reverse stampede of IRS agents.

The drumbeat was suddenly all around them.

Doom doom doom doom doom doom doom . . .

That was when they got a clear look at the author of the incessant sound.

A HUMAN BULLET, Remo Williams catapulted down the corridor, every sense focused on the elusive sound of a beating drum. He whipped around the corner like a slingshot, saw nothing and let his Sinanju-trained senses carry him after the sound.

His senses took him to the stairwell fire door. Remo spanked it out of his way. It blasted off its hinges and went cartwheeling down the concrete stairs.

Remo went over the tubular rail, alighting on the next landing a split second ahead of the tumbling steel door. Whirling, he batted it away. It went over the rail to crash far below.

The drumming continued down the stairs. Remo jumped again. The second-floor landing absorbed the shock to his powerful leg muscles.

Out of the corner of one eye, Remo caught a glimpse of something pink. It was low to the floor and moving toward the green wall. But when he whirled, there was nothing. Just wall.

Chiun's squeaky voice called down. "Remo! What have you found?"

"I don't know," Remo called back, "but it's on the other side of this wall, whatever it is." He hit the fire door.

The door came off its hinges as if hit by a high-pressure fire hose. It struck something meaty and flopped flat.

Remo jumped over the squirming plate of steel from which arms and legs waved helplessly. His heels went click on the floor when he stepped off.

IRS agents were still recoiling from the flying door, their senses not quite taking him in, when Remo spotted the pink creature.

It was barely a foot tall and stood on its hind legs looking up at him, a tiny drumstick in each paw. In alternating rhythm, it was beating the toy drum strapped over his potbellied stomach. It looked up at Remo with a confident, almost bemused expression on its whiskered face. One floppy velour ear dropped doubtfully.

Then it spun in place and started back toward the stairwell.

Big Dick Brull shouted, "What the fuck was that thing?"

"It's the Polarizer Bunny, what does it look like?" Remo snapped, jumping after it.

"That's what I fucking thought it was," Brull said in a disbelieving voice.

Remo chased the plush pink cartoon bunny back up the stairs. The bunny had short little legs, but it wasn't using them. Yet it took the steps as if it was on wheels and the staircase was a flat ramp.

Coming down the steps, the Master of Sinanju saw it scooting back up. His hazel eyes exploded in astonishment.

"Remo! Do you see this thing?"

"I not only see it, I plan to wring its little pink neck. I *hated* those commercials!"

"I will catch it," said Chiun, squatting down to gather up the speeding apparition in his long-nailed hands.

Beating its drum, the bunny twirled, reversing itself.

"I got it," said Remo.

"Do not hurt it, Remo!" Chiun squeaked.

"No promises," said Remo, lunging low. His hands came together like a vise. But when they clapped together, there was no bunny.

"Where did it go?" he blurted, looking around.

"It is between your legs, blind one," Chiun squeaked.

Remo looked down. He brought his heels together with a hard final click.

The bunny was not where Remo's heels met.

Remo blinked. He was fast enough to pace a car, snatch an arrow in midair or dodge a bullet. No way was a battery-powered windup bunny rabbit faster than him.

"I will catch it," Chiun repeated. "Come to me, O annoying rodent. I will not harm you."

There was no chance of that. The bunny scooted between the Master of Sinanju's sandals like a ray of pink-colored light, all the time pounding on its toy drum.

Doom doom doom doom . . .

Chiun gave out a shriek of pure frustration.

"What'd I tell you?" said Remo as they raced up the steps after it.

It led them out into the psychiatric wing once more, past the cell rooms and Harold Smith's gray-and-shading-to-bone-white face, to the ladder leading to the roof hatch.

The bunny was not equipped to climb a full-size ladder. Not with its legs permanently bent and its hands full of drumstick.

But as Remo and Chiun closed in on the ladder, it shot upward as if jerked by an invisible string.

The pink bunny melted through the closed hatch as if the hatch were a screen permeable to tiny hot-pink bunnies.

Remo went up the ladder and knocked the hatch aside. Chiun floated up after him, his face furious.

The plush pink bunny twirled in the middle of the roof, as if seeking shelter.

"We've got it now," growled Remo.

"No. The honor of defeating the hitherto-invincible Polarizer Bunny is mine!"

And the Master of Sinanju executed a flying leap that carried him to the pink apparition. One black sandal struck the exact spot where it stood on the roof asphalt with a thud.

"Hah!" cried Chiun, lifting his foot. He looked down. There was a crater in the asphalt, but no pink splotch. His face fell.

"Try behind you," Remo said dryly.

Doom doom doom doom ...

Skirts swirling, Chiun whirled. His cheeks puffing out in frustration, he extended his long killing finger-nails like a pouncing tiger and flew at it.

The bunny spun, feinted, doubled back and almost succeeded in tricking the Master of Sinanju into leap-ing off the roof in pursuit.

By that time Remo was moving in on the elusive creature, too. The bunny skated between their legs, circled around them, all the time beating its drum unhurriedly.

"Go for the battery!" Remo shouted. "Maybe that'll stop it."

Chiun slashed, failed to connect and began stamping every place the energetic rabbit seemed to be. But the bunny was too tricky. Each time Chiun stamped empty air. But inexorably he maneuvered the thing in Remo's direction.

Blocking its path, Remo tried for the battery. His hands swiped empty air futilely.

"Is that the best you can do, sluggish one?" Chiun snapped.

"I can't help it. It just keeps going and going, just like on TV."

The bunny stopped, its plush head going from side to side, as if taunting them with their impotence.

"I got an idea," Remo said, fists clenching.

"Remo, look!"

The Master of Sinanju was pointing skyward. Remo looked up. And forgot all about the impossible pink bunny.

So low over their heads that they could see the menace in their eyes, circled the three shadowy birds of prey. Only now they were no longer shadowy and indistinct, but very near overhead.

They were purple and bony. Their hatchet faces twisted as they peered down at Remo and Chiun, leathery wings flapping, soundless and unreal.

"Terror birds!" squeaked Chiun.

"Pterodactyls, you mean," said Remo, face hardening to bone.

One purple pterodactyl broke off and, beak yawning, made a snatch at Remo. Remo backpedaled easily. Then he caught himself.

"What am I doing? It's not real."

"Do not take a chance, Remo," warned Chiun.

"You know what this is," Remo said to Chiun, circling the roof. "It's no more real than that stupid windup rabbit."

The Master of Sinanju stood rooted as a second purple pterodactyl fixed its beady eyes upon him. Wings folding, it broke off its lazy spiral and went for Chiun's upraised arm.

Chiun wove a web before his face with his fingernails. The pterodactyl's face should have been clawed to ribbons. Instead, it twisted, wings straining to their utmost, vaulting back to rejoin the circle, face unscathed.

"See?" said Remo. "It's not real. None of them are real." He strode over to the pink bunny. "Not even this little guy."

The bunny was zipping around in broken circles, beating its drum in agitation, the name-brand battery on its back clearly visible.

"Forget it, Purcell," Remo shouted through cupped hands. "We know it's you. You don't fool us."

The pink plush bunny continued its crazy weaving pattern, while the purple pterodactyls swarmed so close their claw-tipped wings dipped within reach.

Remo gave one an angry swipe. Remo's hand seemed to disappear into the thing's skin. The batlike creature flew on, unfazed.

The Polarizer Bunny suddenly halted and started spinning in place. It became a whirling top, then a cone that grew, changing color as it expanded. Pink became purple in which other colors made streaks of flesh, yellow blond and neon blue.

When it stopped spinning, the purple-robed figure of the Dutchman, Jeremiah Purcell, stood tall and proud. He gave a toss of his long corn-silk tresses and fixed Remo with his electric blue eyes.

He dropped into an attack crouch. His lips split into a taunting smile.

Remo executed a perfect Sinanju Heron Drop, snapping into the air from a standing start. It took him to a point over the Dutchman's head, both legs coiled under him to deliver a double death blow.

Chiun's shriek of warning came too late.

Legs uncoiling, Remo dropped straight down.

And landed on flat asphalt.

Remo snap-rolled to his feet, turning toward the sound of a beating drum.

Doom doom doom doom . . .

As he completed his turn, the drum was suddenly behind him. Every time he twisted, Remo just missed his tormentor.

"Face me, Purcell!"

Chiun's voice called. "He is gone, Remo."

"What?"

"There is no one there. Only sounds."

Remo came out of his fighting crouch. His hands relaxed slowly.

The drumbeat faded into nothingness.

The Master of Sinanju padded up to his pupil. "You could have killed yourself with your uncontrolled anger."

Remo frowned. "Come on, Little Father. Let's get to the bottom of this."

Remo turned toward the roof hatch. Poking up was the incredulous face of Big Dick Brull.

"What are *you* looking at!" Remo barked.

"Nothing," Brull gulped, his head dropping from sight like a gopher retreating into its burrow.

WHEN THEY GOT OFF the ladder, Big Dick Brull and his IRS agents were standing about looking pale and foolish.

"This place is a madhouse," Brull said weakly.

"It *is* a sanitarium," said Remo.

Harold Smith said, "I could see everything from here. Pterodactyls, were they not?"

"*Purple* pterodactyls," corrected Remo. "You know what that means."

"I do," said Smith.

"But I don't," barked Big Dick Brull.

"Remo, remove these men while we get to the bottom of this."

"With pleasure," said Remo, abruptly turning. He took Big Dick Brull by the collar and lifted him completely off his feet. Remo set him on the ladder and said, "Either climb up or I'll fling you up there like a bag of manure."

"But—there are pterodactyls up there."

"And there are angry taxpayers down here. Take your pick."

Brull started climbing.

The other agents needed more motivation, so the Master of Sinanju padded up to them and began pinching earlobes between incredibly sharp fingernails.

The unbearable pain sent the IRS agents scrambling up the ladder. The hatch clapped shut.

"Come on," growled Remo.

They went to Purcell's cell.

Remo was saying, "We know Purcell's favorite trick was to create illusions to frighten people. Purple pterodactyls were his favorite. Don't ask me why."

They looked through the window.

Jeremiah Purcell lay on his back staring at the ceiling, unmoving.

"Time to shake him loose," said Remo, lifting the latch bar.

Chium warned. "Do not harm him, Remo. Remember the legends."

"Screw the legends," said Remo, kicking the door in.

Jeremiah Purcell didn't flex a muscle as Remo moved in on him. His fixed stare never left the high ceiling.

Not even when Remo reached down with both hands to grab the front of his straitjacket.

Remo's fingertips brushed the jacket front and kept going.

"What the hell!"

Chiun leaped to his side. "Remo, what is wrong with your hands?"

"Nothing."

But they had disappeared into the Dutchman's recumbent form as if into a pool of milk.

"An illusion," Remo said after fishing his hands around in the opaque human form. "He's not really here."

"The Dutchman has escaped!" shrieked Chiun. "It is a calamity."

Remo pulled his hands out, saying, "He couldn't have gone far. Not if he's making those images appear. He's somewhere near. We just gotta find him."

They checked every room. The ones that weren't empty held only ordinary patients. Except the cell containing Uncle Sam Beasley. He sat at his drawing desk, pretending to ignore them, but with his head cocked at a tilt that said he was listening to every word.

Remo, Chiun and Smith stood outside that cell, talking.

"Maybe Beasley saw something," Remo suggested.

"That is not Beasley," said Chiun very suddenly.

Remo and Smith looked at him.

"What do you mean?" asked Smith.

"Listen to his heartbeat."

Smith grew puzzled. Remo shut his eyes, listening.

"Normal heartbeat," said Remo. "So what?"

"That is impossible," snapped Smith. "Uncle Sam Beasley was outfitted with an animatronic heart after he was brought out of suspended animation."

"Then that's not Uncle Sam," said Remo.

"If not, then who is it?" asked Smith.

The glass in the cell door suddenly wavered as if it were a TV screen or a porthole shimmering in water.

When it cleared, Uncle Sam Beasley was gone. In his place stood Jeremiah Purcell—the Dutchman. He regarded the three startled faces with his neon blue eyes and began giggling.

"Let me at him," said Remo, lunging for the door.

"No," cried Chiun, blocking the way with his tiny body. "Do not let him taunt you into killing him and thus yourself."

"I remember what he did to me," Remo snarled, face twisting with emotion. "To Mah-Li. It was my wedding day and he took her place, the rat bastard. I stood beside my bride-to-be, not knowing that she was already dead and he had taken her place, using his mind tricks."

"That is the past, Remo," Chiun said, trying to catch his pupil's gaze and hold it.

"Shove it," said Remo. "Look at him. He wants me to come in."

"Yes! In the dimness of his mind he understands that if you strike him dead, you too will fall and he will have his revenge in death. Yours and his."

The Dutchman stood looking at Remo through the window, wild-eyed and expectant. He tittered.

Smith spoke up. "Remo, as your father, I order you—"

"Stuff it," Remo said sharply.

"If you will not obey your true father, stubborn one," Chiun said, "obey your adopted one."

Remo just looked at Chiun and Smith, as if doubting their sanity and his own. The tension began going out of his face.

"We can't leave him here," Remo protested. "He could break out at any moment."

Smith shook his gray head seriously. "If he had that ability, Remo, he would have done it."

"But he did. We hauled him back, thinking he was Beasley."

"Did he resist?"

"Well, no," Remo admitted.

"His mind may be coming out of his autistic phase, but apparently not enough for his Sinanju skills to return."

"Only a matter of time," warned Remo, not taking his eyes off the Dutchman's wan, taunting face.

"All in due time."

"What say we check?" Remo said tightly.

"Master Chiun will examine Purcell."

Reluctantly Remo stepped aside.

The Master of Sinanju strode into the cell. The Dutchman retreated. Chiun stalked him about the room until Jeremiah Purcell found himself trapped in a corner covered by drawings.

A quirk of fear came into the Dutchman's pale face. He trembled from head to toe, setting his long corn-silk hair shimmying.

Without warning, Chiun spun Purcell in place, exposing the brass hasps that pinioned his sleeve-wrapped arms to his back. A slashing fingernail broke them in a vertical line. The canvas sleeves dropped loosely at his sides.

"Strike me," Chiun dared.

The Dutchman only giggled.

Chiun began weaving lines and circles before Purcell's pallid face. Each feint brought a flinch, but no return blow.

Chiun paused, frowing. When his fingers licked up to squeeze a nerve on the Dutchman's shoulder, there was no resistance, no blocking blow. The Dutchman wilted, unconscious.

"No mind that retains the sun source," Chiun intoned, "would allow the body it controls to be touched in anger."

His arms disappearing into his kimono sleeves, the Master of Sinanju emerged from the cell. "He is harmless, except for his crazed mind," Chiun added solemnly. "Let us go."

They walked away, Remo reluctantly, after Harold Smith barred the door.

Remo snapped his fingers. "Wait a minute. If that's Purcell, where's Beasley?"

"Escaped," said Smith, his voice flat.

"Damn! That must have been Beasley in the car that tried to run us over."

"We will undertake the search for Beasley later," said Smith grimly. "I must deal with the IRS first."

"Want me to fetch them?"

"Just Brull. The others can cool their heels on the roof."

"Maybe it'll rain," said Remo. "And the IRS will get soaked for a change."

33

They were in Harold Smith's office. Smith threw himself into his high-backed chair behind the desk with the black glass top.

"I have explained that this is a FEMA site," Smith was saying. Big Dick Brull stood nervously between Remo and Chiun. He was staring at Chiun, who still wore the black kimono with the orange markings that made him resemble a monarch butterfly.

"You're the butterfly," Brull blurted out.

"And you are the taxidermist."

"I'm no taxidermist."

"You got that right," said Remo. "A taxidermist leaves the skin."

Brull swallowed hard.

Smith was working the telephone.

"This is Smith. My password is Site Forty. I require independent confirmation of wire transfer number 334 to the Grand Cayman Trust emergency account."

"One moment," a crisp voice said loud enough for everyone to hear. Smith had engaged the speakerphone function.

A moment later the crisp voice said, "Confirming wire transfer number 334 to Grand Cayman Trust.

Date is September 2, this calendar year. Amount is twelve million and no change."

"Confirm transfer fully authorized by FEMA," said Smith.

"Fully."

"That will be all. Thank you," said Smith.

He looked up, regarding Big Dick Brull coldly.

"Those are just voices," Brull said defensively.

"You now have the FEMA wire-transfer locator number to take to your superiors. If you dare."

Brull swallowed hard.

"Of course, since it was the unreported twelve million that showed up in the Folcroft bank account that precipitated the seizure of Folcroft Sanitarium, it might be more expedient to pay the director of the Lippincott Savings Bank a call. I am certain he will confirm that the money was transferred in error and does not belong in the account. They will wipe it from their computers once this has been established to the satisfaction of everyone. And if you are smart, you too will wipe it off the IRS records."

"I can't promise that."

"You have already seen too much."

Brull tossed his head in either direction, saying, "I see these two doing impossible things. I see lavender pterodactyls and pink cartoon rabbits that don't—can't—exist in real life."

"You sound like you need a long vacation, pal," suggested Remo. "You're imagining things."

"Don't give me that! You saw them, too!"

Remo shook his head in a slow negative.

"I see only a liar," Chiun said coolly.

Big Dick Brull seemed to shrink into his shoes. His shoulders sagged. "I make no promises," he said grudgingly.

"And I make no guarantees," replied Smith. "Remo."

Remo Williams reached up and gave Dick Brull's neck a squeeze that brought a flush to his face and made him feel as if his eyeballs were about to pop from their sockets.

"You have breached one of the most secure installations in America," said Smith, his voice stretched drum-tight. "You have behaved as if you are above the law, with the result of many unnecessary deaths." His glasses began to steam again. "And you have violated my home and my wife. Only your high position with the Internal Revenue Service and your uselfulness to us in resolving this outrage without further publicity is keeping you alive."

Brull lost all facial color.

"And don't forget," added Remo, "we know where you work."

"You can't threaten a Treasury agent like this."

"You haven't been paying attention," said Remo, lifting Brull off his feet and sweeping him around like dangle-footed puppet. "We already have."

At that, Harold Smith came out from behind his desk. His face might have been a skull scraped raw. His eyes were hard. He held one fist at his side, a trembling mallet of bone.

Stepping up to Brull, Smith let fly with a round-house punch.

Brull saw it coming, but his arms refused to lift in his own defense. He took Harold Smith's bony knuckles on the point of his jaw, his head snapping half around.

"Show him out," Smith clipped.

"My pleasure," said Remo.

Ears ringing, Dick Brull was sent skimming along the corridor on the seat of his pants, out of the office and toward a particularly unforgiving-looking wall. Unable to stop, he closed his eyes as the wall came rushing into his face.

Somehow he made a sudden impossible right-angle turn and found himself in the elevator, stopped short by the hard impact of his heels against the rear of the car. The doors rolled closed. Dick Brull didn't bother getting up. He just reached up for the button marked 1.

Standing up was awkward just about now. He was sitting in a warm puddle he was certain had originated in his frightened bladder.

REMO, CHIUN and Harold Smith stood looking at one another with doubtful expressions.

Smith cleared his throat as he adjusted his tie.

The Master of Sinanju looked bland and expectant.

Remo broke the silence.

"You," he said bitterly, "are not my father."

"Would that it were so," said Chiun, closing his eyes in pain.

"What's that supposed to mean?" Remo snapped.

Chiun looked ceilingward, avoiding his pupil's eyes. "It is an ugly truth. Emperor Smith is your true father. I have known this for many years."

"Bull!"

"Look closely. You have his nose."

Remo pointed at Smith's patrician nose. "That's not my nose. My nose doesn't look anything like that!"

"Remo," Smith said awkwardly, "I understand your discomfort."

"He can't be my father," Remo continued hotly, "because if he's my father, then his wife is my mother. And I've seen my mother. She's a beautiful woman."

"—who told you that you knew your father," Chiun added.

"Maybe," Remo said defensively.

Chiun indicated Harold Smith with a graceful sweep of his arms. "Behold your true father, Prince Remo."

"Don't call me that!" Remo said angrily. "None of this is real. It's gotta be one of the Dutchman's freaking illusions."

"There is a way to prove this," said Smith. "I can call my wife. She will confirm what I have already related."

Remo hesitated.

"Afraid of the truth?" Smith asked.

"No. Go ahead."

Smith returned to his desk to make the call.

Out in the corridor, the elevator dinged.

"Someone comes," Chiun warned.

"Someone with a gun," growled Remo. "I smell residual gunpowder."

Remo and Chiun took up positions on either side of the door and waited for it to open.

The gun barrel entered a full breath ahead of the gunman.

Behind the desk, Harold Smith stiffened.

"Winston!" he breathed.

Then Remo's and Chiun's hands flashed out in unison.

"No!" Smith cried.

It was too late.

34

Winston Smith saw his Uncle Harold the moment he entered the Folcroft office. He had rehearsed the speech all the way across the Atlantic, in the belly of the MAC C-130 he'd stowed aboard. He had it down pat by the time he'd slipped unseen from the cargo bay at MacGuire Air Force Base and grabbed a taxi.

But with his Uncle Harold blinking numbly at the muzzle of the BEM gun, his mind went blank and all the rage of rejection drained from him.

Then the gun in his fist began clicking like mad. It happened so fast it took Winston Smith's breath away. He hadn't so much as caressed the trigger.

When his eyes stopped blinking, Winston Smith saw that the Lucite spokes of his ammo clips had disappeared completely. He lifted the weapon to his face. The clear drum was gone, too. So was the banana clip in the heavy grip.

It was then he realized he was flanked by two men.

One was short and very, very old. An Asian. The other was tall and lean and looked vaguely familiar. Both were holding fistfuls of Lucite clips in their hands, their postures casual.

"Nice gun," said the tall one.

"Screw you," Winston growled, directing the big muzzle toward him. "There's still one in the chamber."

"We always give a freebie," the tall one said with a hard smile.

"Don't mess with me. I'm a trained SEAL."

"That so? Let's see you balance that toy on your nose while clapping your flippers."

"Your mother," Winston growled, squeezing the trigger.

The BEM convulsed. It was at point-blank range, and there was no way he could have missed. No way at all.

But as the gun sound stopped echoing, the tall guy with the dead-looking eyes and insolent smile stood his ground, unhurt. He should have gone down with a hot round in his thigh, but all he did was fold his arms smugly.

Winston Smith blinked. Was it his imagination, or was there a suggestion of a blur around the edges of the guy? As if he had stepped out of the path of the round and back again too fast to be seen?

"So much for your freebie," the guy said coolly.

"Your mother," repeated the kid in the camouflage outfit and tiger-striped face.

Remo looked more deeply into that face, blinked and said, "You do kinda look like my mother. Around the eyes."

Chiun abruptly seized the kid and spun him around.

"Who are you?" he demanded, searching the green-and-black planes of his face.

"Winston Smith. What's it to you, gook?"

"If you are Winston Smith, why do you wear Remo's face?"

"Who's Remo?"

"I am," said Remo, spinning the kid back again so he could get a better look at him. "He doesn't look like me at all."

"Look more closely, Remo," said the shaken voice of Harold Smith. "And you will see the resemblance."

"I don't see any such thing," Remo snapped. "This is your nephew, right? The one you had me mail the kiss-off letter to?"

"Damn right," said Winston Smith bitterly.

"Wrong," said Harold Smith.

"What?" said Winston Smith.

"He is the proof that I am your father, Remo," said Smith, coming out from behind the desk. "He is my grandson, your son."

"You told me you were my uncle," Winston Smith blurted.

Smith shook his gray head gravely. "A lie—told to conceal from you the truth of your parentage."

"I don't get this," said Remo and Winston in unison.

"Aiiieee! Remo has a son!" Chiun wailed.

Smith said, "I thought you always wanted a son for Remo, Master Chiun?"

"Yes. One to train in Sinanju. A suitable heir to the House. Look at him. He is even whiter than Remo. He smells of hamburger and alcohol and he thinks he is a sea lion."

"SEAL," corrected Winston Smith. "It means Sea Air Land—"

"And he carries a boom stick so ridiculous it is a wonder he has not shot himself dead," Chiun wailed in conclusion.

"Don't think it hasn't crossed my mind," said Winston, glaring at Harold Smith.

Remo, his mouth hanging slack, said, "This kid isn't my son. I never had a son."

"Correction. You never had a son that you knew about," said Smith.

"You're my son?" said Remo, his voice flat.

"If I am, I plan on shooting myself," growled Winston Smith.

"You might as well," moaned Chiun, throwing up his hands. "It is already too late. You have been ruined by uniforms and guns. You can never achieve Sinanju."

"What's this gook talking about?" Winston asked Remo.

Chiun stepped up and seized an earlobe. Winston Smith tried to defend himself with judo. His hands were slapped numb, and he was brought to his knees by the sudden white-hot needles of pain in his right earlobe.

"Aaahhh!"

"It is just like the old days," Chiun told Remo. "Before I taught you respect."

"This is crazy!" Remo said, white-faced. "This isn't happening." He pointed an accusing finger at Harold Smith. "You're not my father." The finger swung around. "And this Navy squid isn't my son!"

"Owww! What—oww—watch you say about the Navy, dickhead!"

"I'm a Marine, swabbie."

"Jarhead. Owww!"

"Speak to your father with proper respect, seal-that-barks."

"Owww!"

"Wait a minute. Wait a minute," Remo said suddenly. "This isn't real. It's gotta be more of the Dutchman's illusions."

"Which?" asked Chiun, cocking his bald head to one side.

Remo thought hard. "All of it. Him. Smith. Maybe even you."

"Why am I an illusion?" Chiun asked curiously, not releasing Winston Smith.

"Because you're backing Smith's stupid story that he's my father," said Remo confidently.

"It is true," Chiun admitted. "I am very sorry to have kept it from you all these years, Remo. But it is true."

"Bullshit!" Remo yelled.

"Denial is the first stage of parenthood," retorted Chiun.

Remo stopped, closed his eyes and listened for heartbeats. He counted them. Three. Smith's checked out. Chiun's came through clear and strong. And the kid's heartbeat, too. It wasn't the Dutchman's heart sound. Remo knew that. So the kid wasn't Jeremiah Purcell cloaked in an illusory sheath. The kid was real. And he had the eyes of Freya and the mother Remo never knew.

Remo opened his own eyes, saying, "No way this is real. It can't be." His voice shook with doubt.

Harold Smith cleared his throat noisily. "It is time to clear the air," he said somberly. "For all of you."

Everyone looked to Harold Smith expectantly.

"When Remo first came to Folcroft for training," Smith began, "it was assumed that his life of service might be short. The work was difficult and dangerous."

"What work?" asked Winston.

"Hush," said Chiun.

Smith asked, "Remo, do you remember a Folcroft nurse named Deborah Dean?"

"No."

"Small wonder. You were sleeping your way through the nursing staff in those days."

"Sue me."

"I saw this pattern of behavior, and knowing that the…ah…organization would have a long-term need for an enforcement arm, paid Ms. Dean to carry your child."

"Liar. I used rubbers in those days."

Smith looked uncomfortable. "Artificial insemination. We took a semen specimen the first day you came to Folcroft. Winston was the product. He spent his formative years as a ward of Folcroft, his adolescence in military schools and for the last few years served with distinction as a Navy SEAL."

"You can stow the distinction part," Winston Smith said sourly. "I went AWOL when I got your get-lost letter."

"Unfortunate. Perhaps your error can be rectified."

"Up yours," Winston Smith snapped.

"The hamburger does not fall far from the tree," sniffed Chiun, regarding Winston Smith unkindly.

Coloring, Smith went on. "Winston was never told the truth. Only that his parents had died and that I had been appointed his guardian in their absence. If anything were to happen to Remo, the organization would have an operative after Winston's SEAL training was complete."

"Why was he not given to me?" Chiun complained.

"I assumed Remo would object to allowing his son to undergo Sinanju training. And frankly, after all that has transpired over the years, I was looking for an agent who was more...er...controllable."

"You got that right," said Remo. "You already ruined my life. I wouldn't have let you ruin his." Remo caught himself. "Not that this squid is any son of mine."

"You do not know that."

"For one thing," Remo said, "no son of mine would wear an earring."

"Goat-fuck," Winston Smith said. "Owww. Why does he do that?" Winston asked nobody in particular.

"Chiun enjoys inflicting pain," said Remo.

"What do you mean by agent?" Winston asked. He was ignored.

"A Navy SEAL seemed the next-best thing," finished Smith.

"You insult Sinanju," Chiun said coldly.

"And you insult the Navy," Winston retorted. "SEAL Team Six is the best there is."

"You have a lot to learn, sonny," said Remo.

"You have a lot to learn, sonny," a new voice said.

"Is there an echo in here?" Remo wondered.

"Who said that?" Smith demanded.

"My gun," said Winston Smith in a strange voice.

"Your gun talks?" said Remo skeptically.

"It's configured to my voice," Winston blurted. "It only repeats what I say. How come it recognizes your voice pattern?"

"There is your proof, Remo," Chiun cried.

"Since when is a talking gun proof of paternity?"

"Why did you return in defiance of my express wishes, Winston?" asked Smith.

"To pay you back, you cold mother."

"How have I wronged you? I raised you, supported you, saw that you had opportunities in life."

"And you dumped me in military schools as soon as you could get rid of me," Winston Smith said hotly. "I thought you were my uncle. I thought you were proud of me. Now I come to find out I'm some kind of fucking guinea pig. My whole life is a lie."

"Join the club," said Remo. "You should see what he did to me."

"What?"

"I've been dead for twenty years."

Winston looked as blank as his camo face would allow.

Smith cleared his throat. "Winston, the circumstances that forced me to write you off have turned out to be temporary. I regret the cold tone of my letter, but it was in your best interests. You were a loose end that needed tying."

"Thanks a heap."

"The crisis has passed," Smith continued. "It is in my power to return you to your unit with minimum disciplinary repercussions."

"Who made you admiral of the fucking fleet?"

Smith winced. "More than that I cannot say."

"Thanks but no thanks. I'd rather bail."

"So bail," said Remo, opening the door for him. "No one's stopping you."

"What about this guy?"

Chiun withdrew his fingernails from Winston Smith's earlobe. Smith got up, recovering his pistol.

Remo looked Winston Smith in the eye for a long time. "No way he's related to me," he said flatly.

"That goes double for me," Winston said.

"I'm sorry that both of you have had to come to the truth so abruptly and without preparation," said Harold Smith. "But the facts remain. Remo, I am your father, and Winston, you are my grandson, Remo's son."

"Prove it," said Remo, folding his arms.

"Yeah," said Winston, copying Remo's posture. "Prove it."

Chiun grasped the puffs of hair over both ears in frustration. "They are both blind."

"We can begin where we left off before we were interrupted," said Smith. "I will call my wife at her sister's home."

Smith sat down and began dialing.

"This is Harold. How are you? Is my wife staying there? Thank you. Put her on."

Smith engaged the speakerphone function.

Mrs. Smith sounded shocked. "Harold! Where are you?"

"Folcroft. All is well again. The IRS have gone. It was a simple misunderstanding. We should be able to go home tomorrow, if not tonight."

"Harold, it was horrible. They threw me out into the street!"

"I know, dear. But it is over. Maude, I would like to go over our discussion of last night."

"Discussion?"

"Yes, you remember. You came to Folcroft last night."

"Harold, I was here all last night, frantic with worry. I tried calling the hospital, but no one would give me any satisfaction."

"Excuse me?" said Smith, gray eyes blinking rapidly.

"Harold, what are you talking about? Are you well?"

Flustered, Harold Smith said, "It is nothing. It must have been a dream. I will be home as soon as I can."

Smith abruptly hung up. "Er," he began, "it appears there has been a slight misunderstanding."

"Hah!" said Remo. "I knew it!"

"But Maude came to me last night," he said dully.

"Yeah," Remo said. "And we all saw pink bunny rabbits and purple pterodactyls. None of them were real, either."

Smith made long faces as he sat thinking.

"We *did* have a conversation about the search for your parentage within hearing of the Dutchman's room," Smith went on. "It *is* possible that he could have created the illusion of a visit from my wife, to sow confusion and dissension among us."

"Who's the Dutchman?" asked Winston Smith.

No one bothered to reply.

Smith continued. "Then it was all concoction." His face was almost comical with realization.

"Right," said Remo. "I'm not related to you and you are not related to me. End of freaking story."

"There is still this one," said Chiun, indicating Winston Smith.

"Forget him."

"He wears your face, Remo," Chiun pointed out.

"I don't believe it."

"Neither do I," said Winston Smith. "I'm bailing."

Smith spoke up. "I am afraid we cannot allow this. You know too much, Winston."

Winston Smith started backing out of the room. "I don't know jack shit. Except that you're a fraud."

"If you will not return to your unit, some provision must be made for you. Chiun, render him unconscious, please."

Chiun shook his aged head. "He is not my son. He is Remo's responsibility."

"I offer him to you for training," Smith said quickly. "Since Remo has made his intentions of leaving the organization clear, we have need of a new Destroyer. I put him in your hands."

"Don't I get any say in this?" Remo and Winston said in unison. Their heads snapped around, and their gazes locked.

After a beat Remo suddenly advanced on Winston Smith. Smith drew a combat knife from a boot sheath. Remo stopped. Suddenly he tossed Winston a set of car keys. He caught them.

"What's this?"

"There's a blue Buick parked down the road. Take it. Change your name. And don't look back."

Winston Smith's camouflage tiger stripes gathered up in confusion. "You're giving me your car?"

"Once Smith gets his hooks into you, he'll never let go. You have a chance for your own life." Remo gave Harold Smith a hard look. "Which is more than I ever got. Take it and go."

Winston Smith smiled cockily. "Thanks, jarhead."

"Don't mention it, swabbie."

And he was gone.

Smith rose from his desk. "Remo! We cannot—"

Remo kicked the door shut. "Forget it, Smitty. Your story may be true or not. Either way, the kid deserves a decent break after the raw deal you handed him."

"Here! Here!" said Chiun.

Smith settled back into his chair, features haggard.

"And what kind of a name is Winston?" Remo demanded.

"I told you before. A family name. It happens to be my middle name."

"You ought to be shot just for naming an innocent kid after a cigarette," said Remo.

Smith made a lemony mouth and said nothing.

The Master of Sinanju floated up to the glass-topped desk and plucked something out of one voluminous sleeve. He laid it on the black glass.

Smith squinted.

"If it is still your wish to end your life," Chiun intoned, "there is the means."

Smith took up the white coffin-shaped pill, regarded it with an impassive expression and without a word slipped it into the watch pocket of his vest.

"The crisis has passed."

No one said anything for a long awkward moment.

Then Smith said, "I have many loose ends to clean up. Staff to rehire. Patients to calm down. Strings to pull with the IRS and DEA."

"What about the Dutchman?" asked Remo.

"His medications will have to be changed. His mind is clearing and the danger is growing. At the moment I am more concerned with Uncle Sam Beasley."

Smith pulled closer the worn attaché case that Big Dick Brull left on the desk. He worked the combination that disarmed the explosive latch charges, exposing a portable computer and telephone handset. He booted it up.

"The basement computers are inoperative but may be salvageable, even if the data stored on them is not. In the meantime, I will undertake a search for Beasley."

"Don't forget my mother," Remo reminded. "I'll make you a copy of the drawing."

"I will do my best as promised," said Smith absently.

"Do better," warned Remo. "You have a lot of sins to make up for."

Harold Smith said nothing to that. He was already lost in cyberspace.

"Come on, Little Father. Let's go panning for gold."

Hazel eyes widening, the Master of Sinanju followed Remo out of the office.

35

Remo Williams led the Master of Sinanju down to the Folcroft basement. They walked in silence, lost in their own thoughts.

There Remo raised the corrugated loading door.

"Remember when the DEA stormed ashore that second time and you tore into them?" he asked Chiun.

"They were fools and died fools."

"You made a lot of noise."

"Striking terror into one's enemies is never wasted," sniffed Chiun.

They were standing on the rust-stained concrete loading dock.

"It covered the whizzing very nicely," said Remo.

"What whizzing?"

Remo had picked up a crowbar along the way. He drew back, letting fly.

It seemed a casual gesture. But the crowbar whizzed once it left his fingers. It kept on whizzing as it arced high out over the sound. The noise it made splashing was too far away to make much impression on their eardrums. But their sharp eyes easily detected the eruption a mile out on the sound where it struck.

"You threw my gold out to sea!" Chiun cried in horror.

"No," said Remo. "I threw everyone's gold out to sea. I threw high and far so no one noticed. Not even you. Of course, I had to work really fast and one ingot spun out of control and sank a DEA boat. But I figured they had it coming."

"What if my gold rusts?" demanded Chiun.

"You know that gold doesn't rust. Like I kept telling you, it's safe as soap."

Chiun puffed out his cheeks while his wrinkled face smoldered. "You will recover every dram of gold or you will never hear the end of it," Chiun said in a flinty voice.

"Done," said Remo unconcernedly.

"Any gold missing from my share will come out of your share."

"Fair enough."

"And any missing from Smith's share comes out of your share, as well. Unless, of course, Smith does not notice it—in which case, it goes into my share."

Remo blinked. "How is that possible?"

Chiun levered a quivering finger at the choppy waters of the sound. "Do not think. Swim. I will not endure the thought of the gold of the House of Sinanju lying wet and untended at the bottom of this barbarian bay."

"Next time let's use a bank."

"Pah! Banks are untrustworthy."

"How is that?"

"They accept your gold and money with smiles and promises of safekeeping. But when you demand it back, they are full of lies and excuses."

Remo looked puzzled.

"They never give you back your own money. It is always someone else's," sniffed Chiun.

Laughing, Remo started down toward the water. Chiun followed, gesticulating in anger with every step.

Once they reached the water, Chiun noticed the pleased cast of his pupil's face.

"What are you thinking of?" he asked.

Remo took the police sketch out of his pocket, carefully unfolding it. "I know what my mother looks like. She talked to me."

"She was an illusion."

"No. It was her. The Dutchman is good at projecting illusions, but he couldn't have cast one a whole state away. It was her. I don't know her name, but I know her face and her voice. It's a first step. And my father is out there, whoever he is." Remo stepped out of his shoes. "And I intend to find him."

"Do not get your hopes too high," Chiun warned.

Remo looked up from the drawing. "You seemed awfully eager to go along with that crap about Smith being my father. What was that all about?"

Chiun shrugged. "A mistake. Like your sending that noisy youth away."

"You think he's my kid?"

"He wears your face."

Remo shrugged. "Hard to tell under all that camo paint."

"I notice you did not wipe it away, the better to see the truth."

"Maybe I didn't want to know the truth."

Chiun smiled. "You are a good father, Remo Williams. Even if you have been woefully negligent in the past."

Remo handed Chiun the folded drawing for safe-keeping and without another word slid into the water. It swallowed him without a ripple. After a moment there was no trace of his existence.

Down the road a car started up.

The Master of Sinanju stood looking at the regathering water, listening to the fading engine sound as his wizened features pulled tight and concerned.

Behind him the purple pterodactyls flying low over Folcroft Sanitarium on tiring wings slowly faded against the cobalt sky until they were no more.

36

Big Dick Brull showed up at the Lippincott Savings Bank unannounced later that day. That was the way IRS usually hit a bank. Without warning. That way no one could bury records, pretending to misplace them or stonewall in other ways.

Striding through the staid lobby, his head swiveling like a radar dish, confident as only a man who worked for the federal government and had a fresh change of underwear could be, Big Dick Brull made a beeline for the director's office.

"Richard Brull, IRS, to see Jeremy Lippincott."

"Are you expected?" asked the secretary.

"Not if we can help it," said Brull.

"What shall I tell Mr. Lippincott this is in reference to?"

"The Folcroft Sanitarium account and a matter of twelve million dollars."

The secretary dutifully conveyed the information to Jeremy Lippincott by intercom.

Lippincott's amplified voice was grating. "Confound it! I have already explained the mistake to the IRS. Twice. Why are they sending more people to annoy me?"

"Because," barked Big Dick Brull into the speaker, "IRS takes no answers at face value, and no prisoners at all."

"Sir! You can't go in there!" the secretary protested.

Big Dick Brull barged in anyway. He crossed the threshold, and behind his desk, Jeremy Lippincott froze in midnibble, eyes startled, the raw carrot dropping from his poufy pink fingers.

Both men froze for an eternity that lasted barely thirty seconds. Lippincott gulped guiltily.

Big Dick Brull lost the contents of his bladder before he lost consciousness.

THE NEXT THING he knew it was hours later and he was in hospital being looked over by a team of doctors and his immediate IRS superior, who was looking very displeased.

"You have a lot of explaining to do, Brull."

Brull did his best to explain. "It was a big fuzzy bunny rabbit. It followed me from the hospital. It's been following me for days, beating its drum. I don't think it likes me."

"I received a call from the Almighty. She is very upset at me. In turn, I am very upset with you. It seems you seized a private hospital without going by the book and managed to screw us up with DEA, FEMA and no one knows who else."

Big Dick Brull looked at his naked toes peeping out from under the bed sheet. "A bunny wabbit stole my shoes," he said in a tiny voice. "Pterodactyls ate my paperwork."

"There, there," he was told by one of the attending physicians. "No need to repeat it all. We heard enough while you were under. Why don't you rest?"

"Dickie wants to go home," Brull said in a whiny voice.

"That's not possible right now. In fact, we're thinking of moving you to a place where they know how to deal with people who see pink rabbits and purple pterodactyls."

Big Dick Brull looked blank.

"Yes. It's a marvelous facility. Not very far from here, in fact. Perhaps you've heard of it. Folcroft Sanitarium?"

Big Dick Brull opened his mouth to scream. All that came out was a mousey squeak. Then they injected the needle into his forearm.

TAKE 'EM FREE

4 action-packed novels plus a mystery bonus

NO RISK
NO OBLIGATION TO BUY